Advance praise for Linda Villarosa and
Passing for Black

"*Passing for Black* is *Kissing Jessica Stein* meets *Good Hair*.
The characters are outrageous and real and heartfelt. Linda
Villarosa has written an important, entertaining debut. Brava!"
— Benilde Little, author of *Who Does She Think She Is?*

"*Passing for Black* weaves issues of identity and sexuality
into an engaging tale of love, passion and family. Finally the
story we've been waiting for, delivered in page-turning, finely
written prose by one of my favorite writers."
— E. Lynn Harris, *New York Times* bestselling author

"*Passing for Black* is a lively page turner that follows the
complicated process of coming out as African American and
female and middle class. It is a sweet, romantic, and sometimes funny tale, brushed nicely with issues of race, class, and
sexuality. As Angela tumbles along her journey to self discov-
ery, I found myself rooting for her to find the way."
— Staceyann Chin

PASSING
FOR
BLACK

LINDA VILLAROSA

KENSINGTON PUBLISHING CORP.
http://www.kensingtonbooks.com

To my mother. Please call her Mrs. V.

Acknowledgments

I am deeply grateful to my agent Barbara Lowenstein and her staff for unwavering, tireless support. Many thanks to everyone at Kensington, especially John Scognamiglio. It's wonderful working with such a receptive and attentive editor. I promise to return the favor by learning to pronounce your name.

I owe big thank-yous to friends who provided hand holding, cheerleading, suggestions, ideas and even dialogue: Allison, Benilde, Bridgett, Erin, Hilary, Nina, Sarah, Staceyann and Toshi.

Many thank yous to several generous and thoughtful readers: Jackie, Jana, Jayme, and, especially, Kera Bolonik and Stephanie Grant, who gave the manuscript the twice over and more. Special thanks to the members of my writing group, past and present, who read bits and pieces at various stages.

Thank you to my mother and sister for all kinds of love, including the tough kind, and to the Sunday dinner crew—Jackie, Juliet and Jane—for great food and better friendship. I am grateful for the children in my life: Toshi, Tashawn and, especially, Kali and Nic, though this book is a little racy for you. Special thanks to my extended family: Carrie, Faye, Lorry, Tracey, Vickie, Arielle and the crew in Texas and Oklahoma.

Above all, thank you Jana, for listening and loving.

She wished to find out about this hazardous business of "passing," this breaking away from all that was familiar and friendly to take one's chances in another environment, not entirely strange, perhaps, but not entirely friendly.

—From *Passing*, by Nella Larsen

Prologue

A chorus of raspy moans and high-pitched screams ripped through the thin walls of the delivery room. I clamped my hands over my ears to blot out the sounds of pain. Hadn't the hospital heard of soundproofing? Though my baby wasn't coming for another couple of hours, I felt like joining in. I wouldn't be screaming in pain, but terror.

With contractions every two minutes, I knew it was way too late for second thoughts. It wasn't that motherhood didn't interest me. But a baby hadn't been anywhere near the top of my to-do list. Learning to play the guitar, kayaking down the Colorado River and a trip to Brazil were much higher. Motherhood was in my future—someday, a long way off. I guess my idea was to start reproducing in my late thirties after accomplishing career goals—like being the editor of my own magazine or writing a book of essays. I didn't believe all the alarmist crap about a woman's eggs drying up at thirty-five. That was just another ploy to make women who loved their work feel like un-pretty losers, waiting to shrivel up and shuffle away.

But all of this was academic. In the concrete here and now, there was a baby—my baby—banging its way out of the womb and into the world.

Chapter 1

The day I met Cait, a passing breeze stirred up the warm, thick air as I walked through the campus of New Amsterdam University. That cool undertow, weird on such a still, sunny fall day, felt like a sign that something was about to happen.

As I pulled open the heavy door of the Humanities building and turned down the hall toward the Kenneth Clark African-American studies wing, that's when I saw her. She was standing on tiptoe tacking a flyer onto a cork bulletin board. It read: "Lesbian Sex Conference: We Want You to *COME*," followed by an off-campus location and a date a little less than a week away.

Putting down the flyer, she turned and looked at me quizzically. Then she smiled, raising one eyebrow, a dimple denting each cheek. I stopped, midstride, and took a deep breath, inhaling a bouquet of Sharpie and pine cleaner.

She was strikingly androgynous, and looked like an older version of Ethan, the beautiful fifteen-year-old boy I had been obsessed with one summer at sleep-away camp in New Hampshire. Her light brown hair was parted boyishly on one side, and flecked with bright blonde streaks. As she turned toward me, I could see Pam Grier doing a Foxy Brown high kick on the front of her T-shirt. Sleeves cut off, it tugged tightly across her breasts.

"I'm Caitlin Getty." Staring at me, her eyes clear gray and steady, she took my hand. Her appraisal was brazen. Thinking briefly about the ring on my finger, I shoved my left hand in my pocket.

"I'm Angela, uh, Wright." I could feel her fingertips against my palm as we shook hands lightly. I tried to ease my hand out of hers, but she held it. Mine was warm and damp, hers, cool and dry.

"Angela, may I give you a flyer?" She spoke with the trace of a British accent; from her mouth, my name sounded like dessert. "I'd love to see you on Saturday at the sex conference."

Finally she dropped my hand and plucked a flyer from a stack next to her foot. "Actually, I would just love to see you. My e-mail address is on the bottom."

As I studied the flyer, I felt a mild electric shock travel from the tops of my thighs and through my crotch, before settling somewhere in the pit of my stomach. I was feeling a pull toward this woman so urgent that it was difficult to nudge aside.

But I had to push away these feelings, as I always had, starting the summer after Ethan. I had been even more obsessed with Adriana, a junior counselor who had a tiny tattoo of a butterfly on her shoulder and wore thick white socks that bunched at her ankles. And in college, when I had had a crush on Laura Chin-Loy, the RA in my freshman dorm. And a few years ago, when I had taken the same photography course twice so that I could stand next to the instructor, Genevieve Britton, in the darkroom, our upper arms touching as we dragged photo paper through pans of developing fluid.

All of those feelings had been free-floating and vague, like a nondescript snippet of music, muffled in another room. I let them drift away; they were un-returned, barely examined. But this was stronger, more urgent. A violent, dangerous delight.

"Yeah, thanks," I said, stuffing the flyer in my bag. As I walked away from her too afraid to look back, I clutched the top of my arm and pressed my nails into the soft skin, nearly drawing blood. *I am not gay-lesbian-bisexual-questioning. I am a straight heterosexual American.* I repeated these thoughts until they crowded out the others.

By the time I slipped into a seat at the back of Keith's classroom I'd gotten right again. Blinking, I focused on my fiancé, who was wrapping up his lecture. Standing in front of the thirty-odd students enrolled in his "Twentieth Century Black Experience" seminar, Keith lifted his palms from the podium, spreading his arms to make a point. He reminded me of the stately prime minister of a Caribbean island. Keith took a breath, mopped his brow with a handkerchief, and looked at his watch. "We're out of time for today." Their heads down, the students noisily began to gather their jackets and backpacks.

"Excuse me." Keith raised his voice to be heard over the sound of students moving out of black history and returning to present. "Let me remind you that by next class, you should be finished with the assigned reading, *The Conspiracy to Destroy Black Boys*. And remember that the African Diaspora Society will hold its monthly meeting tomorrow at five P.M. in this classroom. I hope to see some of you there."

I picked up my coat and bag and walked to the front of the classroom. Keith was involved in a passionate discussion about the global mass marketing of black culture with a student. I wished he were just a good friend or even a cousin. Then I could look at him fondly without creeping panic as I imagined myself tethered to this man for the rest of my natural life.

Keith was a good man, really, but secretly, I sometimes tacked on "enough." He looked good enough, and, in fact, he looked pretty good, compared with other unmarried black men in their mid-thirties who weren't dogs or players or on the down low. The few others left had pillowy bodies, scuffed shoes and frayed collars. When they looked at you their watery Bassett-hound eyes seemed to say *feed me*—and while you're at it, do my laundry, scrub behind my ears, and then tuck me in.

Keith made good enough money with his professor's salary and fit on the edges of my social circle as my slightly older, straight-laced but cute big-Daddy boyfriend. He impressed my friends by translating the fine print 401K lingo of their employee benefits packages into plain English and explaining why every black person must have a mutual fund in order to move the race forward. And my mother loved him. She nodded her vigorous approval during his toasts at family gatherings, centering on "bettering our people." My cousins called him Malcolm Gen-X behind his back.

After five years, we fit together like a pair of worn slippers, one stuck inside the other. Each night I felt his belly burrowing into my back, his soft penis pushing against my thigh, and my body softened sleepily against his. He made me feel safe, protected from the feelings like the ones I had had with Caitlin Getty.

"Good lecture, sweetie." I reached up and placed my hand on his neck and kissed his cheek lightly.

"Thank you for coming," he said. As he looked down at me and smiled, Keith's stern *Dr. Redfield face* faded and the shallow trench between his eyebrows disappeared. I smiled back at him, or at least I tried to make the corners of my mouth turn upward. He was relaxed, in his element and happy to share it with me. I felt suffocated and had a fleeting feeling of wanting to shake things up, make a mess.

As we prepared to leave, the door swung open, and I felt

breathless again. It was that Caitlin woman, the flyers tucked under her arm. But something was wrong. Keith had taken a step toward her and was standing uncomfortably close. A vein ran from his jaw down the side of his neck bulging, large, blue and ugly. The purple kente bow tie I had bought him at an African market uptown looked tight around his throat.

"Hello, Dr. Getty. I see you continue to appropriate African-American culture." His voice was tight and thin as he looked at her coldly, a white woman splashed in Pam Grier.

"Dr. Redfield, you don't own Foxy, just because she's black. She's a woman too, and, if anything, probably a lesbian." Her smile was mean, and her dimple looked less playful than menacing. The accent was stronger, and she pronounced "anything" like "enna-thing."

"Don't be absurd." Keith seemed to congeal into that spot. Only his fist opened and closed stiffly before he shoved the hand in his pocket.

"So, Keith, what's new in African-American History? Oh, right, nothing's new since it's, um, history, a time way before the present when scientists have determined that biological races do not exist and that race is simply a social and political construct that the world would be better without." She said it in one sentence, like she was reciting something she'd written. Keith took a step back. The two of them looked like dancers in a vinegary interracial tango.

"Dr. Getty, how's everything in Gay, Lesbian, Bisexual, and, what is it, Transgender Studies?"

"Transgender hasn't been officially added to our department." She frowned, folding her arms across her chest so they rested lightly on Foxy's oversize afro.

"Well, I think Transgender should be a part of gay and lesbian studies, and at the next department meeting, I plan to vote for adding it," he said, leaning toward her, his arms rigid at his sides. "Or maybe instead we should have courses in bestiality or pedophilia. Or we could make it easier and rename the whole department Perversity Studies."

She rolled her eyes and turned her body away from Keith, toward me. "Keith, you're so rude—hi, again, Angela." Staring at me, her eyes a clear gray, the color of a storm, she took my hand. Keith looked confused.

"This is my *fiancée*." He pulled my hand away from hers and put his arm around me. I felt his grip hard and tight on my shoulder. "Angela, I see you've met my colleague, Dr. Getty."

"Really nice to meet you, again." She continued looking at me, giving me a barefaced appraisal. Why the hell was she doing this? What did she see in me? I squeezed myself closer to Keith. *Get the message now? I am a heterosexual woman, locked to my better half.* Balling my hand into a fist behind my back, I dug my nails into my palm until it stung.

"Dr. Getty, what do you want?" Keith took a step away from me and shoved a stack of papers into his worn, leather briefcase.

"Here, take some flyers to give out to your classes," she said as she peeled several from her stack and handed them to Keith without touching him. "We want to make sure the turnout at our sex conference is diverse—as you've instructed us to strive for at campus-based events."

"Black people aren't interested in this."

He held the flyers with two fingers. "And nice seeing you—good-bye." He dropped the flyers into the trash can.

"That's not very collegial, but I wouldn't expect anything less." She turned toward the door. "See you at the Humanities cocktail party, Dr. Redfield. And please bring your beautiful fiancée." As she opened the door, she turned and caught my eye, flashing me her mischievous grin.

"What was that about?" I asked. At that moment, I felt confused by everything that had just happened, but especially baffled by Keith's behavior. Generally, he tempered his emotions at the U, careful not to ever "show his ass."

"I don't like her," he answered stubbornly, snapping his briefcase shut without looking up.

"Honey, why—" I stopped. I didn't want to hear what he had to say about her, and I wished I hadn't seen their nasty exchange. I preferred to remember the feel of her breath on my cheek.

"It's not because she's gay, if that's what you're thinking," Keith answered, looking at me coldly, and shifting back into Dr. Redfield mode. "And I would never condone discrimination of any sort."

"Yes, I know that—"

"But, you've never had to be in meetings with people like Cait Getty, for God sakes." His voice had risen and he was grinding the toe of his loafer into the tile floor. "Comparing our Civil Rights to their sexual rights."

"Keith, you sound like Bull Connor."

"Angela, every time I hear gays whine about being discriminated against and appropriating the language of the Civil Rights Movement, I want to vomit."

"Okay, I think you made your point," I answered quietly, taking his arm and steering him toward the door.

"No, I haven't," he said with a note of finality. Grudgingly, he allowed himself to be pulled. "It is blasphemous to compare the rights of homosexuals with the struggles of our people. They were never kidnapped from their homeland, forced into chattel slavery, their women raped, their men hung from trees, babies slaughtered. Period. Let's go."

Now that the lynching and chattel slavery cards had been pulled from the race deck, there was nothing more to say. As I followed Keith out of the room, I remembered the dangerous feeling of touching Caitlin's hand. Slipping my hand into my bag I lightly fingered the fold of the flyer.

Chapter 2

The next afternoon, I wound my way through the brightly lit tables, keeping my head down to avoid eye contact with any of the other magazine editors, flitting like sparrows through the Brice-Castle Publishing cafeteria. I found a table and put down my tray, looking impatiently for Mae to join me. I hated sitting alone, and I was beyond starving. I pulled a tube of lipstick in a shade called Dubonnet from my jacket pocket and applied it as best I could without looking. I didn't really want Mae to give me a hard time about "fixing up."

Appraising myself realistically, I had some nice features—smooth, even skin; brown, slightly slanted eyes; straight, white teeth thanks to braces and a retainer; thick, curly hair. My legs were long and, I thought, cute, and I had a pretty good-looking butt. The package was almost beautiful, though I lacked the bearings, style or attitude of a beautiful person. Despite the intense pressure to look good, beaten into anyone who worked at a fashion magazine and had the guts to sashay through this cafeteria, I never quite pulled it together. I didn't understand makeup, so I avoided all but lipstick. My clothes, despite Mae's constant coaching and cajoling, were never hooked up correctly. I was always a couple of seasons behind.

I generally thought people who were fashion forward were simply strange, until I found myself—and the rest of the planet—wearing their previously avant garde pieces a year later. My hair was a disorganized tangle of thick curls, springy and random.

Mae had paused for a moment, buttonholed by a woman whose black dress hung off her, like a garment slipping from a hanger. She and Mae were actually wearing the same Calvin Klein dresses, size 2 and 16, respectively. Mae's dress was orange since she had given up wearing black, because it was now "tired." The hanger stood on her tiptoes and whispered something conspiratorially into Mae's ear. "I heard that," she said, clapping the hanger on the back heartily, nearly knocking the dress off her thin shoulders, before moving on.

Mae was my best friend, my only real friend, at work. She was an associate features writer at *Vicarious*, a celebrity fashion magazine. I was an associate editor at *Désire*, another publication in the Brice-Castle stable. We had started at the company the same week and had been seated next to each other at Brice-Castle's mandatory new employees' welcome lunch.

"Oh no, they put me at the black table," she had said loudly as she sat down next to me.

"Welcome, my sistah," I had replied, smiling at her and ignoring the uncomfortable looks of the other three women and the man seated with us.

Mae had thrown back her head and answered with a raucous, full-on laugh. Right away, her gummy, gap-toothed smile and crinkly eyes felt like home.

Everyone liked Mae. She had created a kind of universal "you-go-girl" black woman persona. She was a magnet to the wispy women and gay men who peopled our company: they were drawn by the confidence and good cheer that clung lightly to her like a misting of cologne. Many felt close to her, though she managed to keep the more textured aspects of her persona secreted away, like an intricately folded dollar stuffed into her brassiere.

Mae had grown up in Iuka, Mississippi, and no amount of New York sophistication could drive out her Southern roots. She was definitely country fried Prada. Two weeks after we'd met, on our way to getting bent on vodka martinis neither of us could afford at the Oak Room in the Plaza Hotel, Mae had revealed to me that just before her fifth birthday, she had announced to her mother that once she was eighteen, she was "outta Dodge." She vowed to someday live in New York City in an apartment high in the sky, all by herself.

"The first time I said it, Mama wiped her hands on her apron and said 'uh-huh,' " Mae had confided in me, dragging out the uhs and huhs for five full seconds. "By the second time I said it, she told me to 'stop the foolishness.' But when I was still saying it two years later, she said that 'if you see yourself there, you're as good as there.' "

The day she graduated from Barnard, her family was there. Ten of them had piled out of an Amtrak sleeper car, greasy shoe boxes of fried chicken and deviled eggs in tow. They spread themselves out on the Lehman Lawn, screaming and holding up signs and banging on noisemakers when Mae walked up to get her diploma. Ignoring the chilly stares of her classmates and their parents, she waved and flashed her gummy smile and shouted "I love y'all," as she tottered past the podium on itty bitty high-heeled shoes.

"They were so fucking country, but I loved having them there." Her eyes had gotten round and watery as she told the story, and mine did, too.

After several years in publishing, Mae had finally grown tired of trying to explain her accent, tone down her loud laugh, and justify how some 'Bama had crashed her way into the ranks of Manhattan publishing. Rather than reinvent herself—again—she began to simply withhold parts of herself.

Several years ago, she had limited her vocabulary around our co-workers to three phrases: "I heard that," "I know you're right," and "I'm scared of you." People found her wise and a little mysterious.

"Hey you," she said, her tray clattering onto the table. The four plates of overpriced haute cuisine must've cost her close to thirty dollars. I loved to eat but hated to pay, so the small, expensive portions the cafeteria served were a source of irritation. I secretly believed that the editors at the company's magazines suffered from disordered eating, so bigger portions made them nervous. They actually preferred to pay more for smaller portions. The few who weren't anorexic were bulimic, ordering double portions, then sneaking off to a bathroom on another floor—oh God, not their own—to throw up in the afternoon. Until last year, they had favored the fifth floor, inhabited by the company's accounting department. After several numbers crunchers complained about the smell, HR issued a clumsily worded memo and the problem ceased.

"I got you the salmon Nicoise with extra potatoes and the balsamic chicken and mango stir-fry," Mae said. She reached into her orange and yellow Pucci tote and pulled out a large bubble-wrapped package. Carefully, she uncovered two pieces of china, delicately painted with green leaves; two sets of silverware; two checkered green napkins and two cocktail glasses splashed with white magnolias, Mississippi's state flower. She insisted that the "insulting plastic mess" would ruin our meals. I had long ago decided not to be embarrassed by this over-the-top display of decorum.

"Hey, what's up with you, today, you okay?" She moved two tidy servings onto our plates and poured bottled iced tea into the glasses. She added an extra packet of sugar to each.

"Yeah, I'm cool," I said, piercing the chicken with my fork, and popping a large, juicy piece into my mouth. It was oddly tasteless.

"Oh no—not again," she said, ignoring me as she chewed a mouthful of tortellini. "Have you set the date?"

"Not yet." I shifted my eyes away from hers.

"Angela, I love you, but, okay, stop it!" Mae said, nearly shouting. Two hangers stopped pushing their food around their plates and looked up at us.

"Please . . ." I didn't want to get into this with her. There was so much she didn't know.

"No, PLEASE! Keith is a good man. He's awright-looking for an academic, and he loves you and wants to marry you," she said, ticking off Keith's strong points on her left hand. "The boy's romantic, you've got to give him that. Remember your engagement?"

After four years together, I had mentioned to Keith off-handedly that I longed to go to Africa. "By the time I see the motherland, I'll be a grandmother," I had said as we climbed into bed one night. A month later, he surprised me with a ten-day trip to South Africa. After visiting Johannesburg, Cape Town and a lavish game lodge in Kruger National Park, we ended up in Franschhoek, South Africa's lush wine country. Over dinner on a terrace with a view of Table Mountain, Keith said to me, "Angela, 'you make my life fine, fine as wine.'" Then he smiled. Langston, his favorite poet. "Will you marry me?"

Looking way beyond corny down on one knee, he presented me with a 4-carat diamond ring, an heirloom passed down from his grandmother, Lottie. It looked as big as a suitcase on my finger. Between the ring and the poem, and the motherland and the ice-cold Sauvignon blanc, I started sobbing uncontrollably.

Crying, too, Keith had stroked my hand. "Uh, 'baby, I'm never gonna give you up, so don't make me wait too long,'" he said, deepening his voice. Barry White, his other favorite poet. Even more cornball. Through the tears and giggles and second thoughts, I managed to sputter out a "yes."

"Besides that fantastic proposal, get real," Mae said, reaching over and stabbing a bite of salmon from my plate. "He's a man, he's black, and he's got hair and vital signs."

"Okay, okay." I pushed a piece of salmon and an olive onto my fork.

"There is a SHORTAGE, I know you know that—catch up." She snapped the fingers of her left hand, pushing a stray piece of asparagus onto her fork with her pinkie.

"Oh, knock it off," I said, grabbing her hand to stop the irritating snapping. "I'm not rushing into marriage because of your crackpot scare tactics."

"RUSH, you've been with this man, what, six years? Plus, you do love him." This was not a question.

"Yes, I do love him," I said, raising my voice, too. "But, Mae, how do I know that Keith is my soul mate?"

"Shut up—PA-lease. No one marries their soul mate, except for lesbians, and they can't get married." She widened her eyes and stared at me. I felt my heart jump, lurching out of sync for a beat as Caitlin Getty's face flashed in my mind.

"Break up with him, then," Mae continued, taking her napkin from her lap and dabbing at a bit of stray sauce from the corner of her mouth. "Then see how easy it is to find your so-called soul mate. Forget the stats; look around at black women who are thirty, your age shortly. Where are a bunch of eligible black men jumping in line to date us?" she said.

"I just read an article in one of the black magazines that said sisters have our expectations too high and that we need to date bus drivers, rather than wait for a man on our level. You know what, that tired advice doesn't even work anymore. I was eating up at Amy Ruth's last week, and I heard two women fighting over a guy—who was in prison. Now, you do the math: If there are two women fighting over every guy in lockdown, that means four are fighting over every bus driver and eight are fighting over every college professor, and God knows how many are fighting over an investment banker."

"And your point is?" I asked, wishing she'd pipe down.

"You know what—I turned the page in that magazine," she continued, waving her fork. "And I was advised to draw a hot bath, light a candle and marry myself. Why would a magazine tell you to marry yourself if there was a living, breathing person to actually marry?" She was getting very worked up.

"I get it," I said. I wanted to get her off this subject.

"No, you don't," Mae said as she stuck her fork into a neat mound of risotto. "Miss Wright, where are you going to look for Mr. Right? Here? You work at a friggin' women's magazine company. Do you see any men here?; well, any that won't be on the 3:50 train to the Pines ferry on Fridays?"

"Okay, if things are soooo dire, why are you always so picky?" I looked at her pointedly, raising my eyebrows.

"Girl, please, I am not picky, I'm discriminating."

"Girl, please yourself." I was irritated, talking much more black than usual. My "black woman voice" seemed to have more authority.

"Listen, Mae, maybe I'm scared, okay?" I said, feeling tired and shaky. I reached across the table and gripped her hand. I wished I could tell Mae about my secret desires for women. But I was afraid. I didn't know if I'd ever be able to tell her. Maybe after I was safely married to Keith. Or maybe this wasn't the kind of thing I would ever tell my best friend. These were thoughts that I would always savor and later punish myself for.

"Mae, I'll be okay. I just need more time."

"I know, I know, of course you are, of course you do," She moved her hand from underneath and rested it on top of mine, squeezing lightly. "Everybody gets scared before marriage."

"Yeah, you're right."

"So have an affair." Her smile was playful, her voice matter-of-

fact. "Men do it all the time. They get jittery before they're supposed to get married, so they find some bimbo to screw. Have
you thought of that?" She grinned; her gap looked large enough
to walk through.

"Now you really are insane." I stood up, holding the tray.
"Listen, I'd love to sit here and continue this crazy talk, but I
have a meeting with Lucia in ten minutes and I'm not too prepared."

"It doesn't matter, it's more important to look pretty. Here,
put on some lipstick." Mae pulled a tube from her purse and
pushed it toward me. "You ate off whatever you applied earlier
to try to impress your ho in chief." Mae couldn't stand Lucia.

"That wasn't for her, that was for you, silly." I went around
the table and kissed the top of her head, before tugging my
own lipstick from my pocket.

Chapter 3

I walked into Lucia's office a few minutes late, hoping she had gotten juiced about something this week, since, for a change, I was light on ideas. I had been preoccupied thinking about Cait Getty and then willing those thoughts away. Twice a month I met with my boss to help her brainstorm ideas for her editor's note, "Deep Désire." It was an odd duty: Most editors at my level would kill for private meetings with the editor in chief of the magazine and were not in on writing an editor's note. But most editors of my level were afraid of Lucia, our brilliant diva of a boss. And most weren't gifted at spinning out magazine ideas. I was the Stephen Hawking of ideas, much to the irritation of my peers.

Lucia Bravo appreciated my skills. She was widely considered a quirky genius and "Deep Désire" had a large, dedicated following. She had reworked the prudish "Tips for Girls" column inherited from the previous editor into a no-holds-barred, monthly sex romp—with tips. Most columns featured Lucia's own escapades or those that she said were hers. In her younger years, she had slept with dozens of men, in hundreds of different locales, and tried numerous, often highly gymnastic, sexual positions. She had also used every fruit and vegetable as a sex toy, had licked various dessert toppings and pie fillings off sex partners, had threesomes, foursomes and hosted orgies.

But now, after several years, Lucia was running low on racy anecdotes. Most of her adventures had taken place at the height of the sexual revolution. Now in her early fifties, she had tired of the legwork to come up with new ideas.

That was up to me. Now she would hear or read a snippet about some sexploit that interested her and send me out into the field to bring back the story for her column. I was used to taking her ideas—communicated through slurred, late-night voice mail messages; messy, handwritten faxes; and scribbled Post-it notes of all shapes and colors—and translating them into neatly typed article ideas. She could've, of course, done this herself, but she couldn't type.

"Good morning, Angela," she said, looking up from a stack of magazines and peering at me over the top of tiger-striped reading glasses. She spoke with the flattened vowels of Upstate New York. Because she thought Botox caused lymphoma, her face was sturdy and lived in, age forming a gentle network of crevices.

"What've you got?" She spoke in her "impatient voice." A white cord hung from her left ear, and she thumped her fingers to the pounding base of 50 Cent. I paged through a wire-bound notebook I used to jot down ideas. Ghost-writing a sex column didn't come naturally to me, though I was pretty good at it. I was sexually inexperienced, having slept with only two other guys, in college, before Keith.

Making love with Keith wasn't honing my skills in bed. It was like plopping down into a comfortable armchair in front of the TV. I felt at ease, unpressured, and knew what to do and what to expect, but not much in the way of passion. It was harder and harder to remember the times when Keith and I made muffled, messy love on the floor of the graduate library, under stacks of books about the years of slavery, before Columbus. Was it really us who, during an overnight road trip to Florida, pulled our rental car into a darkened driveway in a Charleston suburb and had sex in the backseat, too overwhelmed with lust to make it to a rest stop?

Making love with Keith was more interesting when I didn't control my thoughts. Not thoughts exactly, but one thought, a memory that wouldn't go away. Two years ago, at a drunken bachelorette after party, after the other guests had thinned out, I found myself alone with the bride, my sophomore roommate. Lying on her bed, me dressed in my butt-ugly bridesmaid dress, her in the elegant strapless gown she was to get married in next month, we swigged a bottle of warm champagne.

"Lana, why would you make me wear this ugly thing?" I said, kicking my legs in the air, and letting the shiny, peach-colored skirt fall stiffly to my waist. "I look like a Southern madame . . . of a whorehouse. Why do you get to wear Badgley Mischka, and I'm stuck in the frigging Belle Watling collection?"

"Cuz, I have to marry Conrad Moore and you don't." She burped loudly.

"Bee-otch." I smacked her playfully and handed her the bottle.

"Here, let's trade. You be Mrs. Moore and I'll be Miss Jezebel," said Lana, slurring. She set down the bottle and began clumsily unzipping her dress.

We stood looking at ourselves in the full-length mirror on the back of her bedroom door, heads together, laughing until we cried. She looked ridiculous—as anyone would—in the bridesmaid train wreck, which was way too tight, especially the bust. I swam in her gown, my breasts too small for her size 38 C cup. When she reached around me to grab the champagne, we both fell over, giggling wildly. Somehow in the mash up of raw silk, chiffon and taffeta our lips crushed together. We kissed hungrily, me on top, until Lana finally sighed and passed out.

"Lana?" I touched her face lightly, and she sighed again more deeply. She was fast asleep.

Disappointed, I carefully tugged her out of the bridesmaid dress and hung up the two dresses. Squished next to each other in the closet, they looked like two pretty girls in love. After pulling Lana to the bed and easing her under the covers, I watched her sleep. Her mouth was parted slightly, a half smile on the lips I had kissed, sucked and bitten. After an hour, I slugged down the rest of the champagne and left.

Lana and I never spoke about what had happened, but for a year, I savored the memory of the kiss. It made sex with Keith much more interesting. Until shame began to replace the sweet-sour taste of champagne on her tongue, the fruity smell of her shampoo and the cushiony feel of her lips. Now whenever I thought of that night, I'd squeeze my fists tightly, digging my nails into my palms and force it from my mind.

Despite my own sexual history, I enjoyed my work. Studying sex and all of its freaky excesses for Lucia made it a curiosity, like an interesting subject I wasn't majoring in. And I liked Lucia and envied her bawdy openness. She really loved sex, and her column was neither a cheap publicity stunt nor a transparent ploy to lure readers. The sexual revolution had been the high point of her life, and she didn't want to let it go. She wanted to share her joy of sex. She was the fast girl in seventh grade who taught you how to prop your heel on the edge of the toilet seat and insert a tampon or flick your tongue to

French kiss. She wasn't a sex freak; she was trying to be helpful.

"Lucia, here's my idea: 'Honeymoon Surprise.'" I began flipping through my notebook. "I'd like to interview a guy I met who's into cuckolding."

"Hmmm, what's that? she asked, absently fingering an unlit, hand-rolled cigarette. She had quit smoking two years ago, after her father died of emphysema—a story she trotted out early and often. She was always jonesing for a smoke, and that cigarette had become her talisman, as familiar as Anna Wintour's sunglasses. All of us on staff knew that when she stroked it, she was thinking; if she actually put it in her mouth, intrigued; and if she put it down, she was bored silly.

"I guess it would be easiest to explain it as interracial polygamy," I replied, crossing my legs under her desk.

"Gawd, no." She moved her hand from the cigarette and fiddled with her iPod. "You know we've covered polygamy ad nauseum. Neither of us is welcome in the state of Utah."

"Wait, here's a better way to describe it," I said quickly, keeping my voice calm. "This is a married white man who hires a black guy to have sex with his wife while he watches. I guess 'cuckold' describes the husband."

"Geez, Angela, you always surprise me. Where the hell did you hear about this twisted antebellum fever dream?" she said. Ha—the dark-chocolate stud was my fourth cousin, putting himself through Stanford. At our family reunion, I had asked how he was paying for B-school, and he had guiltily spilled his guts. Lucia picked up the cigarette and rolled it between her thumb and index finger. And smiled.

"I don't know where you come up with this shit, since you seem like a prude. But I like it."

Before I could savor the moment, she barked, "What else?" The cigarette was back on the desk blotter.

"Well, let's see." I flipped through the little notebook again. Then I raised my head and said the one thing that made my stomach lurch.

"I was thinking about covering this lesbian sex conference thing that's being put on by some women at New Amsterdam University where my fiancé teaches." The words tumbled out quickly, before my superego was able to snatch any of them and stuff them back inside.

"Lesbians again—bor-RING." She feigned a yawn. "Didn't I just write about having sex with my ex-boyfriend's sister? And I definitely did a review of lesbo porn videos already."

"Well, this is a bit different," I insisted, squaring my shoulders and staring down Lucia. "This is a lesbian sex *conference*."

"Conference, that sounds extra bor-RING," she said. I looked at her hand; her index finger was touching the cigarette. Thank God. I wanted to go to this sex conference and see Cait again, but I needed a reason. I was going to make Lucia give me a reason. "What do lesbians have to confer about?"

"I see this as more of an issues-oriented gathering," I said, my voice rising an octave. I pulled the flyer Caitlin had given me from between the pages of my notebook and glanced down at it. There wasn't much information there. I noticed the words "closed to the press" printed in small letters in the lower right corner. I folded it quickly and stuck it back into the notebook. "It'll be, you know, political since it's college students."

"I don't know about this, Angela." She stroked the cigarette and furrowed her brow slightly. "Will it be arguments about butch/femme, pro or con—that sort of thing, you think? Maybe fights about whether bisexuality is a betrayal or is it political to use a dildo? Insider gossip about celebrity girl-on-girl action? Give me something to work with here."

"Lucia, I just need to send one e-mail." I spoke firmly in a tone my mother used. I put extra emphasis on her name. "I can get you some real information about this and pitch it again."

"Yeah, fine." She put the cigarette down and switched from 50 Cent to the Dixie Chicks. Clearly, I was dismissed.

Chapter 4

To: cgetty@newamsterdam.edu
From: angela_w@brice-castle.com
Subject: sex conference?
CC:
BCC:
Attached:
   Caitlin: I met you the other day at New Amsterdam. I hope you remember me. I'd like to find out more about your sex conference. Sincerely, Angela Wright

To: angela_w@brice-castle.com
From: cgetty@newamsterdam.edu
Subject: re: sex conference
CC:
BCC:
Attached:
   How could I forget? Call me Cait. Let's get together tomorrow at Cookie's. Does 7 P.M. work? I have a break between classes and meetings. –C

To: cgetty@newamsterdam.edu
From: angela_w@brice-castle.com
Subject: re: re: sex conference
CC:
BCC:
Attached:
  Yes, good. I look forward to seeing you. Angela

To: angela_w@brice-castle.com
From: cgetty@newamsterdam.edu
Subject: re: re: re: sex conference
CC:
BCC:
Attached:
  P.S. Don't bring your fiancé.

Chapter 5

I walked up to the front of Cookie's at about 6:45, horrified to be arriving early. That seemed so utterly eager and desperate. But maybe it was better to have Cait walk in and see me sitting back, relaxed and cute, than for her to spot me pacing up and down Columbus Avenue looking anxious, disheveled and crazy. I wanted to seem cool—not too excited—but my real feelings were betraying me.

Cookie's was a funky dive uptown not far from that other university. It served small vegetarian meals, herb tea, wine and beer, and sometimes featured folky live music. It had a definite lesbian vibe, which was why I usually avoided it. I had been dragged there a few years ago with Oz, a friend from college. He lived on the Upper West Side and had been on a health kick and had stopped eating meat altogether. Over seiten stir-fry, mashed sweet potatoes and two glasses of syrah, Oz confessed that he thought it would be very hot to do it with two women. I'd been secretly wondering what it would be like to do it with one woman. He had giggled and looked at me expectantly.

"Oz, you need to pick up two women here then, because

I'm not going to be one of them." I had laughed nervously. He'd always felt more like a brother than anything else. I'd hoped he wasn't flirting with me. "You see anyone or any two you like?"

We had both looked around. No good prospects for him. Or for me if I had been seriously looking, not just playing this secret, silly little game with myself. This was not exactly the *L-Word* crowd. Oz had shrugged sheepishly and we'd both laughed.

Oz wasn't with me tonight, though. I was alone in a lesbian-centric restaurant. Was everybody staring at me? I walked quickly through the small restaurant hoping not to attract attention. When I lifted my head and looked around briefly, I realized how well it was working: No one was paying me any mind. A group of college-age men and women were crowded onto a paisley couch in front of a tableful of books. They were drinking coffee and quizzing each other for an exam of some sort. Next to them, two women sat in thick, dark wood chairs, sharing a sandwich and staring lovingly at a baby in a bouncy seat on top of their table. Nearby a group of women, a sports team I guessed judging from their bloody knees and mud-smeared faces, was drinking beer, jabbing each other and talking loudly.

I made my way to the back, which was dimly lit by a small antique lamp. I sank down into a puffy sofa, and tried to look natural as I waited for Cait. I pulled out a magazine—oops, my own—then shoved it back into my bag. I didn't want her to see me reading *that*. Or any magazine. Cait and her crew didn't seem too keen on the "press." It was a little dark for reading anyway.

Thankfully, I didn't have to wait long. Cait strode in, a few minutes early, looking as fresh as first thing in the morning. She was wearing a light blue sweater, low-cut jeans, her hair slightly damp. Walking through Cookie's, Cait's stride was comfortable and confident as she looked around for me. She stopped briefly to touch the shoulder of one of the girl jocks, probably a student of hers. Then she spotted me in the back. She smiled big, her face genuinely joyful. As she hugged me tightly, I devoured her scent—Ivory soap and hand-washed laundry hung outside to dry.

"You are beautiful," she said, looking me up and down, in a way that was appreciative rather than lascivious. There it was, "beautiful." For a moment I felt just that. "I'm glad to see you." I was surprised, because she meant it. She was stripped of pretense—no air kisses or sarcasm or prideful holding back.

Her directness was startling and refreshing. I wasn't used to that, even from men, who tended to use tired pickup lines cribbed from R Kelly. Before Keith, the kind of men I had dated pursued their attraction in some circuitous, careful way. Keith had been mannerly and cautious, taking correct baby steps into our relationship. Before him, I had used an intermediary, a yenta of sorts. "Find out if he likes me before I like him." After that, I had fallen into one or two relationships almost by default or by accident with a couple of men in college. We had been too polite to admit that sex should've been a one-night stand, rather than drunken, accelerated intimacy turned into ill-fitting, three-month couplings. Nothing was wrong with any of these men, but nothing was exactly right either. *It's not you*, I wish I could have told each of them at the awkward end of the affairs; *it's your gender.*

"Thanks." I felt shy, giddy and goofy all at the same time.

"Can I get you anything to drink?" Cait asked, looking at me with the directness that seemed her trademark. I noticed the suggestion of her British accent again.

"Uh, yes, I'll have . . ." and then I stopped. I couldn't think of what to say. This should've been the easy part, the drink. Not THE DRINK. But the decision seemed suddenly weighted. A few seconds passed. Cait tilted her head to the side, staring at me with amusement.

"Um, yes, I'll have a scotch. On the rocks. With a twist of . . . lime." At least I had said something, but why that? I didn't even like scotch. Did people drink it with lime? Why was I ordering some old man's brown drink? I sounded like my own grandfather.

"Well, they don't serve hard liquor here, but they have this great homemade beer." Cait spoke smoothly, helping me through the uncomfortable moment. "I'm having one; I'll get you one, too, if that's okay."

"Sounds good."

As Cait went up to the bar to get the drinks, I was starting to feel much more nervous. My forehead and underarms were damp with sweat, and I seemed to have developed a slight tic in my right eyebrow. I felt the hiccoughs coming on. Get it together, girlfriend. Girlfriend? Calm down and don't call yourself girlfriend. This does not mean you're a lesbian. This means nothing. You are doing research. With a woman you are attracted to. For an article your boss may not want about a conference the media is barred from. Relax. Do that deep breathing exercise you wrote about in your magazine. In through the nose, out through the mouth, in through the nose, out through the mouth.

Oh no, I was doing it too quickly. Blinking, I thought, *Oh God, I'm hyperventilating; Cait is going to come back and find me passed out.* I needed something to breathe into. A paper bag? Where the hell would I get a paper bag now? I pushed my face into my purse—Kate Spade, real; I'd gotten it at a sale at work—and sucked in air that smelled like lipstick, sugarless gum and a piece of chocolate cake left over from a lunchtime birthday celebration. The cake was wrapped in a napkin next to my engagement ring. Phew, that was better. I pulled my head out of the bag and looked around to make sure Cait hadn't seen me, but she was exchanging niceties with the beer tender. *Okay, more slowly, in through the nose, out through the mouth.* That was much better.

Cait returned to the table with two beers that looked thick as stew. "Here you go." She put the sweating, oversize mugs in front of us. She looked at me more closely. "Are you okay? You look a little flushed."

"Yes, I'm warm." I removed my jacket and fanned myself like one of my great-aunts having a hot flash in church. I was wearing a stretchy sleeveless turtleneck and felt self-conscious and semi-naked.

"You have lovely skin." Cait ran the back of her hand from my shoulder to my elbow. This was not helping me relax, but I didn't want her to stop touching me. I needed to get hold of myself. It took the willpower of several people for me to gently pull my arm away.

"Well, er, I wanted to ask you some questions about your conference. I mean, what is a lesbian sex conference, anyway? Is lesbian sex so complicated that lesbians need to share tips? Is it informational, for straight women?" I was speaking so rapidly that I could hardly understand what I was saying. Why was I talking like a member of the White House press corps?

"Which question should I answer first?" Cait rested her cheek on her hand and looked at me intently. Her cheeks were flushed, too, and her eyes that bright, gunmetal gray. I shut my mouth, and smiled.

"Yes, the sex is so complicated that lesbians don't even agree on what lesbian sex is, so there are endless areas of debate." I liked that she was funny. But more, I liked sitting so close to her that I could feel heat rising from her skin as she spoke.

"Why don't you join us next weekend, and you can find out for yourself?"

"Will I need lesbian ID to get in?" I looked at her suggestively and felt a flutter of excitement. I liked this playful, sexy me.

"If you dump your fiancé, I don't think you need one." Her gaze remained direct. With the mention of Keith, the light moment had passed. I felt nervous again. Why was I doing some provocative Tracy-Hepburn verbal back and forth with a woman? Actually, with *anyone*. I wasn't the flirty type. I was more quietly straightforward. You had to peel off layers to get to my soft, sensual center. Outside of my job as "sex reporter," when the vibe became even vaguely sexual, my sense of humor generally left the building.

"Listen, just come on Saturday and find out for yourself." She smiled, and I noticed small lines around her eyes. I had called them "crows' eyes" when I was a child. I wondered how old Cait was. A little older than me. Thirty-five-ish, I guessed.

"I'll try," I said, taking a breath and smiling back. Cait took a swallow of beer, and set the empty glass back on the table.

"Good." Her voice was velvety and low. We made small talk for a few minutes more before she leaned toward me and brushed her lips very lightly against my cheek. A whisper kiss, like a secret. I moved my face back slowly, and looked into her eyes and lingered for a moment. I felt hot all over; even my hair and the tips of my fingernails were on fire.

"I'll see you Saturday." She stood, turned and walked away, moving quickly, with a wide-legged stride. I even liked the way she walked. There was something forceful about it. Not exactly masculine, but not feminine either. She didn't have that distinctive New-York-City-get-the-hell-out-of-my-way walk. It was something different. She looked purposeful, like she knew where she was going. As I stumbled dizzily out the door, I was the opposite. I looked like I had no idea where I was headed.

Chapter 6

I tugged open the door to my apartment still thinking about Cait, wondering if she was thinking about me. Our duplex, on 128th Street and Adam Clayton Powell, was the envy of our friends. Keith's prescient uncle Carlton had seen Harlem's potential in the '80s, and had cashed out his retirement savings to buy the apartment after the crash in 1987 when the market was in a slump. Since then, he had retired to the Cayman Islands, leaving us the live-in landlords of the roomy two-bedroom.

Keith had insisted on decorating our place. Though I liked bright colors and funky, eclectic furniture and artwork that didn't quite go together, Keith preferred things simple and spare, just short of monastic with lots of white walls, dark wood and shiny floors. He did enjoy collecting African-American memorabilia, including sculptures and paintings, scattered touches of Afrocentricity without looking like a Senegalese bazaar. He scoured yard sales and flea markets for African-American photographs. His prize was the 1894 graduating class of Meharry Medical College, all spit-shine and promise.

As I took off my shoes and placed them under a bench near

the door, I smelled her before I heard her voice—my mother's ever-present scent, the Blue Nile musk that she dabbed on her throat and behind her ears. That unmistakable fragrance made me think of her pushing through the busy African market at 116th Street to buy it, haggling in pennies and charm with her favorite Ivory Coast vendor. What was she doing here?

"Look who's finally home," my mother said as I walked into the living room. She was sitting next to Keith, practically on top of him, perched on the wide arm of our leather chair. At least I think he was in the chair; my mother's bushy, iconic hair was obscuring most of his face.

For the past decade or so my mother, Janet Wright, had been known as the Rosa Parks of hair. In the early '80s, after many years as anchorwoman of the *Five at Five News Hour*, and in the waning days of the Black Power Movement, my mother had decided it was time for the viewers to see the real her. No more shiny pageboy lacquered in place. "I don't need white women's hair to be legitimate," she had said to Daddy and me, as I sat dangling on the edge of his lap, my head buried in his shoulder.

With that, she had left the room, Daddy and I trailing her into the bathroom. She leaned over the sink, and we watched as her pressed, bone-straight hair disappeared and unruly curls sprang to life.

"This is me in all of my black womanness," she had said, using a pick, price tag still on it, to shape her damp, newly minted 'fro. That evening, she appeared on camera sans straightened hair, wearing a black and gold dashiki, the defiant afro crowning her face. Her hair filled the screen as she read the events of the day, sending shocked viewers to their telephones. After the first break, WHTV, the parent company, panicked, removing her from the air and triggering a three-minute blackout, the longest dead-air stretch in local news history. Though callers were equally horrified and thrilled, my mother was suspended indefinitely.

"Screw them," my mother had said when she got home that evening, her body brimming with energy and excitement. "I sent The Man a message." She disappeared from the room, and raced to the phone, spending much of the evening calling her network of "sister colleagues," and asking them to kick into action.

The next day, a nearly defunct local chapter of the Black Panther Party re-energized itself and organized a protest known as the Black Blackout. African-American viewers—or Afro-American as they were called at the time—and their allies turned away from Channel Five in droves. After two weeks of sinking ratings, my mother was grouchily reinstated. She became famous for that moment, frozen in time as a militant hair revolutionary. "It's MY damn hair," she had insisted, and this became her slogan printed on the fronts of T-shirts, posters and buttons. The hair that had made her famous, now streaked with wiry gray, was still wild and alive.

"Hi, Mom, hey honey." I leaned down and kissed my mother's powdery forehead, and patted Keith's cheek. "What are you doing here?"

"I was in the neighborhood, visiting Nona, so we thought we'd stop by and holler at you and Keith." She threw her arm around his shoulder and pulled him close to her. Keith grinned, resting his head on her arm. They looked bizarre, like some mismatched May–December couple.

"Aren't you gonna give me some sugar?" Nona asked, leaning her face toward mine. She was my mother's sister-girl from eons ago. She was clad from head wrap to toe ring in African accessories.

"Nice to see you, Mizz Nona." I pecked her cheek warily. My mother had met Nona back in the day on the first Sailing with Soul Cruise on the Mexican Riviera. They'd been friends ever since. Though I sometimes liked spending time with the two of them, tonight I wanted to be alone to replay my rendezvous with Cait.

"We picked this up for you; some nice man was selling them on the street," my mother said, handing me a small, old-fashioned straw broom with a carved tree-limb handle.

"Thanks, Mom, Nona, I'll pass this along to Cinderella, so she can use it to sweep our hearth," I said as I stood the broom against the corner of the end table.

"Ha, ha, dear. Of course that's for you to jump over. At your wedding. To Keith. Your fiancé. Now let's get out our calendars and set some dates." My mother, Nona and Keith looked up at me expectantly.

"WE aren't setting any dates, Mother," I said, nudging the broom with my foot and knocking it to the floor. "Keith and I will choose a date, and we'll let you know. When WE are ready. Right, Keith?" I shifted my eyes toward him without turning my head.

"Angela, do not speak to your mother in that disrespectful way!" Keith's voice was full of affront. He poked his head around my mother's hair and glared at me.

"Mrs. Wright is a big girl; she can take care of herself. Don't be a suck-up. She doesn't need you to defend her." My mood was worsening. I hated this pressure.

Feeling bullied and bulldozed by my mother had long been a source of irritation. I had gone into journalism because of her. Like everyone else, I was in awe of her—her bravery, her convictions and her activism. But rather than paying my dues as a reporter as my mother continually urged me, I had balked at her pressure. Instead, I had allowed myself to be recruited by the glitzy Brice-Castle human resources department as part of the "diversity initiative" and went to work for Lucia at *Désire*.

Did I really enjoy being the eyes and ears for Lucia's sexploits? Not always, but I had become extremely skilled at standing perfectly still. I was the "I-shall-not-be-moved" girl, giving no ground to my mother and her thinly veiled disappointment that I wasn't "living up to my potential." She had always pushed me, propelling me toward the next level—the one *she* wanted me to reach.

In kindergarten, she had rushed me to read, sinking her top teeth into the fleshy part of her bottom lip to fight back impatience as I struggled, slowly and painfully, through endless *Amelia Bedelia* easy-reader books. But the more she pushed me toward excellence, the more determined I became to hover around just-slightly-above-average. I felt she was pushing me not ahead, but away. I watched as she drummed her fingers as I dutifully recited the events of my day and scratched out addition and subtraction problems, eager for me to fall asleep so she could move on to bigger things—making the world a better place for millions of black women having bad hair days.

I had long ago stopped trying to keep up with her brisk, clipped pace. I fought back with inertia. My mother and I were stuck in some kind of dance of control, only I had willed my feet to stop moving. She could not make me set that damn date. And for a different reason, neither could Keith.

"Kids, kids, now shush," Nona said, waving her mannish hands in front of her. "Get me some more of this fine Courvoisier, would you, Angela baby?" She pushed her empty snifter toward me.

"Angela, Nona was just telling us about her upcoming lecture at your mother's church," Keith said, taking a sip of his drink and glaring at me. I stood up, and carried the decanter into our kitchen/alcove at the far side of the room.

"I know you've got a man, but I'd love for you to attend one of my workshops, dear," said Nona, raising her voice to make sure I had heard her.

In her Too Black, Too Strong lectures, Nona chided women—who were petrified by the constant threat of the black male-female ratios—for being too career-focused and scaring away black men. On her popular *Too Black, Too Strong* AM radio show, Nona reminded her listeners that while "career success is *all that*, you can't get ahead if you leave your man behind." Her favorite quip was "take a break from the fast track and spend more time on your back." She was Helen Gurley "Black" toting a "Sex and the Unhappily Single Black Girl" line. Nona's dirty-girl lectures were standing room only, and she was on the verge of signing a book deal.

"Nona, no disrespect, but as a feminist—" I began, my voice rising to meet hers.

"Child, please. Black women don't need none of that; that's for the white girls," she said, kicking off one shoe and tucking her leg under the folds of her wrap skirt. "Sisters don't have the luxury of being mad at our men. We have to stick by them for the good of the community. Black men have been beaten down by the white man. We have to support them, build them up, not tear them down."

"I hear you, sis," my mother chimed in. "Besides, I'm not burning this bra—I paid good money for it." They slapped five at the old, stale joke.

"Keith, help me here." I glowered at him, exasperated.

"Well, whites do accept you sisters more easily," Keith said. He took another swallow of his drink, raising his chin as though he were in front of a class. How dare he slide into Professor Redfield mode? "They're afraid of black masculinity. You know, intimidated by our walk, our strength and even our voices."

"Not to mention your big black you-know-whats." My mother caught Nona's eye and they both dissolved in hysterical laughter.

"Mom, Mizz Nona, come on!" As they continued to laugh,

I opened the bottom cabinet and pushed aside the fifty-dollar bottle of Courvoisier VSOP Keith and I had bought at duty free on our way back from a long weekend in Puerto Rico. I pulled out a twelve-dollar liter of E&J from the package store around the corner, and quickly poured it into the decanter. No business wasting the good stuff on tacky Mizz Nona.

"As soon as black women leave our men and join up with the white women's libbers, you know what happens?" Nona continued, holding out her glass. "Some white woman turns around and snatches up the brother."

"Yep, that *other* white meat," my mother said under her breath, nodding.

"Besides, you know, most of those so-called feminists are lezzies—except for the ones who are stealing our men." Nona shook her head so vigorously that her earrings, shaped like "the Motherland," clattered loudly. My mother nodded in agreement.

"I hate the word "lezzzbian," my mother said, finishing off her brandy and slamming down the snifter on a coaster.

"Mother!" Though I wanted to make her shut up, I didn't like the word either. It sounded sordid, like a part of the female anatomy you weren't supposed to say out loud. I thought of my sexy banter with Cait earlier in the evening, and knew that this conversation was too close to home.

"Mom, please stop sounding so narrow-minded—you have gay friends. What about that guy, Aaron, who did your TV makeup for so many years? Or Donny, your hairdresser?"

"As the Bible says, 'love the sinner, hate the sin,' " Nona added before my mother could answer. "But please. I am so sick and tired of hearing about gay people."

"Uh-huh," my mother chimed in.

"They have a choice," Nona continued, adjusting her head wrap. "They can choose to be gay or not, and even if they are gay, they can choose to pass."

"How are we going to hide this chocolate skin, this hair?" my mother said, grabbing a handful.

"As black as I am, I know I can't pass." Mizz Nona and my mother slapped five again.

"Sister Janet, look at the time," Nona said finally, looking down at her watch. Thank God. "We've got a reservation at Jimmy's at nine. Then we need to get you on the last train back to Mt. Vernon."

"Bye, Mama, Mizz Nona," I said hurriedly, pulling away from Keith as they stood up to leave. "Say hi to Daddy."

"Think about what we talked about, Angela—the date," my mother said. As she wrapped her arms around me tightly, I closed my eyes. Her hair brushed against my face.

"I love you, baby girl," she whispered into my ear.

"I love you back, Mama," I said as she walked out the door. The bouquet of Blue Nile remained in the air, clinging lightly to my clothing and stinging my nostrils.

Chapter 7

I slipped out of the house early Saturday morning, after explaining to Keith that I was attending a workshop on African-American women's empowerment. A little black lie.

"Excellent, now that's the kind of thing you should be doing." He kissed me sleepily. "Let me go with you; it sounds good. I might learn something."

"No, sweetie. I'm on assignment." I pushed his head back down on the pillow and pulled the covers over him. "Besides, it's a sistah thing. You know, we black women need our own space sometimes." Sistah? I didn't sound natural using that word. I seemed stilted, like I was speaking awkwardly in a language I hadn't mastered.

"Yeah, okay, I hear you. And, don't forget, we have that party to go to tonight," he called out as he turned his back and tucked the covers under his chin. I slammed the door of our apartment, itching with excitement. No matter how many times I dug my nails into my palm or forearm, I couldn't stop thinking about seeing Cait again.

The event was being held at the Jordan-Rustin Gay Lesbian Bisexual Transgender Community Center. It was brand-spanking new, converted from a rundown Presbyterian church less than a year ago, according to the Web site. It was an alternative to the more established gay center in the West Village. Mae was joining me, though I wasn't sure that was a good idea. I had tried to discourage her, but she had been pushy, asking too many questions and insisting that she loved my "freaky little fact-finding work excursions." Finally, she wore me down. She and I had planned to meet at a coffee shop on DeKalb Avenue to map out our strategy.

I had been standing in front of the coffee shop for a good fifteen minutes, and was starting to feel a bit annoyed at her for being late. She had acted so excited about going, so why not be on time? I had no idea what this conference was going to be like or what to expect, so I wanted to arrive early to get a feel for the setting and the scene. And look for Cait.

I liked the city post-dawn. It was interesting to see who was out and about. Not many people at this moment, save for a few families getting an early start on the day's activities; some cheerful drunks, stumbling home; and a portly working girl— a woman with a huge afro, oversize Jackie-O sunglasses, knee-high heeled boots and a tiger-print micro miniskirt. I wondered what she was doing in this neighborhood at this hour; maybe a breakfast booty call. From a distance, she looked clean and healthy—unlike the wasted, tore-up sex workers I had seen trolling 10th Avenue in Manhattan offering blow jobs to truckers en route to New Jersey. As she got closer, I realized that the oversize afro was most likely a wig, and that girlfriend was most likely boyfriend. Then, to my surprise, sister-guy waved, and flashed a gummy smile.

"Oh God, who the hell are you supposed to be?" I gasped, my jaw dangling open.

"I am incog-Negro," she said, looking at me over her shades. "This could be a hoot, but I still don't want anyone at this lezzie sex conference to recognize me."

"Don't worry." I grabbed her arm. Actually, as I examined

her, she didn't look that bad. The whole Foxy Brown cum Divine Brown thing kind of worked. "Come on, let's not be even later than we already are."

The scene at the Jordan-Rustin Center was bustling as we walked through the glass doors to the registration table. The lobby was filled with women of all shapes and sizes and colors, and there was a crackling excitement in the air despite the early hour. We approached the long registration table, manned—wo-manned—by an officious-looking woman about my age—a young Miss Jane Hathaway. Her name tag read "Lindsey." She was flanked by two bulky female bodybuilders, standing sentry in front of the roped off entrance. There was no fee to get in, so I guess the trio was merely providing security of some type, stamping the hands of entrants with two inky interlocking women symbols. The three women were sitting under a lavender banner that read "Welcome to the First Annual Lesbian Sex Conference."

As Mae and I tried to enter, the woman seated looked up.

"Just a sec," she said, smiling nervously.

"Maybe you didn't see the sign?" Looking at Mae, she gestured toward a small piece of paper, hastily taped below the welcome banner: "Women Born Women Only." And "No Penises on the Premises."

"You can get to the Transgender Safe Space by going out that door, and walking through the parking lot and around the corner to trailer A." She spoke quickly before turning her attention back to her registration list.

Uh-oh, I thought. I guess this was their not-so-subtle way to keep men—former and future—out of the conference. My God, why did transgender people need a "safe space"?; was there some danger here? I wondered just how many men who had become women and who were now lesbians wanted to enter. I guess enough to try to exclude them. But why shouldn't they come in? Maybe no one was sure who had what. How did they check? Were they actually going to try and feel up Mae hunting for, what, falsies? Silicone? I prayed that there was no panty check. Mae wouldn't be having that.

Mae had missed the entire exchange, busy watching a pair of punk-looking girls, pierced nearly everywhere except their eyelids, kissing greedily. Noticing the holdup, she looked around impatiently, and asked, "Is there a problem? Because if there is, we are press . . ." she muttered, rifling through her purse for her media ID.

I stamped on her foot, and pointed my eyes to the sign to the left of the welcome banner that read NO MEDIA. I glanced at Lindsey, whose thin lips were pursed, her jaw set in a determined manner that screamed "no way."

"What my friend—SHE—means is that we are *pressed* for time," I said, straightening my shoulders and trying to sound haughty and in charge—like my mother. "Is there someone else we can speak to?"

Now annoyed, Lindsey said, "Wait there," and stood up. Her two black-clad sidekicks stared us down. I felt nervous, praying that we were going to get in. Just then, the two young lovers unlocked their lips and looked up at Mae. One of them, the top of her hair dyed greenish-blue, whispered into her lover's ear, and the two gawked at Mae, eying her with worshipful awe. They stood up and walked shyly over to us. "Miss Gray," one of them said haltingly. "I love your work. 'I Try' is, like, my all-TIME favorite song. Would you autograph my stomach?" She pulled up her wrinkled T-shirt, and handed Mae a black Sharpie.

"Sure," answered Mae smoothly, winking at me. She scratched her name sloppily into the woman's skin just below her double pierced navel. At a very quick glance, Mae Green could pass for Macy Gray.

"Awesome." The woman gave Macy-Mae two thumbs-up.

She and her partner waved at us and walked happily into the conference, whispering excitedly to each other.

Lindsey had seen the exchange. "I am SO sorry, Miss Gray," she said, handing us each a schedule of the day's events. "I had no idea. Please, go in. Enjoy yourself."

"Thank you." Mae raised her chin and walked past them. I rolled my eyes. "You better knock that shit off, Mae. This is how rumors get started. Next thing, Wendy Williams will be giving Macy a 'how you doin'.'"

"Don't say *one* word to me," she hissed as we entered. "I am assuming we are ignoring the whole No Media rule, correct?"

"Correct." I looked around the crowded room, teeming with energy. Small knots of women were drinking coffee out of paper cups and leafing through the schedule.

"Hey, don't we know that woman?" I pointed to a petite blonde wearing tight jeans and a hooded sweatshirt, sharing a corn muffin with another woman. "Yeah, that's Melanie, one of the hangers from our advertising department."

"I don't know if I'm more surprised that she's here, or that she's actually consuming food." Mae pulled down her oversize sunglasses to get a better look at her.

"Who's that she's with?" I asked.

"The beautiful Asian woman that she's now tongue kissing? I think it's your last month's cover model," Mae said, adjusting her "hair."

"Did Melanie see us?" I lowered my head slightly.

"Um, I think the only thing she's seeing is that other chick's tonsils."

I was fascinated by the two beautiful women, making out so hungrily, but mortified that Melanie might recognize me. But at least I had the excuse that I was "on assignment." Neither of the women would know who Mae was the way she was dressed. I nudged Mae to the other side of the room. "Where should we go first?" I glanced at the sheet of paper in my hand.

"Come on, let's shop." Mae pulled me toward a brightly lit room with a sandwich board sign outside the door marked: SEX TOYZ R US.

We walked in and were taken aback by a very, very long table filled with every sex toy imaginable. Excited, Mae even removed her sunglasses. In my travels for Lucia's column, I had seen sex toys before, but never this quantity, and in so many sizes, shapes and colors. I picked up a purple dildo shaped like a whale. Next to it was a green and black camouflage vibrator. It looked like a round tree branch with a pint-sized, buck-toothed beaver sitting in the middle. I flicked the switch on the opposite end, and the beaver's head began to bob rapidly up and down.

"Look, Mae," I said, holding it in one hand, the whale in the other. "Environmentally correct vibrators. Do you think Green Peace is now in the sex toy business? I love it; save the planet sex toys." We both howled.

Still laughing, Mae picked up a thick leather belt, with a hole cut out of the middle and held it up to her waist. "Hey, Ang, how do you think this works?" She clumsily tried to fit a brown dildo through the hole.

"I think this one is more your style," said a voice behind us. Cait appeared, smiling and holding up a leopard-print dildo the size of a bowling pin in her left hand.

"I heard that." Mae giggled even harder. "You know size does matter."

"Hello, Angela." Cait placed the dildo on the table, and leaned toward me. Wrapping her arm around my waist, she moved in to kiss my cheek, but I turned my head slightly—and quickly—and her lips landed near the corner of my mouth.

"Hi," I said nervously, pulling away slightly. I glanced sidelong at Mae. She hadn't missed the intimate way Cait was touching me and stared at us frostily.

Cait didn't seem to notice, and turned to Mae. "Hi, I'm Cait." She stuck out her hand toward Mae.

"She's one of the organizers, a professor at New Amsterdam." I stepped back from Cait as I spoke.

"Charmed." Mae's voice was chilly. She offered her hand tepidly. "So, do you know Kei—"

"Cait, excuse me." A young blonde, whose name tag read "Jules, GALS FREE Coordinator," grabbed Cait's arm. She was flustered but her eyes, locked on Cait, looked glassy and awestruck.

"I'm sorry, but we can't locate the DVD of *L Word* sex scenes that's supposed to be showing in the Chill Out room. I'm totally panicked."

"It's okay, we'll find it," Cait said smoothly as she gave Jules's shoulder a confident squeeze. "Well, duty calls," she said brightly to Mae and me. "See you later," she mouthed as she passed me.

As I watched Cait walk away, I was stunned by longing. I wanted to run after her, touch her, even by accident, and inhale the air she exhaled. This was craziness: Was I coming out after thirty years, woefully late to the party? It was kinda hip to be a lesbian and even hipper to be bi, like I presumably was. So why was I so afraid, punishing myself for these feelings, acting like I had fallen into the "Well of Loneliness?" Women made out with other women on awards shows just to prove they had edge. Yet, as I watched Cait speak into a walkie-talkie before greeting a couple of women, I felt consumed with repressed desire. My feelings felt so raw, I knew I had to hide them. Standing in ground zero of lesbianville, I felt like a heathen walking toward the altar at a church called something like Mount Olive Baptist, somewhere in Alabama, all eyes watching me. The only one really watching me was Mae. She was watching me watch Cait enter a room with a sign out front marked, MORE THAN A TURKEY BASTER: MAKING LOVE, MAKING BABIES.

"What was that all about?" Mae asked.

"What do you mean?" I ignored her gaze, looking down at my hands. "She's the organizer, and I'm here *working*. Remember?"

"Angela, I saw the way you were looking at her and how she touched you."

"Hey, when in Lesbos . . . Anyway, let's go."

"You've got some splaining to do," Mae replied.

"Yeah, yeah. Come on, let's go to some workshops. I think we should split up to cover more ground."

"Sure, okay." She stood behind me, looking over my shoulder at the schedule. "This should be strange, but interesting."

"I think I'm going to check out Pleasure Power: Suzy G-Spot Shows You How to Find Yours," I said.

"I've seen Suzy G on cable access." Mae sounded excited as she peered down at the schedule. "I'm trying to decide between Don't Call U-Haul: The Perfect One-Night Stand and S&M: From Vanilla to Hard Core. What do you think?"

"No, look at this, Mae." I pointed to the workshop on the line below. "Nonmonogamy: A Political Choice?"

"Oh, yeah, I'm going to that," Mae said breathlessly, shifting from one foot to another. "We have that same mess, but the brothers call it polygamy and insist that it's an African tradition that's good for the race. But over here, they aren't supporting a village, but just screwing a bunch of women, having too many babies and not taking responsibility. Why? Because they can." Oh no. I hoped she wasn't going to start with that harangue again. Not here.

"All right, Mae." I shooed her off. "After polygamy and

pleasure—respectively—let's each go to one more workshop and then reconvene at registration later this afternoon."

"Solid." Mae headed toward the Audre Lorde room where her workshop was being held.

The Pleasure Power lecture had started by the time I reached the Melissa Etheridge theater. I had to sit in the front row, taking the only seat left. Suzy G-Spot was in full bloom. She looked like a plump flower, all shiny pink skin and dyed orange-red hair. I had no idea how old she was—maybe mid-forties. Clothed in a short yellow dress with a ruffle on the bottom, her style fell somewhere between Laura Ashley and Laura Ashley's bedspread. She was sitting on a massage table, her plump, freckled legs dangling over the side.

"Every woman has a G-spot." Suzy spoke loudly, with aggressive enthusiasm. "If you want to drive a woman wild, find it." A sign-language interpreter stood next to Suzy, moving her hands with an equal amount of zeal.

"Where is it, Suzy?" shouted someone from the audience. "I've got a date tonight, and I really need to know." The audience laughed.

"Somebody come up here and find mine." Suzy lay down on the table, and yanked her dress up to her shoulders, bent her knees and spread her legs wide. Needless to say, she wasn't wearing matching ruffled panties. "Any volunteers?" she asked, tucking a pillow under her head.

A woman, wearing baggy jeans and a wool stocking cap jogged up to the stage, grinning backward to the audience. "No, darlin', you've done me already. I remember you from my workshop last year in New Haven. Let's get a Suzy-G virgin."

Suzy lifted her head slightly and scanned the room. "You, you with the hair in the front, come do me." I looked around; Suzy was pointing at me.

"No, um, I'm sorry," I stammered, gripping the sides of my seat. My back was pressed so hard against the fabric, I felt like part of the chair.

"Come on, baby, don't leave me hanging. It's just a demo. You don't have to marry me." Nervous laughter rippled through the audience. Everyone in the room started chanting "do it, do it."

As the chanting got louder, I couldn't get out of this. I was too reserved to want to take part in this public sex show, but too polite to refuse. I walked up to the stage slowly, self-conscious and awkward, my backpack still slung over my shoulder. Suzy handed me a latex glove from a box at the side of the table. "Go for it, honey," she said. "You'll know when you've hit it."

I tugged on the glove, leaned down and stuck my index finger gingerly inside of Suzy. *Pretend you're a doctor, on TV, prepping a patient for gynecological surgery,* I said to myself. I kept my eyes locked on Suzy's pelvis. She felt moist but firm.

"Sweetie, I've had two babies, you got plenty more room. Put another finger up there." As the crowd switched to a new chant—"more, more, more"—I slid my middle finger inside of Suzy. Both fingers were rigid, shaking slightly. My backpack slid to the floor.

"Relax. Higher." She moaned slightly, her eyes squeezing shut. I looked away, not wanting to see her contorted "orgasm face."

"Scoot up, toward my navel. Now move your fingers around a little. Ahhhh, you got it, baby," screeched Suzy. I could feel the muscles of her sex organ squeezing around my fingers like a vise. Oh, my God, would I be stuck inside of Suzy? Would we have to go to the hospital, tethered together, walking inelegantly into the emergency room like co-joined twins attached in all the wrong places?

I felt a sudden movement to the side of me. The sign-language interpreter had thrown her head back, and was silently and, unnecessarily, mimicking Suzy, her hands moving wildly. Finally, I felt Suzy's body go slack, and the tightness around my fingers eased. There was no need to ask, "Did you come?" Gently, I pulled my fingers out of her. The signer walked over and held a metal bin marked "medical waste" for me to throw the glove in. Applause swelled around me. For a quick minute, I felt less embarrassed than accomplished.

"Thank you, sweetie," Suzy said, her eyes glazed. She rubbed her buttery cheek against mine and made a kissing sound. "Anybody else want to try?"

That was it? I thought. After the public intimacy, the connection we'd made, just that lame kiss? Not even the suggestion of a shared cigarette? An exchange of numbers? Hmmphf. Though this was highly weird and I was back to feeling beyond embarrassed, I also felt slighted, used, as I picked up my bag and walked toward my seat.

Pushing past me, about twenty women raced to the stage, forming a neat line on the steps. Each one, wearing a latex glove, like so many Michael Jacksons, stuck their fingers inside Suzy, producing shouts of encouragement and gales of cross-eyed squeals. After each woman finished, she politely kissed Suzy's cheek.

Slouching in my seat, my legs extended toward the stage, I took notes furtively, knowing that this scene would bring a cigarette squarely between Lucia's lips. Another great idea to add to the editorial bedpost. In just a little corner of my mind, I worried about the fairness of telling this story, especially knowing that the NO MEDIA signs were there for a reason. Would I be able to explain this weird, orderly and hygienic gang bang? Of course, I wouldn't mention that I'd been a banger myself. Would Cait hate me when she found out that I was a media spy, airing dirty lezzzbian laundry?

I pushed those thoughts into the back of my mind—though

the idea of Cait being pissed continued to worry me. Journalism, even practiced at the highest ethical levels, was a sordid business. That's why the best of the bunch had some line or some deceitful interview technique. Seducing people into revealing secrets and telling tales that were better untold was the goal, and done correctly it always involved dishonesty and sleaze to achieve it. I shouldn't feel guilty writing about Suzy G's escapades; she was putting her coochie out there, into the public domain.

But even as I sat there, thinking about my profession with Suzy G's orgasmic screams in the background, I knew that I hadn't gotten the juiciest tale. What was the deal with those transgender folk, and why were the "women born women" trying so hard to keep them out? Before the end of the day, I needed to take a trip to the "safe space." I stood up, and shoved my notebook into my bag, just as one of Lindsey's thugs walked by. I brushed past her, as she looked me up and down.

Chapter 8

I was still reeling from my Suzy G sexcapade but managed to attend a workshop called "Byte Me! Getting It On Online," before I pulled open the door to the transgender trailer. I walked past a security guard sitting in a chair. She was wearing a crisp blue uniform, the creases of her pants sharp as cut glass. A curly wig, ringlets piled high, was resting uneasily beneath her official-looking cap. The package was incongruous—eyes heavy with liner, she looked like a dancer, back row of the chorus line in Ma Rainey's *Black Bottom*, but costumed like a Confederate soldier. Her name tag read Rhonda. Man? Woman? Not clear. She looked me up and down, and then put a finger to her hat and nodded.

As I moved into the room, I found myself in the middle of a heated shouting match. A ragtag group of six human beings, men, women and some in between had formed a semicircle around Lindsey and one of the security sidekicks, Sheila. The austere white-paneled walls of the trailer created a stark contrast to the brightly dressed people inside. I had to stare pointedly and openly at hair, clothing and bodies to sort out gender. I stuck my hand in my bag, rooting around for my tape recorder. This was interesting; a story. Once I found it, I punched down on the record button.

"The rules are no penises and no 'men born men.' " Lindsey was shouting, her face contorted and eyes bulging angrily. Standing just outside the circle, my mind raced to figure out who was excluded: men in general and any transgender person. That meant no women who wanted to be men or men who wanted to be women.

"I didn't make the rule, but I believe in it," she continued. "Bio women who want to stay that way have a right to attend a conference and not be oppressed by men and their penises."

"Well, girlfriend, I don't HAVE a penis," said a tall woman dressed in a light blue St. John suit, eye shadow to match. Her name tag read "Helen." Dark brown hair teased gently and lacquered into place, Helen had a royal blue pocketbook slung over her shoulder as she walked in front of Lindsey, waving a finger in her face. It annoyed me that she said "girlfriend."

"I am all woman." At about 6'1" she hovered over Lindsey by at least half a foot, and stood about the same height as Sheila. Helen looked down at Lindsey defiantly, daring her to shout back. All woman on the outside, but still a man.

"Helen, which part do you not understand?" Lindsey's voice was shrill, her shoulders rising toward her earlobes. "To get in, you have to be born a woman and not now have a penis—period. You can't just buy a new body then force your way into a lesbian sex conference."

"So you're excluding anyone with money?" shouted a guy or girl of about twenty without a name tag and wearing a T-shirt that read "Boi Dyke." He or she was hyper and fidgety, eyes blazing with excitement and energy. "That's cool. I don't have any money. So I can't get in, but some blood-sucking corporate lawyer can just because she's a so-called lesbian? Please tell me how that is fair?"

"The key is LESBIAN," Sheila shouted back, taking a step toward him/her. "You are not a lesbian if you're trying to be a MAN. This is not a safe space for women-women if it's filled with testosterone, real or synthetic!"

"Lindsey, Sheila, listen to me." A sad-eyed, soft-spoken guy took a step closer to her. Patrick was wearing a plaid shirt, sturdy work pants, and was stroking a straggly beard thoughtfully. Only slightly rounded hips betrayed his past as a woman. "This is my community, the place I call home. I'm not trying to oppress anyone or hurt anyone. Nothing has changed except my body."

"That is exactly what HAS changed—your body," said Sheila firmly. "You are not a lesbian anymore. Go to a men's sex conference. That's where you belong now."

I heard the tape recorder click off in my bag. I turned my back, hunched my shoulders and pulled it out. My fingers were sweaty as I awkwardly punched the buttons. As I began to slip the recorder back into my bag, it slid out of my hand, the metal and hard plastic hitting the floor loudly. Everyone stopped talking and glanced as me, as I scooped up the recorder and shoved it back into my bag. Lindsey's eyes cut to me nastily before she and Sheila stomped out of the trailer. As the flimsy door slammed behind them, the group began to rant and rave at once.

I looked around the room taking in the messy, eccentric jumble of anger and over-the-top personalities. Where did they fit in? Where was their home? Not this tacky trailer. Could they ever just blend? I glanced at poor Helen. She was still new to being a girl, and was overcompensating. She had all the trappings but none of the history, a work in progress as far as her female authenticity. Despite their high-fem exteriors, Helen and the other male-to-females exuded a kind of pushy air of assumption that screamed, "I'm always going to be a man." And Pat, though she had all of the tough-guy accessories of a man, wasn't wearing them well. She and the other female-to-males still possessed a mannered tentativeness that whispered "woman inside."

I think I understood this transgender pain better than most. Though I had been "black born black" for almost thirty years, every day I wrestled with the tyranny of striving for authenticity. Being black—or black enough—was much harder to pull off than being a real woman or man.

Feeling out of place helped me understand the struggle to belong. Growing up, I had never felt really black. Despite having a black "she-roe" of a mother, or because of it, I had spent much of my life being called "white girl." Being black, the right kind of black, was difficult. It was like being in a cult—no—a secret society with rules as fluid as waves. You had to know the right language, the right music, the right dance steps, and, of course, the right handshake. But it all kept changing. It helped to have the right pedigree. The perfect black resume was an upbringing in the hood—South Central, Harlem or the South Side of Chicago—and then an ABC program to get into prep school. That was followed by Ivy League and maybe a master's or law degree or med school, which allowed entrée into a high-paying job in law, finance, publishing, medicine, music or advertising. But no matter how much money you made, you had to give back to the community and visit often, secretly as much to keep up with the music and dance moves as to see your peeps. At home, you easily slipped back into the slang and referred noisily to people you grew up with as "bruh" or "dawg," "girl" or "homes."

You could never forget where you came from and never directly mention where you went to school. If someone asked, you referred obliquely to Boston, not Cambridge; Connecticut, not New Haven; the Bay Area, not Palo Alto, to avoid appearing biggety.

I never, ever spoke of this struggle to be the "best black," afraid that it would sound like I didn't want to be black at all, like those folks who constantly and casually pointed out their "Native American" roots.

I snapped off my tape recorder and moved quickly toward the door. Rhonda tipped her hat as I slipped quietly out of the room in search of Mae.

I walked back into the main building and looked around. I felt someone grab my arm and turned to see Cait flanked by a pink-cheeked Lindsey, Sheila and the other black-clad henchwoman. "What's the deal, Angela?" Cait's gray eyes were ablaze. "Lindsey and Sheila saw you with that tape recorder. The word is that you're a journalist." The way she said it made *journalist* seem like child pornographer or baby killer.

"Tape recorders aren't allowed?" I asked, feeling anxious but also irritated. I was just doing my job here. "Where's the sign that says that?"

"There is no media allowed here." Cait raised her voice. "We don't want journalists covering what goes on. We're trying to do something important here, Angela. What are you doing besides infiltrating?"

"You invited me here, or have you forgotten that?" I snapped at her. No matter how attracted I was to her, *no one* could speak to me this way.

"Not as a journalist!"

"Hey, I was off-site, since that's where you stuck your transgender friends," I said. "And I am covering this, Cait. You can't put up a sign that says no media at a public event. That's against the law, at least according to the U.S. Constitution."

"Give me your tape," Cait demanded, tugging at my bag. "Give it to me now." I pushed her hand away, hugging my bag close to my chest.

"No."

"Give me that—NOW." Her mouth was an angry slash as she tried to strip my arms off the bag.

"Ouch, knock it off." I checked my arm to see if she'd drawn blood.

"Give it to me." She pushed me roughly, clawing for the bag.

"Okay—step off." I rifled through my bag, pulled the mini cassette from the tape recorder and threw it at her. I should've updated to digital. She struggled to catch it before handing it to one of her minions.

"So much for freedom of the press." I looked up at her and felt deflated. Though Cait was still angry, her cheeks streaked with color, her shoulders had sagged slightly. Her eyes were filled with betrayal and disappointment.

"Come on, Cait, can we talk later?" I didn't want this fight to ruin our vibe. Though I was afraid of my feelings for her—and hers for me—I didn't want them to go away. "Can I at least explain?"

"I don't want to talk to you." Cait spoke haltingly, through clenched teeth. "I don't even know who you are. Get out." She turned and walked away, the others in tow.

At that moment Mae came into the room, all smiles and enthusiasm. "Wow, what an interesting day," she said blankly, full of energy. "I went to Butches: Are They an Endangered Species? So interesting, so many issues in common with us. Did you know that butches are in short supply? They're just like professional black men in their thirties, who think they're God's gift. Can you believe that shit? Butchy women playing the fool just like men do. I signed myself up for a Fems Only list serve. We girly-girls have to stick together. Hey, boo, are you okay?" She looked closely at me.

"Yeah, I'm cool. Let's get out of here."

Mae and I walked out onto St. Felix Avenue, as the sun moved through the last moments of the late fall day.

"Thank you so much for coming with me today," I said to Mae, whose sunglasses were somewhere buried in her thick folds of synthetic hair.

"Hey, it was a scream." Her skirt was beginning to edge up, so she yanked it down with a hard tug. "I can't wait to tell somebody about this; I just don't know who yet. But when I describe the scene, I'll do a little editing. I'll make it seem more like one of those girl-on-girl porn videos. Closer to *Debbie Does Diane*, less *Boys Don't Cry*."

"Mae, I didn't get everything I needed," I said, interrupting as we reached the entrance to the subway. "I'm gonna go back for a minute." I had to find Cait.

"You really don't have time for that, do you? We need to meet Keith at Tatiana's party at eight, and you need to change." The party was being hosted by Tatiana Braithwaite, an acquaintance of ours, and perhaps the only right-wing black female member of the media elite. Somehow she was only a few degrees of separation from us. Mae looked at my jeans and long-sleeve tee, turning up her nose. "You know Tati's crowd. Those bougie blacks and corporate white folk will run you out of there if you come dressed like you're coming from Lesbopalooza."

"Yeah, you're right. But I probably won't have time to go all the way home . . ."

"Pass by my place. I'll dig up some little itty bit piece of something that will fit you, and we can go to the party together." I stood on my tippy toes to kiss Mae good-bye. I watched her descend down the subway steps, her afro wig bouncing up and down, before I turned and walked rapidly back to the Center.

I swung open the doors, and looked frantically through the

fast-dispersing crowd for Cait. Instead, I spotted Lindsey, who was standing on a chair carefully lowering the welcome banner. "Have you seen Cait?"

"Oh, for Christ sakes, not you again?" She gave me her back. "Haven't you caused enough trouble already?"

"Lindsey, just tell me where Cait is, okay?"

"She's chaperoning the GALS FREE party, which you aren't invited to." Lindsey shot me a wintry look as she folded the sign.

"Yeah, okay, thanks." I turned and headed for the door, trying to figure out who I could milk for information about the party—whatever it was. I felt a tug on the sleeve of my jacket and turned to see Suzy G, a long red velvet cape thrown over her ruffled outfit.

"Aren't you the journalist?" she asked, smiling seductively. Her eyes were friendly, crinkly around the corners. "I like your style, by the way." She winked at me, and I took a step back.

"Who do you write for, baby doll?"

"I'm covering the conference for *Désire* magazine." No point in being on the "low" about the journalism thing anymore, since the word had gotten out. I moved sideways toward the front door. Though I had had my fingers inside Suzy's major orifice just a couple of hours ago, I felt uncomfortable standing so close to her.

"Ooooh, I love your magazine," gushed Suzy. "Your editor, Lucia is it? I have so much respect for her. She is SUCH a freaking sexual revolutionary."

"Thank you so much." I spoke hurriedly.

"Umm, I'd love to be in *Désire*." She put a hand on my sleeve, smiling broadly. "That whole No Media thing is such bullshit. May I give you my card?" I nodded, looking over her shoulder.

She rummaged through the pockets of an overstuffed garment bag—yes, it matched her cape—and pulled out a tie-dye orange and yellow business card that reeked of patchouli.

"My phone number's there or you can contact me through my Web site. The address is there, www.SuzysGspot.com. Hope to hear from you."

"I'll be in touch." I turned, and began to walk rapidly toward the front door, then stopped short and turned toward Suzy.

"Ummm, Suzy, do you know anything about a GALS FREE party? I guess I missed the flyer in the registration packet."

"There was no flyer. It's a sex party sponsored by the group that hosted the conference, GALS FREE. It's totally underground." Suzy pushed a stray red curl behind her ear. "It's at Suck, you know the club in the Meat Packing District, just off the West Side Highway. It'll get going about ten, eleven tonight."

"So what's the party going to be like?" A conference was one thing, but sex party? Still, I had to get there and make things right with Cait. I'd need to shake Keith and then jet over there after Tatiana's party.

"It'll be hot." Sitting on the steps of the Center, Suzy lit a thick hand-rolled cigarette that she had pulled from her bag. The air around her smelled of cloves. "Stop by."

"Thanks, Suzy. Maybe I'll see you there." Suzy took a long pull on her ciggie, blowing out swirls of sweet smoke, before kicking off her shoes. I decided to get out of there before she took off any more clothes.

"You'll definitely see me, babe. I'm the party motivator. I've gotta make sure every girl gets her groove on."

Chapter 9

Mae and I were sitting in the backseat of a taxi, thighs touching, on our way to Tatiana Braithwaite's cocktail party. Mae was dressed spiffily in a Burberry swing coat with matching hat. I was uncomfortable in a very sheer blouse that was a bit short on tall Mae. She insisted that on me the blouse looked great, a "fun" dress, thrown over the snug, hip-hugger jeans I had on all day. Finished off with strappy sandals at least a half size too large. My feet were ice-cold, perhaps frost-bitten. I tried not to worry about the big lie I would be telling Keith about why I wouldn't be going home with him after Tatiana's party. Thinking about Cait, finding her, explaining what I'd been doing at the sex conference, made me at once nervous and giddy.

"Drop us here." Mae was tapping on the glass, waving a fistful of bills at the driver. He flashed us an irritated glance in the rearview mirror.

"This isn't her block." We were at the corner of 96th and Broadway; I was sure she lived at 98th and West End. "Hello— it's friggin' cold out here. I'm going to need prosthetic toes if I have to walk even one block in these stupid shoes. Plus, I don't want Keith there by himself too long. I'm sure he's there. You know he's compulsively on time."

"Shush." Mae put one hand over my mouth, and handed the bills to the driver with the other. "We need at least two blocks to get out everything we need to say about Tatiana before we get any closer to her place. You know it's tacky to talk about our hostess on her own block. And get your hand out of that bag. You are *not* going to change into sneakers to walk two blocks. This is *not* nineteen eighty-eight."

"All right, all right." I looked down at my feet. My toes were the same lavender color as the nail polish Mae had forced me to apply. "And, you're right about Tatiana. I'll go first: Okay, I hate her—you?"

"I hate her, too," replied Mae. She was struggling a bit in her own fuck-me pumps.

"Are we done?"

"No, we aren't going to enjoy ourselves if we're being phony, thinking about how much we hate her while we drink her liquor and eat her food. Let's get everything out."

"Go on then, Mae—why do you hate her?"

"I hate her icky right-wing politics. But I hate her even more because she's Miss Perfect," said Mae. "She's so good. She's got good breeding, she went to good schools, where she got good grades, she has a good job, she does good for the community, she has a good body, she's got good h—"

"Good what?" I looked at Mae out of the corner of my eye as I turned up my collar and ducked my head against the wind. "What were you going to say?"

"Nothing," answered Mae quickly.

"Yes, you were." I smiled, then stretched my lips to keep them from freezing in place. "You said good 'huh.' You were going to say good hair."

"No, I wasn't; okay, I was." She looked at me sheepishly.

"Come on, you know what I mean. Stop looking at me like that."

"I'm not looking at you like anything." I continued to give her "mock shock," staring straight ahead with my eyes and mouth both opened wide. "I can't believe you almost used the term good hair. My mother would die if she heard you."

"Hair!" she shouted, and we both looked at our watches. "It's been, I think, eighteen minutes. We're early!" We slapped each other five. Our theory that every conversation between any two black women moves to the topic of "hair" within a half hour stood unchallenged. In my mother's circles, it was even sooner.

"One more thing." We slowed a bit as we approached 98th Street, Tatiana's block. I wiggled my stiff toes. "She makes me sick."

"I think that is considered part of the 'I hate her' category." Mae rolled her eyes slightly.

"No, I mean really sick, physically ill."

"Really. You get nauseous or something?"

"Sometimes that, but mainly diarrhea." I was feeling a little embarrassed, sharing my body functions with Mae. "When I'm around her too long, I have to run to the toilet."

"God, Tatiana is your laxative." Mae laughed so raucously that she sounded like she was howling.

As we approached Tatiana's building, we stopped briefly in the lobby to pull ourselves together and apply lipstick. I took a deep breath and wiggled my toes again, while Mae slathered on a reddish-brown lip shade. The doorman pointed us toward the elevator, and when we reached her floor, I rang the bell. Tatiana opened the door and flashed us a brief but dazzling cosmetically enhanced smile.

"Helllllo." She put her arms on my shoulders, leaned in and brushed her cheek against mine. The scent of her custom perfume clung to my skin.

Tatiana was perfectly put-together, as usual. Her (naturally) curly hair was pulled back into a chignon—tight but not so tight that a few tendrils hadn't come free. It was the artfully artless look that took hours, gel, required double-jointed fingers and maybe a personal hairdresser to pull off. Her copper-colored sheath fit snuggly, showing off her slightly muscular arms and complementing her skin and hair. I recognized the dress from my magazine; I had seen it in an issue that wasn't on the newsstands yet. Tatiana looked like a Barbie doll, dipped in creamy milk chocolate. I felt juvenile and under-dressed in my "fun" outfit.

"Enjoy yourselves, please." She spoke cheerfully in her vaguely continental accent, a remnant of two years as a Rhodes Scholar and long periods living in Europe. It was well known that her mother was an Afro-German heiress, her father a diplomat, and that her parents now lived in Amsterdam.

Before I could respond to her greeting, Tatiana had turned her back and moved on. That was how she was: quick, quick, quick. It was the trait she was most known for. I watched her glide over to an older, slickly handsome man I knew to be the host of a cable television magazine show, and was again amazed at her talent for managing up. The room was filled with people who could help her career—TV producers, political pundits, newspaper columnists, people in finance.

Two years ago, at age twenty-seven, Tatiana had created a think tank called the National Legacy Foundation. That plus her very popular blog, The Braithwaite Report, provided shelter and cover for black conservatives like herself. She wasn't rabidly right wing. I thought of her as "right lite." She had a regular spot on *Your Point?*, one of those Sunday morning debate shows. Tatiana was paired with Otis Cousins, a mouth-breathing, scarlet-faced former state senator from Kentucky. Despite his corny drawl and string tie, Otis was clever and deeply progressive. He and Tatiana agreed on nothing; in fact, more than once, it seemed that only his Southern decorum had kept him from calling her an ignorant slut. Neither of them fit into their respective race-gender-regional boxes. When they were onscreen together, the whole black-white/red-state, blue-state thing was totally mashed up.

I looked across the room, and noticed that Tatiana was now deeply engaged in a conversation with Keith, who had come downtown, straight from home. She was gazing into his eyes and smiling. I had brought him to one of her little gatherings last year, and she had taken note of him appreciatively.

"Keith, tell me more about the African Diaspora Society," I heard Tatiana say as I risked my bowels and walked toward them. One of her hands was resting possessively on his arm, while with the other, she was tidying the food table—lavishly spread with sushi.

"Oh, um, it's a group of about maybe twenty-five students." Keith was standing with his shoulders thrown back, head high. He looked handsome, regal, like he was auditioning for Julius Caesar. How disgusting—he was flattered by Tatiana's attentions. I was surprised to feel jealous, given how much I'd been thinking about Cait lately and how much I wanted to find her right now. "We talk about ways to reclaim our power as proud African people." His voice had grown a bit stronger now.

"That's so interesting." She was gushing. I wanted to kick one of her freshly waxed shins. "You've got a new book, right?"

"Well, I've been sketching out some ideas to take to an academic press. You know, publish or perish."

"Uh-huh, right. What I think you need is a platform to get your really smart ideas out in the world. Let's see—reclaiming the power; why don't you call it the *Take Back the Race Movement*?" She raised her chin and a very slow smile eased from one end of her mouth to the other.

"Well, I . . ." Keith dug the toe of his loafer into Tatiana's carpet.

"I love it, and I'd love to interview you for my blog." I couldn't take it anymore and grabbed Keith's other arm, kissing him on the side of the mouth.

"Hi, baby," I said to him, staking my claim. I felt like screaming, "Get your claws off *my* man." Keith looked back at me, and smiled sheepishly. Quickly, his expression turned stern as he looked critically at my boho meets hobo outfit.

"Where did you get this sushi, Tatiana?" I asked, setting my wine down and popping a piece of yellowtail into my mouth. Gliding like I was on ice skates, I positioned myself between Tatiana and Keith. "It's delicious and so fresh."

"Oh, I made it," said Tatiana, looking past me, at Keith.

"You made sushi," said a wide-eyed woman standing nearby. "Tatiana, you do so much, how do you find the time?"

"Sleep is overrated." Tatiana replied. I had heard her say that each time anyone pointed to her huge talent for multi-tasking.

Tatiana was looking just over my shoulder, her gaze pulled toward the more important people in the room. Her eyes were flat and glassy like she was blind. I wanted to slap a pair of sunglasses on her. Actually I just wanted to slap her. Though it was ridiculous, since I had, less than an hour ago, admitted that I hated this woman, I felt slighted.

"I hope you'll keep in touch, Keith. I'd love to talk to you further." She smiled, continuing to look at him coyly.

Before I could hear Keith's response, I felt Mae's hot breath in my ear. "The bathroom's that way." She was pointing her index finger hip level. She was just in time; I hadn't noticed it, but Mae had seen my arm clutching my waist. Tatiana's powers had kicked in.

"Excuse me," I said, and headed toward the john. Someone was in it, so I rushed toward Tatiana's bedroom, hoping she had another bathroom.

In Tatiana's spare bathroom, I looked at my watch and

thought about how I could gently ditch Keith to go to the sex party. I had to talk to Cait. One thing was certain: I didn't feel good about leaving him here alone with that vulture Tatiana.

After cracking the window, I fiddled with my hair for a minute, before morbid curiosity got the best of me, and I opened Tatiana's medicine cabinet. Nothing good; just plenty of high-end cosmetics. I pulled open a drawer, lined with a large, purple satin sachet. I picked it up to get a whiff of lavender, my favorite scent, and underneath were a surprising number of prescription medication bottles. I picked one up. Part of the label had been rubbed off, and some of the lettering was faint. But I could see "deso-something." Was Tatiana ill? Did she have a sick, aging aunt stashed in an attic? Before I could take a closer look, I was interrupted by a knock on the door. I had been in there quite a while.

After I left the bathroom, I scanned the room quickly, and saw that Tatiana had wrenched herself from Keith's side, trading up for a Vietnamese songwriter who had just opened a hot restaurant. Across the room, Mae was keeping Keith amused with God knows what, and examining the sushi carefully.

"Ready to go, honey?" I asked. My face made it clear that I was. "What about you, Mae?"

"No, I think I'll stay for a while." She spoke over her shoulder as she made her way toward a group that included the rapper Hard Tyme and his producer, a Kevin Federline look-alike. "'Bye, kids."

I hugged Mae tightly. "Behave yourself, bad girl."

I looked around, wondering if we should say good-bye to Tatiana. I saw her talking to a small knot of her guests, nodding and smiling occasionally while her thumbs moved furiously over the keys of her BlackBerry.

I pulled my cell phone out of my purse and glanced at it. Though it made no sense, I was hoping for a call or text from Cait. No messages. I'm sure to Tatiana and others in the room, my absurdly out-of-it cell phone seemed as old-fashioned as a butter churn. It was so large that it looked like I had pulled an actual phone from the wall and was struggling to hoist it to my ear. But I didn't care: I secretly thought that people who used BlackBerries were short-attention span obsessive-compulsive workaholics.

Keith and I walked arm in arm up Broadway, not talking much as we sidestepped people heading home to their Upper West Side apartments. "Do you think Tatiana really made that sushi?" I asked Keith, cattily. I wanted him to say something bad about Tatiana. "I mean, she could've easily ordered it . . ."

"Well, she said she made it, so I guess she did." Keith could be such an innocent. Or maybe he was like most men, straight men, who claimed they didn't like to gossip, but actually never noticed anything, so had nothing to gossip about. I would give Mae a call tomorrow so we could really dish.

"Oh, my goodness," I said loudly and abruptly. "Keith, maybe I forgot to mention to you, I need to go back to the Too Black, Too Strong event for a minute."

"What, at this hour?" asked Keith, irritated, looking at his watch. "That doesn't sound rational. It's almost ten o'clock."

"I want to catch the tail end of the, um, empowerment event." What? What was I talking about? I should've thought this through earlier. "Serenity Divine Healing Circle, uh, for Positive Sacred Empowerment," I said, stringing together every "you go, girl" chestnut I could think of.

"What!?" Keith stopped walking and looked at me, very puzzled. "Angela, that doesn't even make sense."

"To you, maybe. But it's a black thing . . . a black girl thing. So you might not understand." I spoke firmly, clear that my mind was made up.

"Well, why didn't you say so earlier, so I could've stayed at the party?" He pulled on a pair of black leather gloves. I saw his mouth set, his jawbone jutting slightly. "Maybe I'll go back."

"No!" I grabbed his lapel roughly. He looked startled. "I mean, no, baby. I won't be long."

I eased my hands from his coat, and put my arms around him. Then I reached up to Keith, and kissed him deeply, pressing my body into his and moaning. "Wait up for me," I whispered hoarsely into his ear. I felt him press against me as he returned the kiss. It was a tacky, low blow, but I needed to get away from him and find Cait.

I stood still, watching until I could no longer see Keith's gray profile striding uptown. Then I turned and headed down the subway stairs toward the sex party and Cait.

Chapter 10

I stopped in front of what looked like a warehouse on West 12th Street, and squinted toward a curling paper sign that had SUCK handwritten in what looked like blood. Walking down a flight of stairs, I could hear the strains of electronic music pumping on the other side of the door. A burly woman wearing a skintight wife beater opened it. "Let me see some ID" She sounded like an extra on *Sopranos* reruns.

After studying my driver's license carefully using a high-beam flashlight, the female Corleone jerked her head toward the door. I walked into a very large room, old couches and easy chairs scattered throughout and dimly lit with dripping candles and several small lamps with scarlet-colored shades. Bright, pastel silk fabric was draped over the sofas, hiding stains, tears and cigarette burns. "Gurl Power" posters hung on every spare inch of the walls. I wondered nervously if this was a fire hazard; could one candle plus all the flammable cloth and posters turn this sex party into an ashtray? Would I end up like so many others I'd read about in the *New York Post* who had burned to death partying in crowded, sleazy after-hours clubs, later identified by my orthodontia?

I squinted through the darkness at knots of women sipping

beers and talking, next to couples making out, some lying on top of each other on couches. Sniffing the air I noticed smoke and looked quickly toward the door, but recognized the scent as a mix of marijuana, patchouli incense and clove cigarettes. At least I knew how to find Suzy. I glanced over my shoulder and saw the ad girl, Melanie, and her supermodel girlfriend squeezed into a dusty chenille easy chair, giving each other periodontal exams with their tongues.

I walked sideways down a short hallway, easing my way by groups of women talking closely or kissing. Women making out—it was weird, but it wasn't. Kind of like a lesbian porn without a stylist. Or maybe this was what a women's college dorm really was like. I entered a large room that had been transformed into a very crowded disco. It was entirely without ventilation except for a hazy undercurrent of sex drifting through what little air there was. Women were dancing close, pressed together in twos and threes, their fingertips caressing each other's bodies. Transfixed, I watched two women of about sixty clutching each other woozily, their wrinkled foreheads touching, as they locked eyes. Wistfully, I envied them for being so in love. In the corner on a raised platform, a dancer ground her hips to the music, eyes closed, her breasts bouncing to the throbbing bass. A few women looked at her from time to time, but only distractedly. She was little more than moving wallpaper. I was disappointed to see that Cait was nowhere in sight.

I noticed Suzy G standing by a staircase at the other side of the room and edged my way toward her.

"Hi, pretty journalist girl." She stroked my bushy hair softly, letting her fingers linger at the bottom of my neck. Lifting my hand, she brought my fingers to her lips, staining them with her scarlet lipstick. Gently, she moved it to her bare hip. Under her cape, she was in the raw except for a bright red satin thong. I tried to pull my hand away, but her grip was firm.

"You like my outfit—it's a Suzy G-string." Her boozy voice was punctuated by a deep, raspy laugh. "You're not bad looking." She cocked an eyebrow and squeezed her lips together into a little bow, gliding toward me. I took a step to the side and wrenched my hand from her doughy flesh, afraid she would try to ease it into an orifice.

"So what's upstairs?" I turned my head toward the very dark room at the top of the steps. I was feeling more than a little freaked out.

"That's our 'back room,' darlin'." She spoke dreamily, moving her hand in a slow, sweeping motion.

"What happens in there?" I asked, though it was screamingly obvious, even to me.

"Lots of love, lots and lots of love." As she spoke, Suzy reached into a little velvet bag that was hanging around her neck on a leather cord. She pulled out a white pill. "Here, have some E; you need to loosen up." I stepped away from her, shaking my head.

"Why so dark?" The room looked pitch-black from here, not even the flicker of a candle for mood lighting.

"Anonymity, baby. You can experience the essence of sensual pleasure without the distraction of some preconceived notion of desire."

"Huh?" Suzy was losing me again. People always thought they sounded so smart when they were high.

"Hon, attraction can get in the way of pleasure. Without any kind of attraction you can be completely free. In total darkness, you're judging your lover using senses beyond vision, so you aren't prejudiced by race or age or hair color or looks of any kind. And no one's judging you, so your self-consciousness melts away. You know what I mean? Unknown flesh is more interesting."

"Suzy, I didn't come here for pleasure—I'm working." I sounded high and mighty even to me.

"Journalistically, this is an experience you shouldn't miss. WWLD—huh?"

"What?"

"What Would Lucia Do?"

"BTDT," I replied. Lucia had already been to a lesbian orgy sometime in the early '90s.

"Just try it. Anonymous sex, particularly with a woman, will ignite your senses; it is pure and intoxicating. And, speaking of intoxicating, here, drink this. You need to relax, Brenda Starr. You're too young to be this uptight." She dug a flask out of her bag, which was tucked behind the staircase.

I took a long pull of cognac, which seared my throat. Well, of course I wasn't going to really have sex or be a part of this Sapphic orgy at all. I was just looking for Cait, but maybe I could get a story out of it. I'd just sit on the side and get an idea of the experience. Just enough to be able to describe it. Anyway, I'd done all sorts of weird shit for Lucia before. I could stay just a few minutes and then go find Cait. Or maybe she was up there chaperoning for GALS FREE.

"Good luck." Suzy patted my bottom, before lighting up another clove cigarette. She closed her eyes and inhaled deeply. "No talking, okay? Don't let words get in the way of your pleasure." God, lesbians had so many rules.

As I made my way upstairs, it got darker and darker. What the hell was I doing here? Maybe this was a bad idea. Why was I deciding what to do based on what Lucia—or Suzy—would do? Well, I was this far, why not just go for a minute?

I pushed past a beaded curtain and then pulled aside another piece of dark, heavy fabric hanging over a doorway into a room swallowed in darkness. It was quiet except for moaning, and stifled grunting and panting, covered by the strains of some kind of sultry world music. The room was cool, and I could hear the whir of a fan in a corner. The smell of sex moved lazily throughout the air. I stepped slowly, carefully, groping my way. I felt fingertips caress my ankle, before I stumbled over someone's bare feet, landing on the floor, cushioned by a soft, forgiving body part. I felt hands touch my arms, shoulders and neck. Alarmed, I tried to sit up and wrench free. But other hands, soft but firm, pushed me down. Lips moved clumsily across my face and landed on my chin, as they eased toward my mouth. Bare breasts crushed against my chest. I moved away, gently, pulling myself up and scooting on my butt toward another part of the room, a bit nearer to the door. As I collapsed against a bare spot on the wall, I felt a pair of hands grip my shoulders, massaging deeply. Ohh, that was nice. I could get into anonymous massage. The hands moved slowly from my shoulders, toward my breasts. I gripped the hands firmly and guided them back toward my shoulders, patting them back into massage mode.

All of a sudden someone struck a match, and moved it toward a fat brown spliff, inhaling deeply. In the dim light, I turned to face the boi from the transgender trailer. His—her?—lips were swollen, cheeks reddened. He smiled at me, as his hands moved south toward my breasts again. I realized that I had had enough of this "experience," and that it was time to get out of here.

"Is someone getting high in here?" A voice, harsh and authoritarian, came from the doorway. "Put it out—now. We don't want to give anybody a reason to shut this thing down." It was Cait—Fire Marshal Cait.

"Cait." I spoke in a stage whisper, detangling myself from the boi. I fumbled my way toward her voice.

"Shhhh—no talking!" Several voices hissed at me in chorus.

"Angela, what the hell are you doing here?" Cait spoke in the same callused voice, as she pulled me through the doorway.

"Cait, stop, we need to talk."

"Shhhh. Take that shit outside." A voice shouted through the darkness and then was muffled, probably by another pair of lips.

"Come on." Cait spoke angrily, yanking me down the stairs. I felt an electric charge where her fingers touched my arm. We passed Suzy G, who was urging a young woman toward the "back room." She turned toward me and Cait.

"Wow, that was fast. You go!" She said it over her shoulder, doing a little "raise the roof" motion with her fleshy arms. I smiled back weakly.

Cait yanked me into a semi-dark hallway and into a tiny room, a storage closet of some sort. She pulled the door halfway closed behind us. The space was tight and dusty and smelled faintly of disinfectant. We stood nearly toe to toe, and I could feel Cait's heartbeat.

"Okay, Jayson Blair, talk—and talk fast before I kick your lying ass out of here."

Cait's gray eyes were flat, and the inviting dimple nowhere in sight. She was wearing low-slung cargo pants and a tight, faded T-shirt that read LESBIAN AVENGERS. She looked more like a student than a professor. Her hair was damp and clung to the sides of her head. I wanted to run my hands through her hair and rake it back.

"Let me explain. Can we at least sit down for a minute?"

"Um, no. We're in a closet, Angela; this isn't a coffeehouse. Just tell me what the hell is going on, so I can get back to work."

"Okay, first, I'm sorry that I wasn't completely honest with you," I began, looking directly into her eyes. "I'm a writer and editor with *Désire* magazine. I came to the conference on assignment."

"A little sexual tourism for the women's magazine crowd?" answered Cait sarcastically. "You can laughingly brag about having five minutes of anonymous sex at a women's party. A lesbian freak show sandwiched between makeup tips?"

"That's not how it's going to be. Our magazine is very sex positive." What did she know about journalism? I took a step back from her, and bumped into the handle of a mop.

"Exploitive is what it is. I'm sure you'll do a really balanced report on the transgender issue—a subject your readers are hungering to learn more about." The sarcasm pissed me off.

"Hey, what's happening with the transgender folks is a legitimate story," I said huffily. She didn't look as cute when she was sounding so imperious.

"Not in your hands," she spat back. "You just want to air our dirty laundry, to make the lesbian community look bad. The right wing thanks you. I'm sure your story will be reprinted in *Christian Coalition Weekly*."

"You just don't want anyone to know that the lesbian nation isn't all that inclusive."

"Why should we include everybody?" Cait drummed her fingers on the edge of a shelf. "Why can't there be a space and a day and an event just for us, for women, without penises all over the place?"

"If you want to get away from penises, then don't sell them," I shot back, picturing those pretty multicolored dildoes all in a row. "What's the message—no penises on the premises unless we can make money from them? You're a hypocrite."

"You're a hypocrite. You're cool with the trans community as long as you're exploiting it to sell copies of your shitty magazine."

"At least I'm allowing them to speak for themselves and tell their story instead of stashing them away in a transsexual trailer park."

"You aren't telling any story, because that tape is becoming landfill as we speak."

"Fuck you." I pushed her as I moved toward the door, putting my hands on her shoulders to nudge her aside.

We were standing so close that our foreheads were practically touching like the two sweet older women I had seen earlier. I could feel heat rising from her, and smell her perspiration faintly.

"Good-bye." I bumped her shoulder with mine. This was turning very playground, sending energy surging through me. She snatched my arm, and I jerked it away. Then she grabbed the back of my neck and pulled my face forward, her lips hitting my mouth roughly. She kissed me, insistent and forcefully, and I kissed back greedily, my tongue bumping against hers. I fell back against the wall as she pushed her loose breasts against mine. I felt a rush shoot from my pelvis, which was pressed against hers, to the tips of my toes.

As Cait first gently, then roughly, bit my lip, I realized that Suzy G was completely wrong. Kissing Cait in this airless closet was better than the anonymous groping in the back room. I knew her just enough to want her more. Not too much, the way I knew Keith, predictable, once every two weeks, sliding his penis inside me, his eyes shut tight. But more than I knew the women upstairs—their minds opaque as they fingered and fumbled in the darkness, driven entirely by the physical.

"Hey, who's in there?" a voice shouted a few minutes later from the other side of the door. Cait and I jumped apart, startled. I looked at my watch.

"I've got to go." Oh, God, Keith. What the hell was I doing? I turned and kissed her again, my mouth lingering on hers, before I pulled away. I steeled myself against leaving her, and without looking back pushed open the door and rushed out. I heard her footsteps behind me.

"Wait, Angela," she said, pulling my arm. "I'll drive you home."

"Should you be leaving the party? Aren't you in charge or something?" I asked, grabbing my jacket from one of the sofas. But I didn't mean it. I wanted to be with her as long as I could.

"They'll manage," Cait said, zipping up her leather jacket and leading me toward the door.

Walking a few steps ahead of me and carrying a helmet in her left hand, Cait approached a lime-green motorcycle that was gleaming under the glow of a streetlight.

"Isn't she pretty?" Cait said as she stroked the black leather seat. "It's a 1973 Honda CB 450. A classic."

I smiled, but didn't answer, not knowing anything about motorcycles or the jargon that went with them. Standing close to me, Cait slid the little helmet over my head.

"It's a skid lid, the lightest helmet they make," Cait said, as she fastened the strap under my chin, tugging gently to squish all of my hair into the top.

"Hop on," she said, throwing her leg over the seat.

"We can't do this, Cait, you don't have a helmet." My voice sounded loud inside my head. "Isn't that against the law, not to mention dangerous?"

"Relax, it's late. I'll take my chances," Cait said as she turned the ignition key, gunning the bike. "I like the feel of the wind."

As she zipped up the West Side weaving around cars and darting through intersections, I clung to her, squeezing my thighs around her hips and pressing myself into her back. Holding her tightly since she was driving fast and a bit recklessly, I lifted my head from the back of her neck and snuck a look at her. She was exhilarated, her cheeks crimson as her hair whipped around both of our heads. As my head, helmet and all, rested on the rough leather of her jacket, I was exhilarated, too.

A block from my apartment, I signaled for Cait to stop.

"This is where you and Dr. Redfield live?" She pointed to the dusty, taped up brownstone in the midst of a renovation.

"Um, not exactly." I swung my leg over the motorcycle, holding onto Cait's shoulder to steady myself. "I'm several houses down."

"Oh, I get it—you're a lady on the low." She smiled as she took the helmet from me and set it on the tank of her bike. I looked down. "Listen, whatever. I am not intimidated by your boyfr—"

I pressed my mouth against hers before she could trash talk Keith any further. I didn't want to hear it or hear her at all. All I wanted to do was stand there, right out in the open, and kiss her. All night.

Chapter 11

Rumpled, my underwear damp between my legs, my hair squashed from the helmet, I pulled open the door to my apartment and prepared for my walk of shame. My emotions were scattered like photographs that needed to be pasted into an album.

When I walked in, I was relieved to see Keith dozing deep in the folds of our brown leather sofa. He had kicked off his loafers and was snoring quietly, a half-full snifter of cognac on the table next to him, PBS buzzing on the TV in the background. Should I just leave him there, sleeping on the couch like an old man? I could avoid breaking the spell of Cait. I didn't want to deal with his irritation about my crawling in so late and his insistent, detailed questions about where I'd been and what I'd been doing. And I really didn't want him to cash that sex chip I had gambled with earlier. I wanted to slide into the bathtub, open a book and stare at the words, while thinking about Cait. Plus, I was such a bad liar, that even these smallish fibs about the empowerment events were stressing me out. I picked up the snifter, leaned down and kissed the top of Keith's head lightly.

As I eased myself into the tub, I felt first guilty then annoyed at Keith. Even if he were awake, I doubt he'd even notice anything different about me. I had just made out with a woman and might be a lesbian, and he was in the next room snoring on the couch. I think if he'd been with some man, I would know. Would he look at me, touch me, smell me and still not know where I'd been and what I'd done? I almost wanted to shake him awake to find out. Did he think I was so utterly conventional that I wouldn't even consider lesbianism? Why did he even believe that crazy story about the "healing circle"?

As I took a sip of his brandy, I knew I was being irrational, working myself into a lather, mad at Keith, to avoid feeling guilty about nearly cheating on him. I sank deeper into the hot water and scrubbed myself with the woodsy soap that Keith preferred. Then I stopped. I didn't want to clean Cait off my body. I wanted her scent on my mouth, my neck, my hands. And I wanted to hold onto my own scent. That smell was connected to a me that wasn't shaped and molded and controlled by Keith or anybody else.

I climbed out of the tub and wrapped myself in a fuzzy, white towel. Tiptoeing, I eased my way toward the bedroom.

"Angela." Shit, he was awake. I stopped walking, held my breath and didn't answer.

"Angela!" He was clearly annoyed. "What time is it? Where are you?"

As I walked into the living room, I could see Keith's dark outline on the couch. In the dim light, I squinted so that his shadow became fuzzy and runny and imagined him dead. With a quiet gasp, his head would flop to the side, and he'd fall softly to the floor in a heap, like a shirt coming loose from its clothespin and floating lightly to the ground. Food poisoning, bad takeout, so sad, his life cut short. My God, I was a horrible person; what was I thinking? Actually, I didn't want him to die permanently, just right now, so I could be alone with my thoughts of Cait.

Instead, without speaking, I pushed him onto his back and began kissing him roughly.

"What the?" he began, but I pressed my mouth onto his, stifling his words. I felt free and wild and aroused. I knew it was tacky and even clichéd to get all juiced up making out with one person—a woman—and then run home and jump your fiancé, but I couldn't stop myself. I needed to first shut Keith up any way I could, but I also needed to have sex—now—while Cait was fresh in my mind and everywhere else. With her in my head, I hadn't felt so excited about him in months . . . or longer. Keith either; he had shrugged off surprise and his body was now taut with excitement. By the light of the window, I could see that his eyes were squeezed shut and he was holding his breath.

Keith practiced what he called "ejaculation control." He had taught himself "sacred sex," based loosely on the principles of tantra. To me, it seemed like blue balls with a spiritual component, but he never complained, insisting that birth control was a form of black genocide, "They," cap T, "have created these chemicals to kill Us," cap U, "and prevent the earth from being overrun with brown children," he explained. As his lips were moving, I had idly wondered where all that locked-in semen would go. Does the body just reabsorb it? I had no idea.

I appreciated not having to deal with birth control, especially condoms, but I also wondered if his passion for me had also waned. Now before we made love, he always took the time to fold his clothing—and mine—and stack them in neat piles on our dressers. I wanted him to burn for me, not tidy up like a fastidious old woman. Part of me wondered whether he was able to control his ejaculation so well because he just wasn't that excited.

But not right now. I pulled at the waistband of Keith's scotch plaid pajama pants, ripping the elastic out of wack and yanked them down along with his boxer shorts. I shook off the towel and straddled him. It took about a minute and a half of rocking and moaning, sweating and even shouting for me to throw back my head as my body shuddered with pleasure. Still panting, I looked down at Keith.

He needed superhuman strength to keep the semen bottled up inside. He was taking gulpy breaths, blowing them out through tightly pursed lips. The whistling sound of his little exhales startled me. I had been so absorbed by thoughts of Cait that I had forgotten he was there. Finally, he exhaled loudly and fully, and his body convulsed and trembled below mine.

A few minutes later, I climbed off him, and stood up. "Hey," he said as he sat up from the couch, fiddling with the waist of his pajama bottoms. "What got into you?"

"I don't know." I shrugged. I didn't want to talk or think or deal. I just wanted to sleep and dream.

"I don't care, but I hope it gets into you again." He reached out and grabbed my hand. "I love you." He said it tenderly, his eyes big and round, slightly glazed.

I didn't say anything back. How could I? My desire for Cait was blocking out any feelings I had for Keith. Though I had loved him—or thought so—at this point, he was merely in the way.

He pulled me back toward the couch and put his arms around me. I could feel need, no, *neediness*, dragging me like undertow. He must've felt the distance and his own vulnerability. It had always been that way with us: When I pulled away from him, he'd crowd me until I reassured him that everything was okay. Then he'd retreat—which was what I wanted right now, desperately. Why the hell did it take so much patience to be patient?

"Maybe next time I won't hold back, and we can make a

baby." He looked at me with little-boy eyes. "And then get married."

"Keith, we've talked about this." Annoyed, I leaned over and picked up the towel and pulled it over my chest. "I'm not ready." He didn't understand the half of it; me neither.

"Shhhh, not now," he said softly. He kissed me, this time using his lips to silence me. "Love me?"

All I had to do was say "yes," and I could savor my privacy. Part of me wanted to scream "I'm not sure anymore."

"Yes, baby," I whispered into his hair, and kissed the top of his head. I felt his body relax as he rubbed his head into my breasts. I stiffened, feeling ashamed and wondering what Cait was doing at that moment.

Chapter 12

To: freegal1@yahoo.com
From: angela_w@brice-castle.com
Subject: hey
CC:
BCC:
Attached:
    What's up? You aren't still mad, are you? Advise. AW,
intrepid journalist

To: angela_w@brice-castle.com
From: freegal1@yahoo.com
Subject: re: hey
CC:
BCC:
Attached:
    Only about you. Can we get together, duplicitous girl
journalist?

To: freegal1@yahoo.com
From: angela_w@brice-castle.com
Subject: re: re: hey
CC:
BCC:
Attached:
  Okay motorcycle-riding mama. When?

To: angela_w@brice-castle.com
From: freegal1@yahoo.com
Subject: re: re: re: hey
CC:
BCC:
Attached:
  Tonight, my house, 124 Sterling Avenue in Brooklyn.
Some friends are coming for dinner. But they'll leave
early. Come around nine. Bring your pajamas. No, don't.

To: freegal1@yahoo.com
From: angela_w@brice-castle.com
Subject: re: re: re: re: hey
CC:
BCC:
Attached:
  Okay. I'll be thinking about you until then. xxoo

To: kRedfield@newamsterdamu.edu
From: angela_w@brice-castle.com
Subject: late
CC:
BCC:
Attached:
  Sweetie, how's your day? Mine sucks. The Too Black,

Too Strong group has organized a Sisters in the Struggle Slumber Party thing. Lucia assigned me a story about the group so I have to go. I'm sure we'll stay up all night trying to figure out you "brothas." Ha, ha. Love, –A

Chapter 13

My hands were shaking as I pushed Cait's buzzer. What was I doing? Coming to this woman's house for what was obviously a booty call. Lying to Keith. I should turn around and take my confused self right out of Brooklyn and back home, to Harlem, to my fiancé, where I belonged. But I knew I wasn't going to. I wanted to be with Cait so badly it hurt. Real physical pain, shooting through the muscles on either side of my groin. I felt pulled to her by some crazy need I had only suspected I had. My voice was raspy as I leaned down to speak into the intercom.

As I walked up the stairs of Cait's brownstone on shaky legs, my sweaty anticipation was fast turning into fear. Did this mean I was a lesbian? Would we make love? I wanted to be near her, touch her, kiss her again and again and again—but sex? What would I do? Would she use one of those multicolored, animal-shaped dildoes on me? Would I use one on her?

Would I eat her? Do you actually consume it? No, I remember the last time Keith went down on me, hungrily, biting, sucking, slurping, devouring. I had been so afraid he was going to actually swallow me whole, that I feigned an orgasm, screaming like Meg Ryan in *When Harry Met Sally*, in order to get him to stop. It was better to lick it, I'd guess, slowly, like eating ice cream melting down the sides of a cone. Would Cait taste like ice cream?

I walked up to the third floor. Cait was standing, grinning, dressed in jeans and a white button-down shirt. Her face was shiny with perspiration and her hair damp and a little wavy. She pulled me toward her and kissed me, and I tasted tequila, tart on her breath. Salsa music pounded in the background.

"Come in." She tugged off my coat and scarf and pulled me into the living room. Two women were dancing joyously, and another danced alone, shaking her hips and moving her arms wildly in the air. I smiled, enjoying their exuberance.

"Dance with me," Cait said. With both of my hands in hers, she guided me expertly. She kept her back straight and her head high, while mine was lowered, eyes fastened to her feet. Cait was a skilled, sure dancer, and I did my best to follow her twisty steps and fanciful moves.

"Look in my eyes." I locked my eyes into hers and was steadied by her confidence. She pulled me closer to her, and I felt her hips gliding from side to side. I wished the other women would leave, so I could be alone with her. "Feel me, feel the music," she whispered.

The last few notes of that song synced smoothly into "Groove Is in the Heart," Deee-Lite's buoyant hit that took me back to my middle school homecoming dance.

"Angela, why don't you get something to drink, while I dance with my favorite girl?"

I frowned. What did she mean by that? She kissed my cheek, and I reluctantly untangled myself from her arms. Cait then walked to the side of her couch, leaned over and scooped up a baby who was sitting in a bouncy seat on the floor. She hoisted the little brown dumpling over her head and twirled her around. As Cait danced around the room, the baby laughed gaily, opening her mouth wide to show bumpy, naked gums. When the song ended, she carried the baby to the couch where a woman was sitting sipping a beer. The little girl gurgled and stuck a brown fist in Cait's mouth. Cait laughed and hugged her tightly. This was a soft, sweet side of Dr. Getty that I didn't know.

"Angela, this is Paulette, and her daughter, the love of my life, Josie," Cait said as she kissed the top of Josie's curly black head. Paulette, pale with Scandinavian-white skin, took the baby from Cait. Josie was a Sugar Daddy–colored version of her mother. "And this is her other mommy, Sara."

Sara had walked back into the room, loaded down with baby accessories. She was very tall, all arms and legs, and wore a wool cap over her short, spiky hair. She picked up Josie and began stuffing her into a pale-blue snowsuit.

"Hey there," they said to me almost in unison, preoccupied with collecting their baby's things.

"Oh breeders, you're flat-leaving without so much as a good-bye to your childless friend?" The woman who had been dancing alone emerged from the kitchen, a tall drink in her hand. Rail-thin with unruly black hair and light brown eyes that matched her skin, she spoke very fast. It was hard to understand anything she said.

" 'Bye, Stella." Paulette blew a kiss at her. "Oh, and you don't have to be childless. You can babysit Josie anytime. I've got my date book; how does tomorrow night sound?"

"You know I don't do babies." Stella took a big sip of her drink. She was wearing a tight T-shirt with "Children Are for People Who Can't Have Cats" scribbled on the front. "They're so . . . sticky. They never keep up their end of the conversation, they don't drink and they can't text."

"Good-bye, Stella, 'bye, Cait, nice meeting you, Angela." I waved at the mommies and squeezed baby Josie's plump thigh before they moved toward the door.

"Good to meet you, Angela. I'm Stella, Cait's ex." She

smiled at me, her teeth big and even, like rows of Chiclets. "You're here for the after party? Am I invited?"

"No. In fact, aren't you leaving?" Cait looked at her, pointing her pinky toward the door.

"No, *in fact*, I'm going to finish this margarita." She sat cross-legged in front of the brown corduroy couch. "No kids at the after party, right? And no mommies, either, I hope. Jesus. Those breeders spend way too much time talking about sleep training and family bed and all of that. So boring; it makes *me* want to sleep. Why do people turn so uninteresting when they reproduce? This whole gayby boom is really putting a damper on conversation."

"Stella, what are you doing after you leave here—in five minutes?" Cait pointed to her watch.

"Lez Be Friends-sponsored wine-tasting."

"Oh God, would you please stop hanging out with those women." Cait frowned at her.

"Shut up, Dr. Getty. You know I'm trying to meet someone. I need to put myself out there."

"What is Lez Be Friends?" I asked as I sat on the couch, sipping the margarita Cait had handed me. Maybe it was the platonic offshoot of Cait's organization GALS FREE. There seemed to be so many lesbian social-political factions to keep track of.

"It's an online 'meet-up' group. Activities for like-minded lesbians."

"More like like-minded *losers*," said Cait testily, sipping from her drink.

I smiled at Stella, and she winked at me. I liked her; she was funny and full of spark. "Do you ever meet anyone?" I took another sip from my drink.

"Well, it's actually usually the same, like, eight women at all of the events."

"Those lesbians like to hang out in packs . . . like wolves. Desperate, friendless wolves." Cait rolled her eyes.

"It's easy for you to make fun, Cait, you've got someone." She flicked her eyes at me. I felt nervous. *Got?* I wasn't hers. Technically, I was actually "his," Keith's. God, I was living a lie. I was a living lie.

"You're just a hater," Cait said. She walked over and sat next to me on the couch. My thigh felt hot where hers was touching it.

"You're right. I'm just whining. And just leaving. Cait, you can stop giving me the 'leave-eye.' " Stella took a big gulp from her drink and put the near-empty glass on the table. She stood up, pulled Cait to her feet and hugged her roughly. They looked like two school-age boys, play-fighting. I liked their close relationship. It reminded me of how I felt with Mae.

"Good-bye, Stella." Cait kissed her cheek at the door.

"Nice meeting you," I called from the couch. The living room was nearly bare, except for the couch and an end table, but felt warm and welcoming. Two thick white candles lit the semidarkness.

The second the door closed behind Stella, Cait set her drink on the table, and eased herself onto my lap, her legs straddling mine. She grabbed the back of my neck and pulled my face forward, her lips hitting my mouth forcefully. She pushed me down onto the couch and eased down my scoop-neck sweater so she could kiss my neck and the tops of my breasts. I heard a moan come from somewhere, and realized it was me. I ran my hands up and down the back of her crisp shirt, and for a second my mind wandered. That preppy, button-down shirt, even unbuttoned to the tops of Cait's breasts, made me think of New Amsterdam University, which reminded me of Keith. Oh God, not now.

Cait had stood up, her mouth still locked on mine, and was

pulling me to my feet. We walked into the bedroom, still kissing. We collapsed onto her bed, still stuck together. I sank into her thick, cottony futon, the soft folds of her white comforter encircling us like frothy waves. No, not here. I sat up, startling Cait's eyes open. How many times had Keith and I made love in a bed—hundreds. Her bed was making me think of him.

"Are you all right?" Cait spoke breathlessly as she struggled to sit up.

"No, I'm not." I tugged at my sweater that felt warm, rumpled and damp and hugged my arms to my chest. "I don't know if I can do this."

"Do what—this?" She put her arms around me and kissed my cheek. "It's just a kiss, that's all. We're just kissing a lot and in lots of places, that's all. Relax."

I breathed in deeply, and the skin of her neck and chest felt warm and soft against my cheek. Still, I found it hard to get a breath. My rational mind was wrestling every other part of me to the ground. Should I let it take over? Whip the rest of me into shape?

"But we don't know each other that well." I felt a sob rising in my throat, and I swallowed hard to choke it back. "Everything's moving too fast."

"It is, isn't it?" She stroked my shoulder. "I don't know much about you, besides the journalism thing. Do you want to slow down and get to know each other better?"

She looked at me playfully as her hand slid down near the top of my breast. Her fingers were bumping up and down to the vigorous rhythm of my heartbeat. My heart seemed to be beating so hard against my chest that my entire body was vibrating. It was much too hard, like a small child, fists balled, pounding on my chest. Would I have a heart attack right here in her bedroom? I closed my eyes briefly, watching tiny lights spark.

"Cait, what does this mean?" I opened my eyes and grabbed her fingers and held onto them tightly.

"Angela, this is what it means. You and I are here together, and we feel something special for each other. At least that's what I'm feeling about you." She kissed my fingertips, and I stopped squeezing her hand so tightly.

"That's what I'm feeling, too." I leaned my head onto her shoulder.

"So we can get to know each other later." She lifted my head from her shoulder and kissed me again. "This is our moment, so let's allow it to happen. Okay?"

"Okay," I answered quietly. The rest of me had knocked my brain senseless. "But here, come here."

I grabbed her hand, and pulled her toward the middle of the room. I sat down on a brightly colored rug and tugged off my sweater. As I lay down, the rough wool felt scratchy on my back. Cait unbuttoned her shirt and threw it in a heap to the side of the room. She had nothing on underneath. All thoughts of Keith vanished when my fingertips touched the soft skin on Cait's neck and back. As I kissed her deeply, listening to her gentle groans, I didn't think I'd ever felt anything that soft, not cotton balls or feathers or the fleshy skin on baby Josie's chubby thigh.

Cait dislodged herself, pulled a pillow from the bed and tucked it under my head. She wriggled out of her jeans and yanked off her underwear, and then roughly helped me pull off mine. As she climbed back on top of me, I felt over-whelmed by the sensation of her body, light but insistent. Everything was moving so quickly. Wasn't making love with another woman a drawn-out affair, all longing gazes and sensual, lingering touches? Something more like the old *Emmanuel* movies, a staple on the blue channels housed somewhere in the upper numbers on my cable remote. Two women not just slow, but actually in slow motion, gauzy as they peeled off layer after layer of filmy linen clothing on an afternoon in Provence.

But Cait was moving rapidly, her longing bordering on desperation. I was so used to waiting and waiting for Keith, careful to avoid knocking off the balance that could trigger his ejaculation. It seemed impossible for Cait to slow down, her wanting was too unfettered. I felt her hands on every part of my body. Her hands were moving so quickly I couldn't tell where she was touching me. Our hips were locked together, hurtling toward something. I felt myself letting go, and forgot about the hard floor, the cool room, the scratchy wool and the fact that Cait was a woman. I blotted out Keith's reserves of restraint, the rough skin on his cheeks and the weight of his body as he shuddered quietly and stiffly in climax. Everything was about my skin and her skin, our giddy friction.

After, we lay apart, sweaty, dozing with our fingers entwined. Strangely, this felt more intimate than her body on top of mine, saying my name over and over. Several hours—and several more sessions of less-frenzied lovemaking later—I glanced at the digital clock on her nightstand. Was it nearly six A.M.? Alarmed, I jumped up, looking around for what was left of my panties.

"What are you doing?" murmured Cait. "You can't just go. It's too early. I don't want you to leave."

"Cait, listen to me." I looked around for my clothes, strewn in small piles throughout the room. "I've got to go. I'm sorry, but I do." I hadn't even called Keith, and he had probably tried my office and my cell several times by now. I needed to get home. I reached down to pick up my shirt, and caught a strong whiff of sex. My skin was moist and musky, the smell of lust and pleasure mingling with sweat. Then I relaxed: Oh, right, it's Saturday morning, and I'm at a slumber party—dishing with the black girls.

When I opened my eyes again, Cait and I were stuck together like two teaspoons as the sun streamed in through her bedroom window. I blinked and looked around the room, really seeing it for the first time. The walls were covered with black-and-white photographs, blown up to nearly the size of posters. An artsy travelogue of picaresque landmarks and lush landscapes, Cait in some of them, others people-free. My favorite was Cait on her motorcycle—no helmet—riding away from the camera toward a mountain backdrop at sunset. Next to it, Stella and Cait were among a group of grinning women, arms around each other, posing knee-deep in the ocean. On the nightstand next to the bed was a pre-teen Cait sitting in a jeep next to a striking woman with long black hair and the same high forehead and cheekbones. The two of them wore matching wraparound sunglasses.

My eyes darted to the clock; it was now eleven A.M. Cait's cat Roscoe was picking at the skeletal remains of breakfast in bed, licking the butter off toast crusts and nibbling cold eggs. I sat up, pulling the covers over my naked body and rooting around for my watch.

I looked over at Cait, sleeping so peacefully. I wanted to nudge her awake, but I was so overwhelmed with emotion that I didn't know what I'd say. Maybe I should just write her a note, take my time, think it through, edit it.

"Cait." I kissed her awake. She looked at me sleepily.

"What could you possibly want that you haven't gotten already?" she asked.

"How about a shower?"

"I'll go with you." She grabbed my arm as she climbed out of bed.

Holding hands, we walked naked to Cait's bathroom and eased into the steaming stall. As I rubbed soap on Cait's back, I couldn't quite believe I was taking a shower with a woman. Generally I didn't like showering with anyone. Growing up with no siblings, I wasn't the best at sharing—either space, soap or hot water. I never liked showering with Keith; he took up too much room. It was weird, being in the small stall, face to face with Cait's slick warm body, the air heavy with steam.

This was also the first time I had gotten a good, close-up look. I felt shy admiring her body without the blurry close-up of lust and lovemaking. She was compact and tight, more muscular than curvy Lana, though I doubted she had the time to work out or any interest in the gym. Her breasts were small and upturned, her nipples two shades lighter than mine. I reached down and squeezed one; it was warm and slippery under the spray.

"Angela, don't start that." Cait looked at me slyly. Then her face turned serious. "What do you want to do today?"

"Uh, Cait, I've actually got to leave," I said, stammering. There was no part of me that wanted to go anywhere but right back to her bed, but I had to get back home.

"Why—Dr. Redfield will be angry?" Cait asked as she lathered her hair with a bar of soap. I was amazed at how some people could use any old thing on their hair. They didn't need the messy concoctions, a sheen of this kind or that, that black women slathered on ours. "I thought you wanted us to get to know each other better. You stayed out all night and he didn't care—why rush off now?"

"I do, but . . ." God, I didn't want to ruin the moment by bringing Keith into the mix. I needed to keep them separate until I could wrap my mind around what I was doing. Get everything sorted out. ". . . I have to, uh, work."

"On the weekend—that sucks." Cait dunked her head under the spray as she spoke. "Do they work you that hard at that crappy magazine?"

"Well, uh, not exactly," I stammered. She wiped the water out of her eyes, blinked at me curiously and slid her slippery hands down my arms. I felt tingles from my shoulders to the tips of my fingers. She soaped up her hands again, and ran them through my hair.

"Doesn't this feel good?" She massaged my scalp gently.

"Ahhh! Stop it—I don't use SOAP on my hair." I pulled her hands from my head and dunked myself under the spray. "Are you crazy! Soap is so drying, and it's not made for hair. Especially Black hair. Don't you have any real shampoo?"

"You are such a girly girl," she said, smiling. "These companies make women feel insecure to sell as many different products as they can. This soap is natural—it won't hurt your hair."

"Don't you have any conditioner?" I ignored her and continued frantically rinsing the soap out of my hair. I'd never be able to comb through this mess.

"Relax, sweetie, I'll get you all the products you need," she said. I felt something well in my throat. Why was she talking about the future?

"So what are you doing today?" she asked again.

"I have to cover a workshop called Too Black, Too Strong," I said, squeezing the water out of my hair. There, I did it. I used Nona's psycho organization—again—to cover my own crazy ass. It was the perfect ruse for my situation. Cait, being a white woman, couldn't probe too deeply, and Keith, being a man, couldn't object too much.

"Can you be either of those things?" Cait asked, pulling me back under the spray. She kissed me, the hot water and her lips making me feel wobbly. Slowly she pulled her face back and looked into my eyes. I put my arms around her slippery waist and held on tight.

"When can I see you again?" she asked as she stepped out of the shower.

"When can I see *you* again?" I asked back, wondering how I was going to keep shuttling between Cait and Keith. There were only so many times I could use the cover of Too Black, Too Strong with either of them.

"I'm pretty free," Cait said, wrapping a thick white towel around her waist. "Oh, except for this stupid faculty brunch for the Humanities Department tomorrow. I have to put in a little face time."

My own towel dropped to the floor. She looked at me, and irritation flickered across her damp face.

"Right. For a minute I forgot that my secret lover is a faculty wifey." She picked up my towel and laid it across my shoulders. There was less bluster in her tone and something that sounded like hurt. "Might you and Dr. Redfield make an appearance? Let me know so I can be ready to pretend I barely know you."

"*Hell* no," I answered as I leaned over and kissed her again. "Why would I put myself through that?"

Chapter 14

I stood in a corner of the room at the Humanities party, Keith's arm around me, his hand thick and heavy on my shoulder. I was riddled with fear, wondering exactly when Cait was going to walk in and kick over my whole house of cards. I had done everything to avoid attending this party—insisted that I had to work, feigned illness, screamed, whined and finally burrowed under the covers of our bed, curling myself into a tight spiral.

"Angela, cut the crap and pull yourself together," Keith had said tersely, tugging an arm out from under the covers. "I have to go to this party and you *promised* to support me."

I burrowed further into the bed, covering my ears with my hands.

"Angela, come on." This time he yanked the covers off and dragged me out of bed. "I need you. You know none of those whities have any respect for African-American studies. I am not going to that party alone."

"Keith, you're being abusive, can't you see I'm ill?" I had shouted, falling back onto the bed. "I don't want to go."

"You are not ill—you're fine," he said, walking over to the closet. He pulled out my old-stand-by little black dress that was tasteful, not too slutty. "Now get up, get dressed, and please do something with your hair."

Now, a glass of pinot grigio in hand, I flicked my eyes toward the door. No sign of Cait—thank God—only Keith drinking himself into oblivion. Despite all his insistence on coming to this party, his mood had changed the second we walked in. He was sullen, getting more and more angry and tipsy, which was in especially poor taste at a brunch. His last trip to the bar, he had ordered two scotch and sodas, and now he reached for the second one, the sweat on the sides of the glass puddling on a ceramic coaster on the bookshelf nearby. Clumps of Keith's colleagues stood near us, engaged in murmured conversation, exchanging bits of department tittle-tattle and other academic inside-baseball and angling to be near the host, Dr. Aravashi Sen, the president of New Amsterdam U.

Craning my neck, I looked around desperately for another black person, someone we could mingle with, at best in another room away from the front door that Cait might walk through any minute.

"See, Angela, see how no one says a God damn thing to me?" Keith was trying to whisper, but rage turned his hushed tones into a shrill, slurred hiss.

"We don't exactly look approachable—let's circulate." I tried to sound soothing, stuffing away sarcasm, but I felt him stiffen.

"This isn't about me, Angela, it's about them." He took another slurpy sip from his glass. "They're such hypocrites."

A bit of Keith's drink sloshed onto the thick Persian carpet near the toe of his spit-shined loafer. I wanted to grind my heel into it to shut him up and then lug him home, just like he'd hauled me here. "They act like they are soooo liberal here with their diversity initiatives and fakey sensitivity-speak. But really they are uncomfortable around blackness, especially black men."

"Keith, I don't thin—" I stopped myself. What good would it do me to point out to him that no one talked to him because he was glowering in the corner and behaving like a social phobic alcoholic? In the conversations I had seen him have with his white colleagues, he spoke far too loudly and aggressively, his already crisp King's English taking on British overtones. When I first met Keith, his rage had seemed exciting. But at this moment, he was just another angry middle-aged man. Absently, I touched my hair, which was patted, smoothed and gelled into a neat little French roll. At least I looked good—like an attractive college professor's soon-to-be wife, but with a hint of something lusty underneath.

I turned my head and spotted two other black professors mingling with colleagues. Although Keith insisted he was first and foremost a "race man," he didn't speak to either Dr. Adrian Thompson, who taught History of the Caribbean, or Dr. Rhonda Wyndom, whose Gender Studies classes were some of the most popular on campus. Several times, I had heard him call Adrian "Uncle Thompson" behind his back and complain that "he thinks he's better than me." He grumbled that Rhonda, whose mother was white, "wasn't a real black woman."

It was really Keith who was uncomfortable with his own blackness, I thought. I pictured him twenty-five years ago, and felt a rush of pity. I wanted to wrap my arms around that sulky little boy I had never known but had seen glimpses of in present-day Keith. I knew it had taken all his courage to once quietly admit to me that at his all-white suburban school in Cincinnati he had never felt good enough. I longed to whisper to him "relax and just be your own best."

Instead, I took another sip of my wine, and felt a pleasant burn as I swallowed. Maybe Cait wouldn't make it after all, and I could instead come up with some excuse to see her later in the week.

A flash of color caught my eye from across the room, and I

spotted Belinda D'or, a chirpy doctoral student and African-American literature instructor. Swathed in a bright African-patterned turban, she waved us over, smiling at Keith and me. I smiled back, trying not to stare at her lazy left eye drifting in a northerly direction behind thick, rimless glasses.

"Hello, Dr. Redfield. Hello, Angela—what a pleasure to see you." Her voice sounded tinkly, like glasses clinking together for a happy toast. I was relieved to see her and happy to be a safe distance from the front door.

"Hello, Belinda, how's your dissertation going?" I asked. I felt Keith's hand loosen on my shoulder. His mood had brightened, as he leaned down and gave her a fatherly pat on the back.

"Well, it's okay, but to be honest, I've been thinking of changing direction." She cocked her head to one side, the turban seeming to weigh her down. "Would you mind if I ran an idea by you?"

"All right." Keith looked concerned.

"Well, you know I've been researching the topic of The Narrative Voice in the Negro Reconstruction Novel."

"Yes, Belinda—post-slavery literature is very important." Keith fingered his glass and nodded encouragingly.

"Yes, I know, but, well, I was thinking of tweaking my topic a bit. To make it, um, more, I don't know—sexy. If I choose the right topic, I can get a book deal and pay down my student loans at least a little. You know what I mean?"

"Sexy? Really?" I said. Hmm. Sexy was a good thing in an academic topic, but I wondered if Belinda could pull it off. Did she have sexy in her? If I looked beyond the lopsided turban and the wandering eye—well, I guess anybody can be sexy to somebody.

"Actually, Angela, since you're a writer, in the, um, mainstream, let me run my new topic by you." She looked at me hopefully. "The Ride or Die Bitch and Other Hip-Hop Iconography in Urban Fiction. What do you think?"

"Umm, provocative." I raised an eyebrow. "Very Modern Language Association."

"Right? I think so. I'm already visualizing the book jacket."

"Belinda, please, you must hear me out before you go forward with this ill-thought-out plan." Keith set his drink down on the coaster. He spoke urgently but patiently, as though explaining something to an unruly toddler. "Go back to your original idea. This kind of thinking isn't good for any of us. As black academics, we must uphold the highest, most serious intellectual standards."

"But Dr. Redfield, I plan to be thorough and rigorous. You know me—I would never sacrifice—"

"Belinda, we have to choose serious topics that are important to the race," Keith said firmly, speaking over her. "So few black professors ever publish—except for vapid mainstream books. Our academics rely on popularity, media appearances and racial politicking to get tenure and respect."

"Thank you, Dr. Redfield. I respect your opinion." Though she looked sincere, I saw an intensity in her eyes and suspected she would barrel ahead with her hip-hop dissertation, perhaps with Adrian or Rhonda as her advisor. But right now, Belinda looked up at him with awe and respect, squeezing his hand gently.

I liked Keith at this moment. He was a woman's man, a surrogate papa to all the young black women in his orbit, who hungered for black male mentors, myself included. My father was courtly and quiet, swept up in the wake of my mother's storm. I loved him fiercely, but I had still ached for the company of a willful, charismatic man who could sweep me in *his* wake. I moved my hand down and entwined my fingers into his. He looked at me and smiled, before he turned his attention back to Belinda. This was fine. I was myself again, back in character.

Keith continued to gently guide Belinda, speaking in soothing, smooth-jazz tones. Good, he was covered, so I could slip away.

"Uh, excuse me a minute, I'm going to get a drink—anyone need a refill?" Keith grunted a no before continuing to explain why selling out was bad for blacks in academia, as Belinda listened intently, debating him gently from time to time. Neither noticed that my wineglass was still nearly full.

I walked into an adjoining room, a glass-enclosed porch, which the Sens used as a sitting room. I savored the warm sun filtering through the ivy-covered roof. Standing alone against an exposed brick wall, I let myself do it: I relaxed and allowed thoughts of Cait to fill my mind. I had promised that when I was with Keith, I wouldn't indulge myself. Instead, I'd hold back, squirreling away the memory of her like Halloween candy to enjoy in stingy little bits. But I was too weak. We had had a phone call and poetry-laced e-mail. Now I ached to see her again, just not here.

But I did. Cait walked in, her eyes darting quickly around the room. She was arm in arm with Cristina, Dr. Sen's wife, smiling, a dimple in each cheek. She looked at me, and then turned her gaze back to Cristina. Then she blinked and looked at me again, her smoky eyes traveling from the sleek hairstyle she'd never seen, down my body. When a man did that it felt piggish and exploitive, but her appreciative gaze seemed both subversive and seductive. Despite myself, I felt a current ripple through my body, mingling uneasily with dread. Holding my damp hands behind my back, I started to dig my nails into my palm. But then I stopped. It didn't feel right anymore, and it didn't help.

"Hello, there." She sounded throaty, like she'd just rolled out of bed. I wished that was where we were. Forgetting about

Mrs. Sen and everything else, I smiled at her so widely all of my teeth showed, even my molars. Cait was wearing a very tight yellow shirt, the first several buttons open, tucked into velvety leather pants. Her red cowboy boots looked peacocky in this room full of gray pheasants. She even outshined the lovely college president's wife.

Equally oblivious of Cristina, Cait picked up my hand, turned it over and kissed the inside of my wrist, holding it to her mouth for more than a second. It was very 19th-century and felt more dangerous than any sex act I'd ever had, even with her. I actually shuddered.

"You look more beautiful than ever." She sounded suddenly formal, more British than ever.

"Well, Cait, I see you've already met Keith Redfield's fiancée, Angela," said Mrs. Sen, smiling and raising an eyebrow.

"Yes, once or twice," Cait answered smoothly. My hand still in hers, she turned it over, and my ring gleamed at her.

"Did I hear my name?" Keith walked into the room, clutching his glass, followed by Belinda. He looked from Cait to me to my hand, still in hers.

"Excuse us," said Cristina, pulling her silk shawl tightly around her shoulders. She glided out of the room, Belinda clumsily in tow. Keith, Cait and I stood in a stony semicircle, him glaring at her, her glowering back.

"What is going on here?" Keith said, his voice hard and flat. He took a step closer to Cait. "Don't you touch my fiancée."

"She wasn't your fiancée Friday night. Or yesterday morning." Cait dropped my hand, her voice a low snarl. So much for her being my lover on the low. "You don't own her."

"Angela, what does she mean?" A glint of fear moved across Keith's face, so quickly that it barely registered. "What is this shit?"

There was nothing to do, no way to squirm out of this, no lie to tell, no little joke to smooth away the tension. My life was about to fall apart. But not here. I refused to let my mess become fodder for a roomful of stuffy academics dressed in bland clothes, gossiping about us in compound sentences.

"Keith, I will explain everything, but I need a minute." I turned and faced him, looking up into his eyes. My voice was firm. "I'll meet you at home."

"Angela, come with me. Now." He pulled at my arm. "Do what I tell you. I'm not leaving you with her."

"No, stop it. I said I'll meet you at home." I turned my body toward his, my voice barely a whisper. I never spoke to him in this harsh tone. He was startled, and took a step back. Despite his anger, he looked like a dog that'd been kicked, retreating to a corner.

Would he let his colleagues see this horrific catfight? Cait didn't give a damn about the other professors, but Keith did. For her this was a triumph; for him, a humiliation. I watched his eyes dart around the room, and knew ego was having a shouting match with disgrace in his head. He then turned toward Cait, and stared at her an uncomfortable few seconds. She kept her eyes locked on his, her lips forming a cold, superior half smile.

"Don't you dare be long," Keith said as he dropped my arm and turned reluctantly toward the door. I watched him leave, his neck stiff and his head high. Only sagging shoulders revealed his shame. Alone in the greenhouse, Cait reached out to touch me.

"Why did you do that?" I knocked her hand away. "It wasn't up to you to tell him."

"Don't blame me; I didn't tell him anything." Cait took a step toward me. "The man's not stupid. Even he could feel the heat between us."

"I thought this whole thing, what we were doing, was cool with you," I said. I took a step back from her. We looked like sparring partners.

"I wasn't going to lie, just because you chose to." Her voice was cold and crisp. "Why should I hide the way I feel about you to protect him? I don't give a shit about him."

"But I do." I was shouting now. "He has feelings, Cait."

"That's your problem, not mine." She grabbed my arm. "Come on, let's go."

"I'm not going with you." I pulled away from her and walked toward the door.

"Don't go home to him—come with me." Cait grasped my arm again. Her fingers dug into my skin as she spoke.

"No," I said, my voice firm. I felt unsteady, like I was about to fall over. "I've got to make it right with him. He is my fiancé."

"You can't possibly think you can make it right with him at this point." She dropped my arm and crossed her arms in front of her chest, I imagined, to protect her own heart. "Please, let's go."

"Cait, stop pressuring me." I looked at her, wishing she'd just be patient. But her face was tight and closed, all of the playful sparkle gone from her eyes. I hated her demands; I wanted to get away from her. "You don't own me, either. Can you give me some time—please?!"

"Yeah, I'll give you all the time you want," she said. A couple who had wandered into the room holding hands and talking quietly to each other, turned and walked out. "Go home—go home to your husband or whatever he is to you."

"Cait, how dare you be mad at me!" I reached toward her, but she moved away, leaving me clawing into the space where she'd been standing. "Please, Cait. Don't do this."

"Go home, that's where you belong." She walked out of the room, but without her usual forceful purpose. Her stride was shorter, her body stooped a little to the left, like she was dodging a blow. Unable to watch her leave, I closed my eyes, and listened to her heels drag, not click, across the glossy floor.

Chapter 15

I hauled myself up the stairs to my apartment, stumbling on the top step, my body heavy with fatigue. What was I doing? What was I supposed to say to Keith? Everything had moved so fast with Cait; I hadn't slowed down to consider this moment.

Part of me still couldn't believe I had cheated on Keith. Mae said that men had affairs because they were addicted to new "punani," a word I couldn't believe Mae actually used. But now that I had had an affair of my own—and new punani—I didn't agree with her. It wasn't just the newness of Cait or the secrecy of the whole affair, or the escape from Keith and our predictable, scripted lovemaking. There was something so seductive about mutual desire. I liked Cait's hunger, for me, bordering on recklessness, and was surprised by my own. The fact that it was fresh and forbidden made being with her even more of a high. I liked touching her, even in passing. The feeling of her skin was alluring, and I knew she felt the same.

Having now done it, I understood why people risk their marriages, their homes and their children for that feeling. It was addictive, like a five-dollar iced mochaccino, crystal meth

or television. No wonder adultery was a mortal sin, an abomination according to the Bible. Otherwise everyone would do
it, jonesin' for those feelings. Thinking about Cait right now
made me want to turn around and take the train to Brooklyn,
get down on my knees and beg her to forgive me.

When I opened the door to the apartment, I noticed that
the shades were pulled, the apartment semi-dark except for a
dim light in the bedroom. I walked over to the window and
pulled open the curtains, sending early afternoon light streaming into the room. I turned toward the bedroom, and saw
Keith sitting stiffly in a chair in the corner. His face was rigid,
his hands gripping the armrests. I stood near him.

"Angela, what is going on?" He was growling. He pulled my
arm roughly, yanking my head into his face. He sniffed me,
like an animal. "You smell different. You smell like her."

"Stop it, that hurts." I took a step away from him, and tried
to pull my arm away.

"Why would you do this to me? To us?" His eyes were wild,
angry. He poured scotch from a carafe on the table next to his
chair into a delicate glass etched with the word "together." I
watched his Adam's apple bob as he took a large swallow. He
looked like a long-necked bird.

"I haven't been happy, Keith." That sounded lame even to
me. My arm was starting to turn an ugly purple where his hand
was gripping it. I tried to wriggle out of his grasp.

"Why didn't you say something?" He let go of my hand,
picked up the glass and took another swallow. "Instead, you
run around behind my back with that vile woman."

"She's not vile . . ." I began. But I felt exhausted and over-
whelmed.

"Are you a lesbian now?" His face went slack, and I saw
some of the anger retreat, replaced by confusion.

"I don't know." I looked down at the floor. My voice was
shaking.

"Jesus." He said it without moving his lips, his body was completely immobile as he spoke. He was still holding the glass, which looked inappropriately festive in his hand.

"You don't know?! You're jeopardizing all that we have, all that we've worked for, our life together, for I don't know?"

The glass in his hand was shaking. At that instant, I realized that I had made a selfish mistake. I should've been more careful. I should've made Cait promise not to say anything. I should've avoided that party at all costs.

Now I was afraid; I wanted him to stop talking. I wanted him to understand. Maybe if I kept talking, if I made him listen, he'd stop being angry. We could go back to the way things were, neat and tidy, except I'd keep seeing Cait.

"I don't understand why you didn't tell me, talk to me, before now."

"I tried to, but . . ." I stopped. I really hadn't tried to talk to him at all. I had planned on marrying him, and accepted that we would have a life together. I hadn't realized that I had been feeling so intensely dissatisfied until I felt the pull of Cait's desire.

At this point, I didn't know what else to say or where to look, so I stared at the glass, shaking in Keith's clenched hand. I watched it shatter, shards of glass falling to the floor and blood dripping down the sides of Keith's hands and staining the tan brushed-suede chair.

"Get out," Keith said quietly, not cleaning the blood or the glass, just sitting, still as a stone. "I never want to see you again."

I stood up and leaned toward him. "Keith, I'm so sorry," I said, reaching down to touch him. Quick as a finger snap, Keith's hand shot out and backhanded me across the face, leaving the imprint of his bloody knuckles on my left cheek. I fell backward, onto the floor, and lay there, sprawled awkwardly. I tasted blood, warm and metallic, inside my cheek.

"Get the fuck out," he said again, not moving. Pain and anger mingled on his face, the skin so tight it looked like it would crack. A tear inched down his cheek, trickling through the fissures of his grimace. His eyes remained unchanged, never blinking.

I rushed out of the living room and into the bedroom. As I sat on the bed, my head in my hands, Keith walked in. "No, out. Get out of my house." His gaze was cruel. I had never seen him like this before. He was unwavering.

"Don't do this, Keith." I was pleading with him.

"I'm not. You did it. Now get out."

I moved past him and back into the bedroom. Hurriedly, I packed a duffel bag, haphazardly throwing in work clothes, shoes, T-shirts, cosmetics and underwear. I was afraid of this Keith, bloody with rage. At the last minute, I tossed in a picture of Keith and me taken four years ago on the ferry to Martha's Vineyard that was sitting on the nightstand and zipped the bag shut.

When I entered the living room, Keith had returned to the same spot, completely still. He looked paralyzed, like he might never move again. I touched his hand, still damp with blood, but he didn't move. I twisted off my ring and lay it on the side table next to him. My hand felt naked and light without it. Closing the door behind me, I left him in the semi-dark room.

As I walked toward the train station, it sunk in that we had just broken up. How could we have been together for years, and then broken up in minutes? I understood why they called it a breakup. A shattering may have been a better word. Even though I had triggered this entire incident, I was shocked by how quickly the whole thing was over. One minute together, the next, shattered, like the etched glass, bits of us crushed underfoot, ground into the rug, then swept up and thrown away. Keith could clean up the mess using the broom my mother had bought us to jump at our wedding.

This was not how I had fantasized our relationship ending. Though I had sometimes imagined Keith dying, more often I had simply fast forwarded, creating an image of a life without him. That he was gone from my day to day without a fight or explanation to my parents and friends, faded out of the photograph of us en route to the Vineyard. It would be just me in the picture, smiling on the ferry. We would still be friends of some sort—like Cait and her ex, Stella—but the details of the detangling of our lives were always sketchy. Not ugly and painful.

In some childish way, I had expected Keith to somehow, miraculously, sense that I had needed something more. In my fantasy, he even understood these feelings, though I hadn't voiced them. He was able to divine that my foot-dragging around the wedding plans and my waning interest in making love was more serious than the excuses I had given him. Part of me, a very irrational part of me, thought he might be happy for me—maybe not the part about Cait—and that he might agree that breaking off our engagement would be best for both of us. He would then explain everything to my parents, so we could get on with our new lives.

I tried to imagine how Keith looked yesterday morning when I left the house, but I couldn't conjure up the face I had stared at day after day. I couldn't shake the image of him immobile and bloody, hurt and disappointment leaving his eyes deadened. He hadn't asked me anything, how long I'd been seeing Cait, if we could work it out. All of his questions were packed into that slap.

Even in these few minutes without him, I felt adrift. I was coming unglued. I had spent so many years being held together by Keith, that I felt like I was falling apart without him.

I thought I would feel relief after I told Keith the truth, but instead I simply felt alone, jarred by the rawness of his hurt. My name felt incomplete without his tacked on the end. Angela andKeith; we had been attached like that—without even a hyphen—for so long. No one ever called us KeithandAngela; that didn't even sound right. Always AngelaandKeith. I wondered how I would hold it together. Where would I live? I had so quickly abandoned our house—or his home, as he'd been so hasty to remind me—in order to get away from that awful, unexpected moment. Now what was I going to do?

Chapter 16

I was relieved to see my father's freshly washed black Volvo station wagon rumble up to the curb of the Mount Vernon East train station. My father, Dr. Wright to everyone who knew him, lumbered out and picked me up, engulfing me in a great big bear hug. His steel-gray hair was parted and brushed down on the sides, and the sparse beginnings of a beard dotted his face.

"Glad to see you, baby," he said, smothering me in his chest. His heavy wool jacket scratched against my face, and he smelled smoky, like the outside. "But I'm always glad to see you. Now, everything's all right, isn't it?"

As soon as he asked, I started to cry. He looked at me worriedly, not sure what to do. Though I felt like he and I were close, we still sometimes behaved like acquaintances, pressed together by nostalgia and history. When I was growing up, he had been overshadowed by my mother's larger personality. We had often sat side by side at our dining room table, listening to her adventures in television-land, appreciative seat-mates at a dinner-theater performance. My father was a soft touch but a tough read. An old-school gentleman, quiet and stoic, he thought

it was selfish and impolite to show emotion. His medical training had cemented his value of privacy.

On paper *only* it looked like, in Keith, I was trying to marry
my father. Part of me did want a marriage like my parents had.
They had met in Idlewild, Michigan, where both of their families summered. My mother was an ambitious secretary at a
Detroit television station, pursuing her dream to be "in the
media," while my father, two years out of his residency, had
joined a small family practice on the south side of Mount Vernon. They were a perfect match. My parents described their
early courtship, with anxious relatives hoping and praying and
cajoling and hovering, as an African-American arranged marriage. The match had worked, and my parents had been together for thirty-some years. My mother provided the spark in
my father's life. He was her steady flame, the pilot light that
never went out. Mae referred to him as Ed—short for "Steady
Eddie."

"Tell me," my father urged gently. "What is it? Is it work?
Did something happen with Keith? Tell me what's wrong."
His meaty hand gripped the leather cover on the steering
wheel as he started up the car.

"Daddy, Keith and I broke up," I said. Even in my hysteria,
I knew not to offer too many details. "We aren't getting married. Everything's all messed up."

"Honey, it can't be that bad." He pulled a hand off the
steering wheel and awkwardly stroked my shoulder. "You two
will fix it. Everything will be okay."

That's what he thought, that anything could be fixed. I
imagined Daddy, with his putty knife and tool kit, patching
together our relationship, gluing the broken pieces back together.

My father turned toward me, concerned. He squinted,
glancing at my cheek. He looked at it closely and rubbed the
back of his hand against the faint, bluish bruise, the same ges-

ture Keith had used to make it. "Keith didn't lay a finger on you, did he baby?"

"No, Daddy, I did that to myself. I messed everything up myself," I said, continuing to cry harder.

"Okay, okay," he said, pulling the car into the driveway. He couldn't stand crying. He got out and opened my door, pulling my duffel bag over his shoulder. Our house, a sturdy, two-story brick, was in the eastern part of the North Side of Mount Vernon. The small Westchester city just north of the Bronx had the distinction of being majority African-American in a predominantly affluent white county. Like us, many middle-class black families had moved from the poorer, blacker South Side in the 1980s.

"Your mother went to pick up some groceries, but she'll be back in a minute. Are you hungry? Let me make you something to eat." That was Daddy's way of fixing me. Something to eat. He lacked the stomach for big emotions and preferred to fix and fuss and mend, which was why he was a good doctor. I was relieved by his presence, quietly in motion.

Inside, the two of us sat around the small wooden table in the kitchen, as he carved thick hunks of turkey and placed them between warm brown bread. Carefully, he cut my sandwich into the neat squares I had preferred as a little girl. He poured me a glass of orange juice and put the plate and glass beside me.

"Thank you, Daddy."

"Don't worry, Angela. Everything's gonna be okay. You and Keith will work things out." He was fidgety, looking for a task. I sniffed and straightened my face, smiling slightly, hoping to reassure him. The back door clicked, and my father's shoulders relaxed.

"Mommy's home, honey. You talk to her about what happened. She'll know what to tell you."

My mother walked in, the heels of her boots clicking across

the tile floor. "Sugar, are you ready for church?" She spoke quickly, rushing the words together.

"Baby, Angela's here." She turned to look at me, raising her eyebrows. Her eyes softened briefly, then narrowed.

"Great, you changed your mind about Nona's lecture." She walked over and kissed my forehead before whisking her pocketbook off the counter. "And you look nice. Thank you for putting in some effort for a change." I was still wearing the little black dress.

"Mom, I, um." What was she talking about?

"Okay, that's fine," she said, interrupting me. "You're here, now, so we can attend the late afternoon church service and then go to Nona's together."

Oh, right. Nona's lecture. That was the very last place I wanted to be. All I could think about was running up to my bedroom, furrowing into clean cotton sheets stretched tightly over the mattress. I needed time to myself to figure out what I was going to do. I imagined the comfort of my room, the flowery bedspread and every inch of the wall covered with posters—Michael Jackson, not black, not white but beige; his sister Janet; a young, healthy Whitney Houston; Kriss Kross and faded *Playbill* covers from "The Colored Museum" and "The Good Times Are Killing Me" stuck to the wall with yellowed Scotch tape.

But that would never happen. My mother was darting through the kitchen, a driver impatiently changing lanes. She'd barely glanced at me since she'd walked in and had no clue that I was coming apart. "Come-on-Angela. Chester, are you coming?"

"Naw, I went to Bible study this week, so I think I'll pass," my father said as he picked up the plates from the table and began loading the dishwasher. "Janet, you need to spend some time alone with Angela."

"Okay, then, good-bye Chester." She gave my father the

same distracted kiss—lips on his forehead, eyes on the door. I stood up tiredly, shuffling out behind her.

My mother was in high spirits as we drove to the church, her voice as cheerful and animated as a Christmas carol. I was sitting pressed to my side of the car, slumping deeper and deeper into the cold leather seat. A car honked as it passed us, and my mother turned to wave at a grinning woman, her white-blonde hair pulled tight to her forehead. That happened all the time, Scandinavian descendents happily misunderstanding the SISTRFND vanity license plate stuck on the back of my mother's late-model Lexus.

I wished I could talk to her, tell her what was going on, and ask her to help me clean up my mess. But that seemed as likely as blondie in the car next to us being full-blooded Nigerian.

"Angela, guess what?" My mother was so excited, her words tumbling over each other. She didn't wait for me to even grunt a reply.

"Remember I told you I applied for that Ida B. Wells fellowship? I got it. Isn't that great, I got it!" She looked over expectantly, her eyes leaving the road completely. I felt the car lurch slightly to the right. With a quick motion, she flicked the steering wheel back into position.

"Great, Ma, that's great." My voice was completely flat. My irritation rose. Me, me, me. I needed to just cut in, to tell her that I really needed to speak to her, spill the story about Keith, without the Cait part. I wanted her to pull the car over and turn all of her attention on me. Why couldn't she sense that something was wrong? She couldn't read my mind, but the more she talked about herself, the more my need for her to understand what I wasn't telling her increased. Tears pooled in my eyes.

"I'm already looking for ideas," she continued, now gushing. She steered the car into the parking lot of First AME

Church of Mount Vernon. "I have to produce three documentaries over the next year. I'm thinking that I'd like to do something a little different than usual, but you know, for and about our people, of course."

"Of course." My mother was too jazzed to notice the sarcasm. I slammed the door to the car. A large crowd was gathered on the front steps of the church, clusters of women dressed in brightly colored coats, most with matching hats. My mother glowed in a white wool belted coat, her hair stuffed into a white fedora. Several women signaled to her, as we walked toward the entrance.

"Angela, pick up your head." She didn't wait for me to respond. "Come on, this isn't a funeral. You don't come to church often, and I know you don't think that highly of Nona, but you could get a story out of it."

"Mother, Nona's message for black women is toxic—can't you see that?" I felt my face grow from warm to hot. I had just gone through some mixture of one of the best and worst forty-eight hours of my life, and I was going to explode. I was either following my passion or completely ruining my life and my mother had no idea. My head pounded as I choked back tears.

"Angela, snap out of it. What is wrong with you?" My mother grabbed my arm. Then she stopped walking and turned to look at me intently.

"Baby, what *is* wrong?" She stared at me, finally focusing. Pain and confusion moved through me in waves, and I knew she could see it. "Tell me, Angela. Tell Mama."

I opened my mouth to pour out an edited version of my sad saga—"Keith broke up with me," no mention of lesbian experience—but was nudged brusquely by a young woman who seemed to be hurling herself into my mother. She was tall with smooth skin, the color of a chestnut horse. Out of habit, I stared hard at her head; I was always mildly curious about the hair of the people who bowed down at the altar of my mother.

Hers was thick and healthy, twisted into cute funky curls, and her smile warm and inviting. She was someone I might like under normal circumstances.

"You're Janet Wright, right?" She grinned as she stepped between my mother and me, awestruck. I hated that Wright-right business. It was so stale; I had been hearing it since second grade. She didn't wait for an answer.

"Yes, I know who you are. You're my hero." She threw her arms around my mother and hugged her tightly. "I love your work. You are soooo wonderful," she sang.

"Thank you, sis." My mother spoke in honeyed tones, giving the woman her polished TV smile. "But if you'll excu—"

"Now all I got to do is find a man. And I know the right one is out there for me."

"Of course he is." My mother patted the woman's back. All right, I'd had enough. I stepped between the two of them.

"Mother, Keith and I broke up—do you give a damn?" My voice sounded shrill. The woman took two steps back, startled by my tone. My mother pulled me to the side of the church, as several sister-girls glanced at us through half-mast eyelids.

"What?!" My mother's eyes widened, and she looked down at my bare left hand. I finally had her full attention. "Why didn't you tell me?"

She pulled me tightly to her, glancing around nervously. Then she looked into my eyes. When I could wrestle her attention away from every black woman with a hair problem, my mother was my soul mate, dishing out insightful advice, always laced with empathy. She was focused as an x-ray, her eyes two watery lamps. I appreciated her attention. It was a gift to have my mom at her best. She wasn't Janet Wright, local TV anchor, responsible for keeping New Yorkers informed. Or Janet Wright, hair activist, helping black women love every inch of their hair whatever the texture. She was simply my mother. Mine, mine, mine.

"Mommy," I whispered hoarsely, drained from my outburst. "Keith and I aren't getting married. He kicked me out of the apartment."

"What? Just like that? Why?" My mother looked puzzled and I could see that she wasn't believing the edited version. She knew how to dig for the truth, and this wasn't all of it.

"We've been having problems. We weren't meeting each other's needs. We're taking a break." I was stuttering. The clichés were rapid-fire.

"Angela, breathe." My mother took a deep breath in and blew it out slowly. I did the same. "That's fine. So you are getting married then, after the *break*?"

"No. I don't know. He's very angry. He won't talk to me."

"Oh, you hate that." My mother held me by the shoulders, her gaze loving and teasing. "Remember the time you locked yourself in your room, you were so afraid of your cousin when she shouted at you?"

"Yeah, I remember." I had always been afraid of anger. I hated the way people lost control when they were mad. It felt like they turned into someone else, some permanently angry person to avoid. Anger seemed like a constant state that you couldn't ever get rid of it.

"Keith hates me." I said quietly.

"No, he doesn't." My mother spoke soothingly and I felt protected by having her on my side. "You've just had a fight, that's all. You'll make up, and everything will be fine. And you won't be mad anymore, either."

"I'm not mad."

"You never like to admit you're angry. I used to say, 'Baby girl, are you angry,' and you'd say, 'No, I'm annoyed' or 'I'm upset' or 'I feel funny.' Funny—when you were mad, you described it as funny."

"What am I going to do?"

"You're going to work it out, for goodness sakes." Her voice now had an edge to it. As the church bells rang, I could feel her impatience sneaking up, pushing my nice, attentive mother aside. "You can't just give up. I'll speak to Keith, and you two can get this worked out. This is ridiculous." She pulled her cell out of the bag slung on her shoulder.

"No." Frazzled, I knocked the phone to the ground. "Don't call him. I'm sorry. You're right—we can work it out." I spoke hurriedly as I leaned over and picked up the phone, feeling all the blood rush to my head. My mother could *not* know I was seeing Cait—if I still was—and that would be the first thing Keith would tell her. I could hear him: *Mama Wright, your daughter left me for a woman. She thinks she's a lezzzzbian now.* God, no.

"Excuse me." I felt a hand on my shoulder. I turned to face a stocky security guard, a young black rent-a-cop with a smooth-shaved face and sad eyes. He was probably there to provide security during Nona's packed-house event. His face was swollen, puffy, a bloodstained butterfly bandage peeling off his forehead.

"Do you remember me?" He looked familiar. I glanced at his name tag—Ronald.

"Have we met?" I asked him, wiping my eyes and taking a deep breath. I was feeling overwhelmed, glad for the distraction.

"Yes, at the Center a couple of weeks ago, do you remember?" I looked at him a little more closely, picturing him in the same uniform, now slightly nubby and pilled, but wearing a wig and eyeliner. Rhonda, the security guard at the transgender trailer.

"What happened, young man?" My mother came up behind me, looking at his face with alarm.

"Got beat up—again." His eyes watered, and his shoulders grew slack. "I got jumped by some guys."

"Did they take your money?" My mother seemed genuinely concerned. She touched his bruised cheek with her fingertips.

"They called me fag . . . I was, you, know, Rhonda that night." Anxious, I studied my mother's face and saw surprise pass through her features, quickly, like a hiccough. Just as fast, she switched to her professional mask.

"Is it common, um, Ronald? I mean, I don't think I know any of our people who are, well, transvestites."

"I'm not a transvestite. I'm in transition. I'm not just *trying* to be a female, I plan to succeed." Ronald spoke stridently, but he looked from her to me, his eyes pleading for understanding. "And I know lots of brothers in my situation.

"You're a journalist, working on a story, right? I'd like to talk to you, but not with my name," he continued, relaxing a bit. So did I. My mother would understand that I had met Ronald in my professional capacity as a journalist, not my newfound personal identity as a lesbian.

"I'm not actually doing a story . . ." I shrugged a little sheepishly, remembering that he had seen me with the tape recorder. But I couldn't back down now after promising Cait.

"Ronald, I'm Angela's mother, Janet Wright," my mother said, using her silky, polished voice. "I'm a television journalist, and I'd love to talk to you. Black on black crime, no matter the circumstances, is always misguided. Your story deserves to be told." She pulled an engraved silver case out of her purse and pressed her card into his hand.

"Thank you." He said it softly, full of gratitude for a moment—even a slick journalistic moment—of acceptance.

"Come, come, Angela, we don't want to miss the sermon—or Nona." My mother tugged at my arm. "Nice meeting you, Ronald, and please call me." She brushed her lips against his cheek softly, and squeezed his arm. Oh, my God: My mother was seducing him. How disgusting, seeing the shtick she used to land interview subjects. How nauseating. However, she *had* been kind and open-minded with Ronald. Maybe talking about my feelings and offering her a "lite" version of the Cait part of the story wouldn't be so bad—down the line.

"Well, that was interesting, wasn't it, dear?" My mother moved her purse to her shoulder as she looked toward the church doors. "I mean, the gay business isn't good for our people. And I don't know about the whole transgender thing. But this could be a great story, so I would never allow my personal views to undercut my professional judgment in any way."

"Mom . . ." I began, but didn't finish. I wasn't sure what to say. At this point, it was better to say nothing.

"Angela, come on, let's go." My mother tapped her fingers on the place between my shoulder blades, and then paused. She took a small inhale, put both her arms around me and held me tightly in her arms. She was my mother again. I sighed, my eyes filling with tears. "I love you and don't worry. Everything will be okay. We will work out this Keith problem."

Chapter 17

I walked into the well-lit lobby of Mae's building at 28th and Madison after working late at *Désire*. I had been shuttling between her place and my parents' for over a week. Cait and I were still in a standoff. Which stung but was also okay; I needed to catch my breath.

Mae's apartment was in a weird, commercial part of Manhattan, but she loved it. I think she loved that she lived in a high-rise building, and was always trying to work the phrase "my doorman" into conversation. Mae was standing in her doorway wearing a pink shortie nightgown and matching pink silk head scarf. She had put on dusty-rose lipstick, even.

"Honey, you're home!" Mae said as she helped me pull off my coat. We sat together on her bed, which was in the living room of her studio. It was really "our" bed now. I had slept badly every night I'd been there, teetering on my edge. Last night was the worst: I had awakened at 3 A.M. with Mae's pudgy hand on the side of my head, a clunky ring wedged in my ear. Her apartment didn't have to be configured the way it was, but she'd chosen a yawning walk-in closet over a bedroom.

"You don't look so great, Ang." As soon as Mae said it, I

started to cry. Worriedly, she stroked my shoulder, and handed me a tissue out of a candy-striped box on her nightstand.

"Mae, I know I look like shit. My life is ruined," I huffed through sobs. "What have I done?"

Though I was raw from my breakup with Keith, it was Cait whom I longed for. I had called her several times, but she had refused to answer when my number came up. The one time she had picked up, I had hung up, unsure what to say. But I hadn't told Mae any of this.

"Ang, explain to me again why Keith broke up with you and kicked you out of your apartment so suddenly." She handed me another tissue. Always a good reporter, she was sniffing around the holes in my story.

I wanted to tell her, to blurt out the whole thing and stop obscuring the details, but I was afraid. Would she be able to handle the gay part? She had lots of gay male friends, and she had made it through the lesbian sex conference. But she also had a Southern black background. I was afraid of the kind of small-town Christian judgment that clings even to sophisticated people long after they've left the South. I couldn't risk losing another person whom I loved.

"You know you're not a good liar; you never were," Mae said, putting her arms around me tightly. "I love you no matter what, right? Now *tell* me whatever it is."

"Okay." I took a deep breath. "Remember how you told me that I'd feel better about getting married if I had an affair?" *Oh God, here goes*, I thought.

"Uh-huh." Mae said, fluffing up her pillows and kicking her feet out in front of her on the bed.

"Well . . ." I stopped and lowered my head, staring at her bedspread, which was splashed with color and embellished with a map of her home state.

"Oh, my God, you're having an affair? Oh, my God, Oh, my

God," said Mae excitedly. "With who? Tell, tell me, tell me now."

"With, um. Remember the woman, Cait, you met at the conference?" I turned to her and studied her face.

Mae didn't say anything. She just stared at me, looking shocked. Her hooded eyes were as big as silver dollars.

"My God—you're like that chick, what was her name? Anne Heche. One minute a straight girl, and then—bam—a lesbian on the red carpet with Ellen DeGeneres. Are you going to lose your mind, too, and start wandering around thinking you're from outer space?"

"Ha, ha, Mae. This isn't funny." I searched Mae's face again, but could detect nothing more than surprise, sarcasm, and confusion. She was still my Mae and hadn't morphed into a dour church lady. "I could be ruining my life here."

As I told her the rest of the story, she listened quietly, save for the occasional "in front of all those stuffy *academics*?" "You let that girl fuck you?" and "No, he did *not*." I left out the part about how Keith had slapped me.

"Girl, you're in trouble," Mae said finally as she tucked her legs beneath her.

"Hey, it's your fault. You told me to have an affair." Seeing that she was not going to abandon me, I was able to smile.

"Yeah, yeah, but I didn't think you would. I thought an affair would be too messy for you. You don't like disorder. I mean, I assumed that cheating would be too sloppy for you. Plus, come on, I had no idea you were gonna get with a woman."

"Are you mad at me?"

"I'm not mad at you for being a dyke or whatever it is you are," said Mae slowly. "I'm mad at you for not telling me sooner. You drag me to that freaky sex conference without letting me know you were doing research for yourself."

I looked at Mae and realized that although she worked for a celebrity fashion magazine, she really did have the personality of a hard-core journalist. She had a desperate need to know, priding herself on being the first on the scene. She secreted away precious bits of information and bartered snippets of gossip like casino chips. She felt betrayed, getting my news in a late edition.

"I'm sorry, Mae," I said, snuggling into the pillow next to her. "I was so afraid to lose you."

"That will never, ever, ever, ever, ever happen." She moved her head over to my pillow, her head nudging mine. "Well, what are you going to do?"

"I don't know," I answered, sitting up. "What should I do? I can't eat, I can't sleep, I can't think."

She sat up, too, and moved in front of me, pulling my arms around her thick shoulders. We rocked back and forth, and I clutched her and buried my head in her back.

"You're a mess," she said finally.

"I know." I sighed, feeling weary, but wired. "I'm talked out, but I'm never going to sleep."

"Here, get comfy, and we can watch a movie until you fall asleep."

She walked over to her gold-leaf dresser, so large and shiny that it looked like it belonged in Emerald City. On top were a line of photographs of Mae, in brightly colored frames, posed in front of different New York City landmarks—the Statue of Liberty; Empire State Building; Sylvia's; and the Brooklyn Bridge. She was alone in each photograph in full makeup, her stance always the same—body turned slightly to the left, her best side, face forward, chin down, eyes up. At the end of the row, she had one last 3 x 5 snapshot of the two of us, tucked into a shiny silver frame. Our heads were sandwiched next to each other, Mae grinning, her lips bright with bloodred lipstick, planted on my cheek, eyes turned forward and locked onto the camera. Next to her, I looked as wan and plain as a Vermeer model. Though I was smiling slightly, my eyes looked serious, lost in thought.

Mae pulled out a pair of pajamas dotted with lavender poodles. "Put these on. Perfect color for your coming out."

I stripped off my clothes and put on the pajamas, which were about three sizes too big but felt warm and cozy. Mae picked up the remote and began shuffling through the crowded cable-TV menu. "Okay, let's see. Our goal is distraction, without getting pissed or offended, and maybe some black people—right?"

"I'm with you."

"Let's try the Independent Film Channel first." She pointed and clicked through the titles and descriptions. "Let's see: noble, wise, uneducated Africans teach an upper-class family that has escaped Nazi Germany to recognize their humanity? God, no!" She stuck out her tongue at the screen.

"Westchester housewife embraces her independence with the help of her wise and noble housekeeper," I read, squinting at the screen. "No."

"An uptight lawyer learns to relax and dance with the help of his wise and wisecracking African-American client, who has recently been released from prison. No, no, no."

"Socialite loses her fortune and discovers her humanity after she becomes a drama instructor-basketball coach at an impoverished inner-city middle school . . . full of wise noble seventh graders." Mae managed to laugh as she scrolled near the end of the selections.

"Repressed army colonel taps into deep reserves of empathy and courage, saving a village of Africans from invasion by an enemy tribe."

"Jesus. Let's try something black with some women in it, but nothing that takes place in the hood, at a beauty shop, barbershop or car wash. 'K?" Mae clicked onto BET's menu.

"Here's one: a bitter, unmarried, black advertising executive discovers her capacity for love when she switches places with a hooker and falls in love with one of her johns." We both hissed at the screen.

"Forget it, let's choose something with no blacks."

"That's easy. Let's find some old Woody Allen and call it a day."

"Yeah, except for the one with the black hooker . . . with a heart of gold, who helps a short, aging, near-sighted nebbish discover his . . ."

". . . . humanity." I filled in the last part of the sentence, slapping five. She clicked around until she found *Hannah and Her Sisters*, about half finished. We pulled Mae's bedspread up to our chins and settled in.

The following morning, I blinked, and felt the sun warm on my face through Mae's sheer rose-colored curtains. It was around 7 A.M., but I couldn't get back to sleep. My mind was reeling; I felt like Elizabeth Taylor and Richard Burton had somehow entered my brain and were stomping through an endless dress rehearsal of *Who's Afraid of Virginia Woolf.* And Mae's room was so bright. I looked over at her, tangled in the sheets she had snatched from my side of the bed, and remembered that she slept with a tiger-striped sleep mask over her eyes.

I maneuvered out of bed and curled my toes into Mae's thick fuzzy rug. Leaning over her, I pushed her scarf aside and whispered, "I can't sleep," into her ear. She grimaced slightly and snuggled more deeply into her dream.

"What should I do?" I whispered more insistently, shaking her shoulder.

"Angela, stop it, I'm still sleeping," she said, irritated. She readjusted her pillow and jiggled the mask from one eye. "But if I were you, I'd get my ass out of here, find that girl and get her back."

Chapter 18

I marched up the street toward Cait's brownstone. I was going to *make* her listen no matter what. I missed her fiercely and was ready to talk—and force her to hear me. As I got closer to her building, I squinted, and saw that she was sitting on the steps, wearing a jean jacket, a wool scarf wrapped tightly around her neck. A pair of wire-rimmed glasses perched on her nose, Cait was shuffling through a stack of papers, occasionally making a mark or jotting down a note in the margins. Roscoe the cat was curled beside her, yawning into the sunlight.

"Cait." I approached the steps tentatively, afraid that she would jump up and run inside. She looked up at the sound of my voice, and I saw her face grow tight and hard. Roscoe readjusted his body, stretching a paw lazily toward Cait's thigh.

"What do you want?" Her voice sounded like a growl.

"Please, Cait, just listen to me—please." I walked up the stairs and sat on a step, one below her.

"Why should I listen to your double-talk?" She picked up her papers and stood up. Reluctantly, Roscoe stood up, too, and slipped through the front door, which was propped open with a damp phone book. "I've heard enough."

"No, you haven't. Please, give me a chance." I reached out

and grabbed her arm. She snatched it away, and walked through the door, kicking away the phone book and slamming it shut.

I banged my fist on the door. I could see her through the entryway glass, furious, but sad around her eyes. "I'm going to do this until you open this door!" I shouted to her.

"Stop it—go away." She hammered her palm hard against the glass, and I could feel it vibrate from my fist through my arm all the way to my chest. I stopped pounding, pulling my fist back sharply, afraid the glass would break.

"If you don't get out of here I will call the cops."

"No, you won't; you know you'd never trust the cops—now open the door!" I spoke forcefully, using a voice and a determination I didn't know I had. I locked my eyes on her through the glass until she turned the knob and opened the door. I followed her up the steps.

Cait sat down at the table, placing her hands on the rough brown wood near a faded water stain. I pulled out a chair across from her and sat down.

"Okay, you've caused a scene and forced your way in here, now talk." She sounded testy and put upon, like she'd rather be anywhere else. But I didn't care. I would make her understand.

"I am so sorry . . ." I began, looking down at the table. I felt much of my resolve dry up and blow away.

"I know that, I know you're sorry," she said, and slammed her hand so hard on the table that a vase of dried flowers nearly toppled over.

"But you should be sorry, too," I said, putting a hand on top of hers. She tried to pull away but I squeezed her fingers. "You rushed me. Why couldn't you just wait for me to catch up?"

"Because . . ." she began. She looked small, teary and stubborn. "I didn't want to wait—not one minute."

I dropped my head into my hands and squeezed my temples. This was exactly what I had wanted to hear, but all of a sudden it felt like too much to handle.

"I don't know how I let this happen." My face still covered, I closed my eyes tightly.

Cait stood up, bracing herself on the table. She was angry again. "You didn't let it happen, you made it happen."

"Yes, I wanted it to happen," I said, standing up, too. I grasped the tops of her arms and pulled her toward me. "I wanted it—you—so badly that I didn't allow myself to think."

"Well, you should've thought about it. But it's too late now: Whatever it was, it's over." She jerked her arms away from me and took a step to the side. I saw her mouth twitch slightly.

"No, please, I don't want to lose you." I stepped toward her, wanting to grab hold of her again, but afraid of the anger.

"Obviously, you never had me. And I truly never had you. And never knew you." She turned and started to walk away. I reached out and pulled her toward me again, clutching her tightly this time.

"You don't know me, because you aren't paying attention," I said, forcing myself to look into her eyes. I tried not to be afraid anymore, and let the truth spew out of my mouth without censoring or editing. "This isn't easy for *me*, like it is for you. Who am I to you, anyway? Just some young thing, probably one of many."

"You don't know that—" Cait began.

"No, I don't. But I do know how much you mean to me, and how much more being with you has meant to me."

"Oh, for God sakes . . ." Cait put up her hand. "Stop being a martyr."

"Be quiet. You said you wanted me to talk, so sit down and listen." I pointed to her chair, and sat down in my own. "I not only risked hurting another person and destroying our future, but making love with you also changed who I was. In the last few weeks, my identity has moved from heterosexual to bi, or lesbian, or confused or something. Whoever I am now is not who I was last month or last week."

"Good for you; now you've got a juicy coming-out story."

"You know what, after our first night and only night together, you probably snuggled back into bed and called Stella to give her the giggly details of our evening." I reached for Cait's hand, and this time she didn't draw it away. "Am I right?"

"Well, yes." She almost smiled.

"I bet you felt light, in a sexy postcoital kind of way." My fingers lightly stroked the top of her hand. "What about me though? I wasn't at all light. I had the burden of our secret.

"And you know what was the worst part of it?" I continued, staring at our hands on the table, fingers interlocked. "It's that I couldn't tell anyone that I'd just had the most insane, divine, amazing, surprising, life-changing experience of my entire life."

"Did you say 'divine'?" Cait lifted my fingers to her mouth, and rested them there.

"Yes," I said, watching her and enjoying the feeling of relief. "But you know what was even more scary? I was deathly afraid that I would never be able to have that divine feeling again."

"You needn't worry about that," Cait said, standing up and pulling me with her. "I missed you."

"Me, too."

"So, let's stop talking and do what we do best." Putting her arm around my shoulders, she guided me into her bedroom.

Chapter 19

I rubbed my eyes open, feeling groggy and disoriented. Where was I? Then I felt Cait's arm curled around my shoulder, her breath warm on the back of my neck. I turned and kissed her cheek, and she smiled slightly in her sleep. She smelled sweet, like the meat of a mango close to the pit.

I had been staying at Cait's apartment for almost a week, and it felt like a honeymoon. All bliss, no mess, but only because I hadn't allowed reality to join us. I refused to let any thoughts of Keith, my parents, or whether or not I was a lesbian spoil the fun.

But the thoughts were there. *What would my mother think about me with this woman—a white woman no less? It would make her sick. And my father?* The thought of his face when my mother inevitably blurted out the news made *me* feel sick. I had to keep this a secret.

Even as I snuggled against Cait and felt the steady throbbing of her heart against my back, I knew that she and I needed to talk. I couldn't just continue to stay with her without some discussion about what the hell we were doing—besides being in love. I wriggled myself out of her arms and sat up on my elbows.

"Cait, hey," I whispered, leaning down to kiss her awake.

"Mmmm, you're still here, I'm not dreaming," she said, trying to pull me back down into the mound of pillows.

"Actually, that's what I wanted to talk to you about," I began, feeling hesitant. "I really appreciate you letting me stay with you . . ."

"Are you kidding, I love it." She smiled, but then she blinked, and I saw something change in her face. She punched up the pillows behind her and sat up.

"Well, there is something I think we need to talk about, too." There was a catch in her voice, and her eyes darted away from mine briefly.

"Don't worry, I'm not trying to crowd you or rush you," I said quickly, racing in. All of a sudden I felt too anxious to hear what she had to say. What was she going to tell me? That she didn't want me here? That she was seeing someone else, who had been out of town for the past week? She was a lesbian, for Christ's sake; didn't they bring a U-Haul on the first date or whatever?

"This could just be a temporary thing, me staying here. Of course I'll pay rent until I find a place of my own."

"No, it's not that," she said. When she looked up at me, her eyes were serious.

"Well, what is it?"

"I want you to stay here," Cait replied carefully. "But there's something else." She stood up and began pacing slowly, touching her hand lightly against the wall.

"What?" I shrugged my shoulders, nervous and impatient.

"I'm planning on having a baby." She looked at me expectantly, running her hands nervously through her hair.

"Yeah, and . . . ?" God, I felt relieved. "I mean, I want to become a mother someday, too."

"No, Angela. I'm not talking about *some*day; I'm talking

about sooner—like now." Cait sat down and took my hand. Hers was shaking.

"What—are you telling me that you're pregnant?" That was freaking me out. One thing was having sex with a woman, but another was having sex with a pregnant woman.

"I didn't say I was pregnant now, but I'm going to start trying."

"What! You're just now telling me this?"

"Angela, you have no room to talk," she replied, dropping my hand. "Not too long ago you had a fiancé."

"Hey, the key word there is *had*," I said. "And you knew that."

"Having a baby is something I've wanted to do for a long time. It was in the works long before I met you." She spoke very firmly, and I didn't like the way her jaw seemed to have locked into place.

"I've had a thorough medical exam and a midwife has been helping me chart my ovulation. My friends and I have been on the Gentex CryoBank Web site narrowing down sperm donors. I want to start at the beginning of the year."

"Ohmigod! That's only a few months away!" My voice sounded shrill. It bothered me that she had had this whole other life—during the last several weeks at least—that I wasn't part of. She had been sneaking around figuring out her ovulation, studying potential donors on a Web site, talking to friends about her *baby*, a baby I knew nothing about.

"What does this mean for me?"

"It doesn't mean anything. It just means you're going to be seeing someone who is pregnant, and then you'll be seeing someone with a baby." She crossed her arms.

I put my hand on my neck and tugged at a tense muscle. I knew this was not true. How was I going to simply go out with Cait, live with her, while all this was going on in her life—first

pregnancy, then the birth of her baby? I felt confused and terrified. A month ago, I was pushing thirty, engaged to a good-
enough guy who, admittedly, I wasn't in love with. Then I
was still that, with an affair tacked on. Nothing too out of the
ordinary, except that the affair was with a woman. Now I was
suddenly someone else: A heart-breaking, home-wrecking
lesbian . . . mother?

"This seems rushed, Cait, I mean—"

"Not to me. I've been waiting for years," snapped Cait. I
was startled by the unyielding sound of her voice, and pulled
away from her even further. I was barely balanced on the edge
of the bed.

"But, Cait, how will you do this . . . on your own?" Though
this was a shock, I understood why she hadn't told me. I hadn't
wanted to ruin our little corner of paradise with the inconve-
nient, messy reality of my life. Homelessness. An angry ex-
fiancé. Clueless parents who would disown me if they knew
about her. Confusion about my sexuality. I had been afraid
that discussing it all might drive her away. That's how she felt
about the truth of her own third party. She had been scared—
she was still scared. I moved a little closer to her on the bed
and rested my hand on her thigh.

"Your life will change, you know, and so will mine," I said
quietly.

"Women have babies all the time, and their lives go on."
She leaned over and picked up the photograph on the nightstand. "My mother did it. She traveled all around the world
and having me didn't stop her. Everywhere she went, I went."

"But Cait, your mom was like Angelina friggin' Jolie. All
the two of you were missing were Brad and the other kids." I
pulled her close to me and kissed her hair, as she continued
staring at the photograph. "Are you going to be able to do
this?"

"Of course I am." She put the photo back on the table and

leaned her head on my shoulder. "I know this is all new to you, but I want you to understand that my child will simply be part of the life I have now—period."

"Yes, I get it, it's just the timing," I said, stroking her cheek.

"The thing is, I want to get going, so, you know, my hormones won't be drying up at the same time my daughter rages into adolescence."

"Or when your son wakes up from the first of many wet dreams." I saw her face freeze at the possibility that a male might spring from the loins of a full-grown Amazon like herself. Despite the angst her news had created, I stifled a laugh.

"But seriously, Cait, I have to be honest; I'm a little freaked out. Keith wanted to have a baby, and I didn't. I'm not ready to be a mother."

"I'm not expecting you to be the *co-mother*." She sighed. "Why don't you start out as the girlfriend of the woman with a baby?"

"So I'm baby mama's other mama?"

"Something like that." Cait smiled, leaning against me.

"This is all so fast." Roscoe sauntered by and rubbed his back against my leg.

"For your education, in Lesbianville, this wouldn't be all that fast," Cait said, putting her arms around my neck. "Lesbians create a kind of relationship shorthand, so lesbian time is accelerated. A week is more like half a year for us. I think there's a math calculation for figuring out 'lesbian years'—like times seven. Like dog years, I think." She smiled and her dimple appeared.

Her arms still around me, I felt the creeping sensation of claustrophobia. My feelings were more than simply mixed; they were totally mixed up. My God—what was I doing? Had I somehow sleepwalked—more like sleepran—from one suffocating relationship to the next? All of a sudden, I felt more trapped than happy and wanted to sprint out of her apartment

and race down the street, just for the feeling of being propelled by my own momentum. But the moment passed as I allowed Cait to hold me. I was tired, worn out from the chaos of
the past month. At this moment, her sturdy arms and the
cushiony feel of the comforter felt steadying and secure.

Chapter 20

I picked up the phone at my desk and hit the speed dial button marked "M." Mae answered on the first ring.

"Hey you—I'm on my way down," Mae said, sounding excited.

Mae was thrilled that we were finally getting to help Cait choose her baby's daddy. When I'd first called to tell her about Cait's planned pregnancy, it had taken five minutes to explain that Cait wanted to have a baby, and another ten to convince Mae that lesbians could, in fact, have babies. When I had finished, Mae said nothing, but I could hear her breathing so I knew she was still on the line.

"Don't you want to ask me stuff?" I had asked. "Why are you so quiet? You don't want to know why Cait is rushing to have this baby?"

"I know why. Because she's about thirty-five, right? She's like every other woman that age, gay or not; that biological clock is pounding in her ears. She can feel her eggs shriveling up."

"Come on, Mae, aren't you going to ask what I'm going to

do with some baby or how Cait and I are going to work that part out?"

"No, there's nothing else to say or ask," she had replied before hanging up. "The bottom line is, your life is totally FUCKED up."

Mae had pulled a chair next to mine and was staring at my computer screen. The Gentex site was colorful and slickly designed. Multicolored double helix danced around a soft-focus blow-up photo of a smiling couple staring lovingly at a baby swaddled in a blue blanket.

"Damn, do couples even use sperm banks anymore?" Mae asked as she sat down. "I thought it was just single career women in their late thirties and early forties and, I guess, lesbians."

"Why bother when you can make your own biological replica in a petri dish," I said, taking a sip of my coffee. I knew from my own magazine that in-vitro fertilization and other kinds of infertility procedures could correct baby-making problems like low sperm count or anemic sperm that couldn't swim in the right direction. So most heterosexual couples no longer had to travel in cover of night to pick up some stranger's specimen when they could go to a clinic in broad daylight.

"This is so interesting," she said, taking a sip of tea. She had switched to herb tea to "calm her nerves." "I love that you can pick your baby's daddy this way. It's so much more streamlined than dating and sex. All right, let's check out the first guy." I clicked open the link to his photo and profile.

Though his profile on the Gentex site was extremely detailed, each part of the in-depth description made the guy seem highly average: A brown-haired, brown-eyed, 5'8"-tall medical student, who weighed 195. A little chunky. I wondered if he had a "problem" with food. I clicked to the next screen, "self-assessment." When asked which popular cele-

brity he resembled, his answer was: "I don't compare myself
to others. I prefer to be happy with who I am."

"Not attractive," Mae and I said in unison. I clicked on his
photograph. Very average-looking. I wondered why Cait chose
this guy. Selecting your baby's daddy from a fuzzy photograph
and a third-grade psychological assessment was weird. But I
guess it was a step up from the condom breaking during a
drunken one-night stand.

"Okay, let's move on." I clicked on number 7451 and went
right to the link for his photo and clicked on it. This donor was
much more handsome, much thinner and much paler.

"Hey, 7451 looks a little like Ashton Kutcher, but Ashton
playing a serial killer," said Mae, staring at the brown-haired
man who was looking uncomfortably into the camera.

"And, actually, a bit gay." I said, scrutinizing the photograph.

"Oh, God: a gay serial killer. Cait's child will grow up to be,
what was that guy's name who killed Versace?" Mae said, slapping both of her hands on my desk. "But seriously, do you
think Cait's kids will end up gay?"

"No, come on, Mae—get out of the Dark Ages. Lesbians
don't necessarily have kids who are gay, too. If kids all had the
same sexuality as their parents, no one would be gay, would
they? Duh."

"Yeah, right. But gay or straight, is the kid going to be
okay?" Mae took another sip of her tea. "You know how mean
other kids are to each other? Are other kids going to torture
Cait's kid because he's got two moms—or one mom and her
girlfriend or whatever?"

"I'm not worried about that," I said, swiveling my chair and
turning to face Mae. "You know who's meanest—black people. Somebody's always hatin' on you or saying they're going
to kick your black ass into next week. Somebody else if criti-
cizing your hair and skin color, or talking about who thinks

she's all that or who's acting white. Add in racism, and it's hard growing up black. But we survived our childhoods, right? Everybody's going to be tormented for one thing or another. You just have to teach kids to be strong enough to withstand other human beings."

"Well, you might make a good girlfriend to a baby mama after all," Mae said, poking me in the side. "Hey, Ang, what are those "P"s next to Ashton's name?" Mae asked, turning back to face the screen.

"Previous pregnancies," I replied. "The guy has three. I think they can have a maximum of five in the same geographical area, and ten altogether."

"So many of his kids are running around! The possibilities for inbreeding seem nearly limitless. And Princeton isn't far from here. Geez, be careful or you'll end up with a seriously retarded grandchild."

"Could Cait's kid end up dating her own brother?" I wrinkled my brow.

"What is this number?" asked Mae, pointing to thirty-five percent, in a column under his sperm measurement.

"I think that's the amount of viable sperm per ejaculate. There are something like twenty bazillion sperm per ejaculation."

"Wow, I can't see how Cait could *not* get pregnant with thirty-five percent of twenty bazillion sperm swimming so desperately to her egg. With so much sperm out in the world, I can't believe I'm not pregnant. Be careful, I think I see some sperm swimming around your desk." She laughed and jabbed at my legs.

"It dies instantly."

"Men are so weak.

"But, serious question—both of these guys are Caucasoid. How do you feel about being the other mommy to a white kid?"

"This is Cait's party. I'm in the wait-and-see mode," I said, putting my elbows on the desk. "But, really, I don't think I could bear being confused as the kid's nanny more than once."

In my few visits to Park Slope, the next neighborhood over from Cait's, I noticed the many nannies, mostly Caribbean, caring for the white babies of women like the hangers we worked with. It was knee-jerk to see pallid infants bundled in snowsuits and tucked into strollers being eased down Seventh Avenue, the main strip, by a klatch of baby-sitters, their lilting island chatter trailing behind them. Maybe I was being a complete classist snob, but the thought of being mistaken as a black worker taking care of some white woman's baby mortified me.

"Let's find a black donor on this thing," I said, clicking through several pages until I found donor 0901. He was a so-so-looking brother, with medium brown skin and a nice smile—though it looked like a tooth was missing on the right side.

"What's with the hair? Is that a flat-top?"

"Mae, the haircut is not genetic. This picture looks old. Check this guy's birth date." She shifted in her chair and leaned toward the screen.

"April 24, 1968. This guy is old. Cait's not gonna get pregnant with some old sperm."

"Let's see what he does for a living," I said, leaning toward the screen. "I guess he's a lawyer. His degree is JD."

"Why is a lawyer donating at a sperm bank? He must not be a successful lawyer."

"How much do they get paid for doing this?" I clicked on the link marked "Information for Donors."

"It says here one hundred dollars for each ejaculate. Wow, the sperm sells for four hundred dollars, not including shipping and handling. That's, what, a three hundred percent markup. That's worse than buying a bottle of wine in a restaurant."

"I vote for the old black man with the ugly hair over the gay white serial killer or Joe Average," Mae said, stretching as she stifled a yawn. "But, is it really fair for a white woman to raise a mixed-race kid?"

"I don't know, but at least the baby will have Josie, a mixed-race cousin."

"Yeah, but how's the kid gonna know about stuff like Kwanzaa?"

"Oh relax, nobody knows anything about Kwanzaa," I said, finishing the coffee in my cup. "What do *we* know about Kwanzaa?"

"Isn't one of the days Kugi-chaga-something?" Mae said, downing the last of her tea.

"I think I have the days on a holiday card somewhere," I said, rubbing my eyes.

"You know, you're right, girl," Mae said. "Let's agree that no matter what happens, we'll teach Cait how to do her kid's hair. That's all our people care about, so if the kid's hair doesn't look jacked up, everything'll be fine."

"Hair!" we said together, laughing and falling onto each other from across the chairs.

"Mae, seriously, do you think this is weird?" Before she could answer, I clamped my hand over her mouth. "I know, I know. I do, too."

"Speaking of weird, guess what my mother's doing?" I clicked onto the *Désire* magazine home page of my computer, watching Gentex fade back into cyberspace.

"I have no idea; your mother is so busy, who can keep up? Talk about a hardworking black woe-mon."

"She's got this grant or fellowship or something to make a bunch of documentaries for television."

"I'm scared of her. Tell her congratulations for me."

"Yeah, it's great and all, but guess what her first topic is?" I looked up at Mae, who shrugged. "Black transgender oppression."

"Okay, you've lost me. I have no idea what you're talking about."

"Transgender people feel like they don't fit in anywhere. Straights harass and abuse them because they're different and some gay people don't want them included in their movement. Remember that whole woman born woman thing at the lesbian sex conference?"

"Oh, right, I heard that," Mae said tiredly. "So now that Mama Wright is making this documentary, she's an expert on the transgender, um, community?"

"Not expert, savior." I felt my anger rise. My mother had a new group of acolytes eating away her attention. "She's deep into it. Just like all those hair nuts, now it's the transgenders, too. She's called me twice to tell me how fascinating it all is."

"Ang, have you said anything to your mom about Cait?"

"Hell, no." I tapped my index finger on the desk nervously. "She's sure Keith and I are getting back together."

"But, Ang, now that she's this angel of mercy to people of different lifestyles and dress codes, don't you think she'd be more open-minded about what's going on with you?"

"No, no, no!" I shrieked, bordering on hysteria. The editor in the next cube over scowled at us to hush up. "Work is work and torturing me is a whole other thing. Being gay is fine for the faceless interview subjects, another thing for her own daughter."

"Right, right, what was I thinking?" Mae said as she stood up to leave. "You okay, sweetie?"

"I'm going to be all right, I think." As Mae picked up her teacup and hugged my shoulders, I hoped I would be.

Chapter 21

That afternoon, I was sitting near the front of Lucia's office, forcing myself to not fidget through our weekly "ideas" meeting with the boss. She hated them, bored by what she thought were the editors' insipid, simplistic suggestions and constant whining. It was a rite of passage to be dressed down by her.

I felt smug since I had plenty of ideas to offer. Plus, sex was an easy sell. My talent at "pitching" always surprised and aggravated the sleek girl panthers seated around me. I had honed my reporting and spinning abilities around the dinner table. I was rarely allowed to watch TV, except the news. My father and I often dined alone, picking apart the events of the day, after watching my mother's segment. On weekends, around the dinner table, small talk wasn't allowed. We discussed ideas. Gossip was grudgingly permitted in small doses, tolerated as a form of reporting. "On your friends," my father had joked. My mother called it a constructive way to explore the psyche of people and understand human frailties as long as it wasn't mean spirited, hurtful or back biting.

Lucia sat at her desk wearing a lavender knock-off Chanel suit with matching reading glasses around her neck on a chain.

Her gold nose ring glinted in the afternoon sun as it streamed into the panoramic window behind her desk. She fiddled with her iPod with one hand and fingered a hand-rolled cigarette with the other.

"What have you got, Catherine?" barked Lucia, turning her eyes toward Catherine Brice, the niece of the company's owner. The young heiress had been assigned to our magazine as a junior editor. Lucia had hinted to me that she thought Catherine was a spoiled, talentless crybaby, and took particular delight in humiliating her. She prided herself on making the girl's lip quiver at least once during every meeting. I felt sorry for Catherine, but was also grateful to be on Lucia's good side.

"Well, I thought we might do a short profile on Erika Allegra," began Catherine, haltingly. "She's a hot new singer with a kind of ska sound . . ."

"Oh, for God sakes, Catherine, get an original idea." Lucia's voice had turned to a snarl. "We're not covering another *O.C.* chippie who is appropriating music from underdeveloped countries and then getting a record deal because she's cute and blonde and thinks she's got rhythm when all she really did was bang some guy on the beach in Montego Bay. That is so David Byrne. The Bo Derek braids she came back with will probably last longer than her career. Why don't you find the guy who told her what ska was and we can do an article on him? Next." Lucia could play the dozens better than any black person. Catherine's lip was trembling, her eyes filling with tears.

"Amanda, maybe you can bring back something this weekend while you're on the mall tour." Lucia gestured toward our beauty editor.

"I'm not going," replied Amanda, tossing her shoulder-length blonde hair. She pulled her arms tightly across her skin-hugging mohair sweater.

I enjoyed counting how many times Amanda did the "white girl toss." Generally Amanda tossed her hair more when she was annoyed, so today I expected that she'd be jerking her head and neck like a Tourette's survivor.

"Yes, you are." Lucia narrowed her eyes at Amanda.

"No, I'm not," Amanda shot back in her crisp Australian accent. "I will *not* spend my weekend in Schenectady, New York, or wherever the hell Marketing wants me to do makeovers on ugly women in bad clothes."

"Yes, you are. Those women are our readers, and you *will* be there. It's good PR for them to see you."

Lucia hated her more than anyone else on staff, and would've fired her if she wasn't also our celebrity wrangler. She dealt with the star maker machinery behind our cover subjects, brokering deals, soothing bruised star egos and screaming at publicists. Her electronic Rolodex was worth almost as much as the pointy, Italian leather thigh-high boots she was wearing.

"They don't need to see me—in person," she shot back, undaunted. Her cosmopolitan haughtiness gave her courage to stand up to Lucia that others lacked. "Why can't they simply see me on the telly?" She made the rounds on celebrity cable shows, yucking it up with the hosts and dishing out fashion and makeup advice.

"Amanda, you will be going, and I don't want to hear any more about it," said Lucia. "One more word, and I will cut off your expense account, and you'll be taking a Greyhound bus to Schenectady." Amanda tossed her hair again, as Lucia looked over the group for her next victim.

"Could someone who isn't mentally deficient please talk to me?" Lucia fingered the cigarette. No matter how abusively she behaved, young editors still lined up to learn from her. Though I was happy to be Lucia's teacher's pet, sometimes I worried that she might turn on me, too.

"Angela, how was the lesbian sex conference?"

"Great." I proceeded to describe Suzy G's workshop. As I had promised Cait, I didn't mention the transgender fiasco. That was my mother's territory now. Listening to the story, Lucia laughed, and my description of the sex party brought the cigarette to her lips. I could feel Amanda's evil eye on my back.

"I love *that*!" she shouted. "I'd like to meet this Suzy G, especially since she has the brilliant taste to admire my work. Ba-hah! Anyway, let's move on to cover ideas. Throw out some names."

"Kirsten Dunst."

"Kate Winslet."

"Reese Witherspoon."

"Ahhh!" Lucia jerked the unlit cigarette from her lips and slapped the side of her desk. "Come on girls—we've had each of those women on our covers in the last year and a half. Isn't there anyone who is not Aryan? Or even a non-celebrity?"

Lucia's last question was met with a stunned, stone-cold silence. Everyone, Lucia included, turned toward Brian Berryman, the research expert who the parent company foisted on all of the editors to make sure they were paying attention to the latest demographic information about readership and cover sales. Lucia despised him.

"Your bestselling covers have been A-list celebrities," said Brian, who was sitting with his legs crossed in a chair next to Lucia's desk. He was vaguely handsome, with prematurely gray hair. But he bit his nails freakishly low and his voice sounded thin and scratchy.

"Blue backgrounds work well for you, and the words 'mind-blowing sex' have been shown to boost your performance on the newsstand."

"Thank you, Brian, I knew you'd want to put your two

cents in. And your insights are oh-so useful." Lucia tapped her fingernails on the desk as she spoke. "Soon editors will be obsolete and number-crunching suits like you can run magazines. But until then, girls, give me some possible non-celebrity cover ideas, please."

"What about a cover on women who shape public opinion?" It was Catherine again, speaking just above a whisper. She had more spunk than Lucia gave her credit for. "You know, political bloggers."

"Oh, yeah, some of these snarky girl geeks are pretty attractive," Darcia, the fashion editor, spoke approvingly, happily picturing cute, sample-size women sitting at computers.

"Hmmm, good idea." Smiling, Lucia moved the cigarette near her lips. "You're sure we can find enough Internet hotties, right?"

Catherine nodded.

"Okay, let's narrow it down to three of them with the working coverline 'Blogger Babes: Do These American Beauties Have the Power to Elect the Next President?' I love it." Lucia slid the cigarette between her front teeth.

"Um, Lucia, I don't think this is a good idea." Brian rested an arm on Lucia's desk as he spoke. "You know the cover rules: young is better than old. Pretty is better than ugly. Rich is better than poor . . ."

"We're okay so far. Please move on." Lucia was now glaring at him, tapping her foot impatiently under her desk.

"Music is better than movies. Movies are better than TV," he continued. "And anything is better than politics and nothing is better than a dead celebrity."

"Shut up, Brian!" Lucia shouted, pushing his arm off the edge of her desk. "Go back into the hole you crawled out of and take the Midwestern housewives from your useless focus groups with you. Somebody get with Catherine and pull up photos of some of these young women. And make sure they're not all white—please. Is there a woman of color blogger?"

Every eye turned toward me. Didn't any of these white women have any women of color in their lives? And for God sakes, I wasn't going to suggest the vile Tatiana.

"Yes, there is—Tatiana Braithwaite." I turned to see Lizette Ng, the only other woman of color in the room, smiling broadly. Shit. "She's a total beauty with a blog and political think tank. She's hot—a thirty under thirty type. Right, Angela?"

I nodded numbly.

"Great, great, great." Lucia almost shouted, rolling the cigarette between her thumb and forefinger. "Make sure to get her."

I felt sick as I walked back to my desk. Uck—Tatiana as a cover girl on my magazine. I'd have to stare at her disgusting face for a whole month. At least I felt a sliver of satisfaction knowing that she was the "affirmative action choice." She'd hate that. I speed-dialed Mae to give her the news of the Tatiana cover debacle.

"I'm glad you called, but what I have to tell you will make you feel worse," Mae whispered into the receiver.

"I'm bracing myself," I said.

"I was in Saks yesterday, and my personal shopper told me that she had seen Keith in there the day before." My eyes widened with genuine disbelief, and I nearly dropped the phone. "I know it's surprising—"

"No, the surprising part is that you were ever up in Saks buying retail," I said. "I'm sure it wasn't him," I added quickly.

"Well . . ."

"No, he hates to shop," I said, straightening a stack of papers on my desk. "He gets everything from catalogs. I don't think he even knows that clothes hang on racks."

"He was buying a suit, Hugo Boss, I think," Mae continued.

"How did she know it was him?" I remained skeptical. Keith rarely wore anything besides khaki and tweed with a few African accessories thrown in. Mae's gossip was generally correct, but she seemed off base this time.

"Ang, he wasn't alone. Tatiana was with him." I could hear her fidgeting as she let out a deep breath.

"She was? What do you mean *with*?" I grabbed a pencil from a cup on my desk and began to twist it in my hand.

"They were in the store together, shopping for his suit."

"Together, together?" I put the pencil in my mouth and chewed on the eraser.

"I don't know, I guess," Mae said, and I could hear sympathy in her voice.

"Are you sure it was *him* and *her* with him?"

"Yes, she knows Tatiana. This girl is Tatiana's personal shopper, too."

"Come on, Mae, you and Tatiana have the same personal shopper?"

"You know that three degrees of separation is all we have in our small black world." Mae was quipping, but sounded worried. "Tati introduced Keith to the girl."

"How did she say he looked?" I pictured Keith with sallow skin, thin, small clumps of hair missing and his body limp from depression, Tatiana trying to help him fix up. He hadn't returned my several phone calls.

"She said he looked kind of good, actually."

"What!" I tried to understand how I could feel shocked, sad, angry and betrayed all at once.

"How could he date *her*, and so soon?" I knew it was irrational since I had broken our engagement, but still. His mourning period seemed inappropriately brief.

"Let's just wait and see, okay?" Mae replied, trying to sound soothing. "Maybe it was nothing."

"Yeah, I guess you're right," I said as I hung up. But I didn't mean it. How dare he move on? I had no reason to be jealous, but that's exactly what I was.

Chapter 22

By the weekend, I was thoroughly enraged by the whole Keith-Tatiana news. Blazing through Harlem on Saturday morning, I needed to burn off some of my anger. I was moving so fast that I looked like some crazed speed walker. I had decided to go over to my old apartment and pick up the rest of my clothes. Keith obviously wasn't that broken up over the breakup and didn't have the right to keep my stuff hostage by refusing to take my calls. It was getting colder, too chilly for the fall clothes I had dashed out of the apartment with the day Keith and I broke up. Plus, I needed something cute to wear next week. I was dragging Mae to a holiday party to fix her up with the host, Rufus Browne. And I couldn't keep patching together outfits using creative combinations of Cait's funkiest clothes, though I had been looking a little bit hipper lately. Several hangers who sat near me had said so.

I paused for a minute, and punched our old number into my cell. I wasn't sure if I wanted Keith to be there or not. I couldn't gauge how it would feel to see him. How would we behave? But he didn't answer, even after I tried several more times. Out of town? Keith wasn't a call-screening kind of guy. It still surprised me to hear the machine pick up with only his voice on it. Our chirpy, coupley message had finally been erased, replaced by his solemn, "Please leave a message for Dr. Keith Redfield after the tone."

As I walked up the steps of my brownstone, I felt a pang of nostalgia for the old neighborhood. I had only been "living" in Brooklyn for a month and a half, but I missed the all-black hustle and bustle of the hood. Prospect Heights was completely integrated—overrun, really, with recent Manhattan transplants who had gentrified the community—and it had a different, more sedate vibe. In Harlem, 125th Street on the other hand, was like a chaotic, colorful outdoor bazaar, despite the proliferation of superstore chains. You could purchase anything on the street—from African fabric to bootleg DVDs to incense and bestsellers. Despite all of the adventurous Caucasian couples and gay men who were supposedly buying up brownstones in Harlem—white faces were still pretty much an oddity.

Keith had been so quick to throw me out that he hadn't bothered to get the key back. Nervously, I pushed it into the lock and clicked it open. At least he hadn't changed the locks. As I walked into the living room, I was surprised to hear the smoky voice of Barry White blasting through the apartment. The music was so loud that the walls shook slightly. Was Keith home or had he accidentally left the radio on tuned to one of those all-70s R&B stations? There were plenty of them that were trying to appeal to black baby boomers desperate to escape from hip hop. Keith wasn't really a fan of either kind of music, though. He preferred classical. As I walked through the apartment, not much had changed. All photographs of me and us had been removed, but everything else remained intact.

The music was coming from the bedroom, but the door was closed. I felt a little afraid as I pushed it open, half expecting to see Keith having a seizure on the floor, which would explain why he was unable to turn off Barry White's too-loud song of seduction.

What I saw was worse. Keith actually looked like he was having a seizure. His head was thrown back and his body shaking. Not illness, but pleasure. Tatiana was straddling him, rocking and grinding, in a nasty-dance of ecstasy. I knew it was her, even from behind: I recognized her back, perfectly muscled thanks to personal training, and every bone-straight hair in place. And her voice; she was actually singing Barry White's words to Keith, slightly off-key and two octaves higher, as she ground her pelvis into his. How clichéd is that? Her clothes were in a heap on the floor in a pile mingled with Keith's, and I squinted and recognized Michael Kors, one of her favorite labels.

Even worse, on the nightstand were not one but two empty condom wrappers. Oh, Tatiana inspired so much passion in him that no amount of tantric power could keep him from ejaculating? And he listened to Barry White with her, while I had to endure Enya or discs of whales masturbating or whatever New Age crap we made love to that helped him contain his sperm? This was the most disgusting thing I'd ever witnessed. And in my own bed! I couldn't believe he'd chosen her—and so soon. I felt ill imagining her dozing in the still-fresh indentation my body had made in the mattress.

Actually, I really did feel ill; my large intestine was rumbling wildly and my bowels had loosened. Even—or especially—screwing her brains out, Tatiana still gave me diarrhea. I ran to the hall bathroom, not even worrying that either of them would hear me above the music and singing and gyrating. I sat on the toilet for a few minutes, sobbing quietly into my hands. I didn't know if I was more mad or hurt or confused. I wanted Keith to have remained devastated by our breakup to prove how important I had been to him. He wasn't supposed to be over me so quickly. Had our relationship meant nothing to him?

I finally got up and walked toward the door, empty-handed. I didn't care about the winter clothes. I was just too drained to deal with it.

"Who's there?" Keith shouted, holding an unabridged dictionary in one hand. He was using his other hand to press a pillow against his crotch. "Angela—what the hell are you doing here? Why didn't you call? You can't just bust in here like this."

"Keith, what's going on?" shouted Tatiana from my bed.

"Nothing. Everything's fine," he shouted back as he pulled the bedroom door closed. "Now, what are you doing here?" he asked me again in his deep-voice stage whisper.

"This was my home, too, and you haven't answered any of my calls, so I thought you were out of town," I said, taking a step back. "I needed some clothes. I didn't expect this freaky peep show."

"Speaking of freaky, how's Dr. Getty?" Keith's face was turning purple. "I wouldn't know since she hasn't had the nerve to be a man—which is what she wants to be—and tell me that she stole my fiancé. Every time I see her stupid, smug face outside her class—"

"Oh, speaking of class—you clearly have none," I spat back. "Do you know how corny you are, listening to Barry White while having sex?"

"Get out—this is my house and you're not welcome." He pushed me toward the door, nudging me awkwardly with the red and white dictionary. "Give me the key—immediately."

"I can't get out of here fast enough." I slapped his hand, and dropped the key on the floor. I stepped over it and walked out the door.

Chapter 23

I lay my coat on the mahogany sleigh bed in Rufus Browne's bedroom and admired his décor. Though I was still depressed about Keith and Tatiana, I was determined to hook Mae up with Rufus.

Looking around the room, I imagined Rufus thumbing through Pottery Barn's fall catalog, stopping midway, then ordering an entire bedroom set, linens, pillows and all. His taste was as tidy and predictable as he seemed to be—except for the snapshot blown up to 11 x 14 on the wall over his bed. Hanging in a frame covered in shiny gold lamé, the black-and-white photograph featured a snaggle-toothed young Rufus, one arm thrust in the air, the other slung around the shoulders of his older brother Elijah, who was now known as the rapper Hard Tyme. Rufus was turned toward Elijah, his head thrown back, and both boys were overcome with body-convulsing laughter. They were wearing T-shirts on their heads, the sleeves hanging down their backs like ropy dreadlocks.

For the third or fourth time I yanked down my skirt. It was a little snug around the hips and thighs. I was uncomfortable, but for the first black holiday party of the season, I couldn't be choosy: I had borrowed the leather lace-up skirt and suede shoes from the fashion closet at work. I hadn't made it back uptown to get the rest of my clothes after the horror of seeing Keith in bed with Tatiana. It was either squeeze into this skirt sized for a supermodel or buy retail at Saks or Bloomingdale's. Happily, the skirt matched a silk shirt I had snagged from Cait's closet.

I glanced one more time at the large box I'd placed on the floor next to the bed. It contained donor 0901's precious sperm. Kirby, the Brice-Castle mailroom guy, had brought the monstrosity to my desk at lunchtime, since it was taking up too much space in the back. "Thank you, Kirby," I had replied hastily, not meeting his curious gaze. "I, um, bought some art-work, and it's easier to receive it here. Sorry for the trouble."

"Sure," he had replied, raising an eyebrow as he set the box down next to my desk.

Mae walked into Rufus's bedroom, and tossed her faux fur coat carefully on the bed next to mine.

"Who's your light-skinned friend?" she asked, unwrapping her scarf from her neck and lifting her eyes slightly toward the box. "Is that your date?"

"No, you're my date—for now. This is Cait's man. It's the baby's daddy," I answered, giving it a gentle nudge with my toe.

"You're kidding? Why is the box so big? How much sperm is in there?" she whispered, walking closer to get a better look. "I've never known a guy to produce more than a couple of ta-blespoons."

"I think it's just a few ounces, but it's stored in dry ice. I think we've got thirty-six hours to get it in Cait."

"Ewwww, spare me any more details, okay?" Mae turned up her nose. "It's the black donor, right, that loser lawyer guy?"

"Yeah," I said, glancing down at the box.

"Thank God," she said as we moved toward the door. "What did Cait say about that? About having a mixed-race kid?"

"She insisted she was a 'post-race' woman and didn't really care," I replied. "I think she was getting overwhelmed with her embarrassment of choices, and was relieved that we'd picked for her."

"Well, that's cool," said Mae, over her shoulder. "The baby will be a cutie, light brown, the color of that box."

As we walked into the main room, I looked around at the pretty people, a holiday splash of colorful dresses, suits, shirts and ties as bright and shiny as Christmas ornaments. Though black folks whined constantly about New York's bone-chilling winter, the cold-weather holidays really looked good on us.

"Stop fussing with your skirt," murmured Mae through the side of her mouth, stepping into the room behind me. "You look just fine."

"Okay, okay," I replied, giving it one final tug. "Hey, where's the host? Let's say hello to Rufus."

"Do we have to?"

"Mae, you promised to try to keep your mind open." I had spent twenty minutes on the phone earlier convincing Mae that Rufus was boyfriend material. She shot me down, point by point, like some captain of the never-gonna-get-a-man debate team. "You said you were ready and wanted to meet someone, so here he is."

"He's fat."

"Shhh. No, he's not. He's thick and healthy. I think you're developing body image issues from hanging out with the hangers."

"He's boring."

"Would you lower your voice?" I looked around to make sure no one was listening. "And he's not boring, his job is boring. But he makes good money doing whatever it is he does. Plus, he's available, and he likes you. And his brother . . ." I began.

I had met Rufus while doing a mini-profile on Hard Tyme for *Désire*. Rufus had stood out since he was quiet, educated and well-mannered, unlike the rest of the tacky, new-money hip hop entourage, clinging to the frayed bottoms of Hard Tyme's baggy jeans. Rufus and Elijah had grown up in Hollis, Queens, though Hard Tyme tried to downplay his beginnings. Rufus had graduated from Middlebury College, and then returned home to hover around the edge of the young, black professional class that we all belonged to. When we first met, he mentioned that he had annual winter and summer solstice parties, so I gave him my card to put on his guest list. Thanks to his good job and famous brother, Rufus could pull in a crowd that sparkled with the Talented Twentieth and a few members of the hip hop nation thrown in for spice.

"Stop. I wouldn't be dating the famous rapper brother. I'd be dating the nothing accountant brother or whatever he is," sniffed Mae.

"You know what, Material Girl, yes, Rufus is an accountant, but for a cable company, so he often has free tickets and passes to screenings and stuff. He brings extra cache to the table."

"He's a player, so he's probably got a lot of women hanging around him. Video hos and rapper trash."

"No, he doesn't. I don't think you can be both a boring accountant and a major player. Come on, Mae, you're just being difficult." She snorted, clearly unconvinced, but lowered her shoulders from her ears as I pulled her toward the middle of the room.

The bar was in Rufus's homey dining room, tastefully decorated in understated African. The host was manning the blender, cheerfully pouring drinks for his guests. Rufus was dark and handsome, with large brown eyes so pretty he could've been wearing eyeliner. He looked sharp tonight in a dark brown suit, pink shirt and red print tie, a cheery little handkerchief fluttering from his top jacket pocket.

"Hey, Buster Browne, hit me with one of those drinks," said a guy I thought I knew vaguely from somewhere. Rufus was the kind of easygoing, fun-time guy who had a lot of nicknames. He was good-humored and made a point of remembering names, the kind of younger kid who finds a way to shine through the star power of his older brother.

"Hi, pretty ladies," he said, grinning, looking past his friend at the bar. He winked at Mae. "You both look lovely."

"I'm scared of you," Mae said, her voice a mix of apathy and sarcasm. I ground my heel into the pointy toe of her right pump.

"Can I pour you drinks?" Rufus's deep baritone was jovial, willfully ignoring Mae's sour tone. I nodded and smiled as I nudged her roughly in the ribs.

"Nice party, Rufus," she said, still being stingy with her smile. "You're quite the host."

"That's so I can pull women like you," he bantered back. Perfect. Mae looked like she was thawing. "Let's get this party started. 'Scuse us, would you, Angela?"

Rufus reached behind him and turned up the music, LL Cool J's "Around the Way Girl." He grabbed Mae's hand and pulled her to the center of the room, as he smiled and mouthed the lyrics. Just then I felt my phone vibrate.

"Hello," I said loudly over the throbbing bass.

"It's me—where are you?" Cait asked.

"Remember, I mentioned that Mae and I were stopping by this party thing?" I cupped my hand over the phone and moved into an empty corner of the room.

"Right, you said it was in Tribeca." I could hear the sounds of the street behind Cait's voice. "I'm feeling keyed up about the insemination. Maybe I'll join you guys. Is there dancing?"

"Yes, but, uhhh, no, honey, I, um, won't be staying long..." I hedged. I couldn't be at this party full of bougie blacks with my white female lover.

"Great, dancing will make me feel better. I'm on the street; text me the address, and I'll jump in a cab." Before I could answer, she had hung up. Reluctantly, I sent the address.

My stomach was doing back handsprings as I walked toward Mae and Rufus who were dancing to "Brown Skin." Rufus was holding Mae, but not too tightly, his eyes closed as he swayed to the music. Mae looked comfortable, and happy, despite herself. The living room door opened, and I felt my chest lurch. Keith walked in with Tatiana fastened to his arm. I quickly pivoted and pretended to join a conversation with a few folks I didn't know, stretching my eyes nearly out of the sockets to keep Keith and Tatiana in my peripheral vision. I had wondered if they might show up, though neither of them knew Rufus very well. I was sure they were just here to torment me.

I hadn't seen Keith, clothed, since the day we broke up, and I was shocked at how great he looked. When I ran into him—naked underneath Tatiana in my bed—I had been too surprised to really notice how buff his body had become. Clearly, he'd been working out; his suit fit him like a latex glove. Were those new titanium glasses he was wearing? With me, Keith had been little more than social wallpaper, but the minute he got with her he had morphed into high-wattage arm candy. And Tatiana was stunning, clad in a made-to-order turquoise halter dress, her hair hanging in dark waves around her shoulders. They looked like expertly matched showroom furniture selected by an upscale decorator. The colors in his tie even complemented her dress.

"Hello, Angela," they both said to me, coldly, in unison. Though Keith's chin was high and his back ramrod straight, something in his eyes softened as he gazed at me. Tatiana's posture matched his. She looked like an aging grand dame who, in a blink, always posed with her head to the right, chin in the air, to tighten her wrinkled neck and show her good side in photos.

"By the way, thank you for recommending me for the cover of your magazine." Tatiana was smiling, but both her voice and eyes were flat. "Are you here alone?"

Standing there in my pieced-together outfit, I felt more alone than I ever had. Before I could answer the door opened. Cait walked in, crimson-cheeked, her face ruddy and wind-burned. She was wearing tight jeans, low-heeled boots and her worn motorcycle jacket. She would've looked hot in context—at Suck or with her GALS FREE mentees—but not here.

"Oh, look, it's Angela's lezzzbian lover." Keith's eyes looked small and mean as he turned his body away from me and toward Tatiana, his smile tight and unkind.

"Dr. Redfield, if I'd known you would be here, I—oh right—wouldn't have come," Cait snapped as she took off her jacket and walked toward us. Her hair, tousled from the wind, was sticking up on top. She looked like she had just crawled out of bed and was on her way to the auto show.

"Come on, hon, let's dance." Keith turned his back, bumping Cait's shoulder as he led Tatiana to the dance floor.

As he put his hands out to Tatiana, the two of them looked almost robotic, like the crudely animated cartoon characters I had watched on television as a girl. This cheered me somewhat. Still, Keith had the upper hand in this small black world.

"Pompous jerk, and he can't dance, either," Cait muttered as she followed my eyes and watched Tatiana and Keith stiffly salsa dancing from side to side. "Come on, I feel like dancing, too."

Cait dropped her jacket into a corner, and guided me to the dance floor. At that moment, it seemed like time had stopped—as though all the light in the room had suddenly dimmed except for two cruel searchlights beaming onto Cait's hand sitting thickly on the small of my back. Her hand felt oversize, like one of those spongy green "number one" souvenirs that fans wave at sporting events. As Cait spun me around showily, I was already fast-forwarding to three hours from now when I would be the subject of ungracious post-party dish. I might've been able to get by with the whole gay thing had Cait been a "celesbian," like Ellen DeGeneres or Sheryl Swoopes. But in the here and now, in the middle of the dance floor, I might as well throw on a scarlet dress and call myself Jezebel.

Thankfully, the song ended and Mae scurried over, smiling nervously, Rufus in tow. Cait, her hand locked in position on my back, moved toward them.

"Hey, Rufus, this is Cait, my—" I stopped, not knowing exactly how to make the introduction. Gay people really didn't have adequate language for their objects of affection. What was Cait? My partner? No, that sounded like a business relationship, like we owned an Internet café together. Companion? I could be describing my seeing-eye dog. Mate? Too scientific; chimps in some Jane Goodall experiment. Lover? Too sexual, that puts you right in the bedroom. Girlfriend? Juvenile, or maybe too "strong black woman." We sounded like Oprah and Gayle. My wife? Technically incorrect given most laws of the land. We all stood there awkwardly for a few uncomfortable seconds. Finally, Mae rescued me.

"We know who she is. Cait's your bitch." Everyone laughed and Cait stood on tiptoe to give Mae a hug.

"Girl, I saw you, you can dance," said Rufus, grabbing Cait's hand. "Come on, take a twirl with me." Before she could speak, he propelled her onto the dance floor, and they rocked and twisted a lively rhumba. Genial Rufus allowed Cait to lead. Thank God.

"Come here," Mae said, tugging me toward Rufus's bedroom. As I turned to follow her, I gawked at Tatiana and Keith, the two of them leaning lazily against a wall. He looked down at her and all of the grouchy anger and professorial stuffiness I had lived with so long disappeared. With Tatiana at his side, Keith looked sexy, comfortable in his skin. I couldn't take my eyes off them, locked in their private moment. I felt surprised and overcome by my continued, raging jealousy. I had seen them having sex, but this stolen intimacy was even more raw.

"Oh, my God." Mae turned, took my chin in her hands and yanked my face away from them. "Angela, have some dignity. Stop looking over there."

We slipped back into the bedroom, and I closed the door behind us.

"I want to go home," I said as I sat down on a fur coat that was thrown across the bed. My voice sounded thin and whiny. "This is too much."

"Relax, everything's cool, though your girl's a bit under-dressed," said Mae, absently fingering the fur. "Besides, we aren't leaving. Not enough people saw my outfit." She did look dazzling. Her dress was bloodred, draping her perfectly, like the scarlet spray of a fender bender between Vera Wang and Lane Bryant, lipstick and nail color to match. I liked that she said "we." Mae felt like the only constant in my life.

"Do you miss him—Keith?" She lay back on the bed, falling on the fur coat, pulling me down next to her.

"Oooh, this feels good." I burrowed deeper into the coat, closing my eyes. "Yes, I do in a way."

"The dick?"

"No, not that. It's kind of a relief not to have that. Penises are so high-maintenance. Is it hard? Is it soft? Then guys have to give them names—my Johnson, Jimmy and the twins, whatever—like they're another person, not a body part. Plus, the mess. Sometimes I think it's easier without a dick in the mix."

"What is it, then?" She sat up and looked at me genuinely curious. I sat up, too.

"It's this part, the social thing. It would be nice to just go to a party and not have it be a 'coming out' party."

"I heard that."

"You'll have a permanent escort pretty soon. You and Mr. Rufus seemed to be getting along fine," I said as I glanced over to make sure the sperm was okay.

"He's a little sugar pop, isn't he?" She was finally shedding the tough-girl act. I was glad to see that she'd even christened Rufus with a nickname. "You know, if you want to leave, it's okay. I'm having a good time here," she said.

"I'm glad." I stood up and pulled on my coat, before picking up the box.

"It's all going to be okay. You know that, right?" Mae walked toward me, lifted the box out of my hands and wrapped her arms tightly around it.

"Yeah, I guess so. Thank you, Mae. Sometimes I feel like you're the only person in the world who understands me." I felt all mushy and sentimental. "Group hug?" I hugged her and the box tightly.

"You're my girl. Now can you please get out of here?" Mae replied, dropping the box into my arms. "You and Cait need to take this box of jizz home and make my godbaby."

Chapter 24

A half hour later, Cait and I were on the 2 train, our box of baby daddy on the seat next to me. I tried to push my feelings about Keith aside as I held Cait's mittened hand inside of her jacket pocket. But my foul mood hung on. Someone bumped my foot roughly, and I pulled my eyes from Cait's to throw whoever it was some shade. Some knucklehead, his fingers entwined with his girlfriend's, sat down across from us, barely mumbling "excuse me." His hair buzzed into a longish crew cut, he was wearing a leather Motocross racing jacket, tight jeans and work boots. Macho asshole.

I glared at him, but he didn't notice. He was looking at his pretty girlfriend with an intensity inappropriate for public display. She leaned over and whispered something in his ear, and he pulled her close and kissed her noisily, laughing into her mouth. That pissed me off even more.

"Cait, it is so unfair that I can't kiss you like that," I whispered tersely, thinking again of Keith and Tatiana. Like this couple, they could make out wherever they wanted to, while Cait and I were reduced to holding hands on the sly. "Stupid heterosexuals and their PDA."

"Who are you to talk?" Cait glanced at me sideways, and

poked me in the side with her gloved forefinger. "You were part of the straight nation very recently. It's always the recovering hets who are the most militant."

"Whatever." I rolled my eyes. "I just wish they'd cut it out, advertising their privilege."

"Angela, I have two words for you: who cares?" Cait had pulled my ear toward her and was whispering. "Plus, they're both women."

"Huh?!" I looked at them closely, studying the jawline of the man. It was milky white and smooth. As he put his hands lightly on his girlfriend's face, I noticed how small they were. Cait was right. Now as I continued to stare at her, she began to look much more feminine. She was only accessorized as a man. I should've figured that out: working at a woman's magazine, I should be able to see beyond accessories. But I wouldn't have known he was a she if Cait hadn't clued me in.

"Cait, you barely looked at her—how did you know?"

"By the way she touched her girlfriend's face, so gently." Cait smiled knowingly at the couple, who were peppering each other with kisses. "Also, now look at them—showing off. Passing women always go a bit overboard."

There was a theatrical quality to their passion. The butchy one was getting off on the passing. Kissing her girlfriend was like flipping the bird. Was this the only way gay and lesbian people were comfortable in the world—by passing? Cait was a bit butch, but she couldn't pass, and she wasn't the kind to start calling herself "boi" or something. I'd never be able to kiss Cait in public; dancing with her was hard enough. We had to stay in character, passing as affectionate friends bumping into each other on the way to the train.

"You know, I would kiss you like that, if you'd let me." Cait turned, moving her face toward mine. I pulled away from her abruptly, looking around again. I patted her shoulder.

"No, thanks, I don't feel like being a statistic."

As I snuggled closer to her, I looked again at the other couple. They were rubbing noses as they got up to leave the train.
For God sakes, why don't I just peck Cait on the lips? It was
such a small gesture, and none of the jaded New Yorkers on
this subway car would blink an eye. Deep down, I knew I wasn't
really scared of any of our fellow passengers gay bashing us—
with what? Creased copies of *The New York Times*? The white
cords of their iPod earphones? I was afraid of being judged,
scared to even brush Cait's lips with mine, because of what
strangers would think if they even noticed us. People with
bad fashion and bed hair who lived in parts of Queens that I'd
never heard of. It wasn't danger that kept me from kissing her,
but propriety. Why should the passing couple and Keith and
Tatiana be the only ones to have the privilege of public affection?

I leaned toward Cait and kissed her full on the mouth in
front of everyone on that train, including the show-off, passing
couple. "I love you," I said hoarsely into her mouth. After a
few seconds, a startled Cait smiled and whispered, "I love
you, too."

Feeling happy and self-satisfied, I looked around as the
doors closed, and the train began to move out of the station.
Over my shoulder, I noticed someone standing on the platform, watching us through the window. Was it . . . oh, God, no,
yes—Nona. It was her—the mud cloth coat and "Body and
Soul" tote bag gave her away. She was pushing a pair of large
round glasses to the bridge of her nose gaping, her mouth dangling open. At this moment, I prayed Cait was butch enough
to pass. It was better for Nona to think I was making out with
a white man—though she insisted that God had created a
brother for every sister—than a woman of any race.

Chapter 25

I washed my hands for the third time, scrubbing the anti-bacterial foam over my arms and between my fingers so hard that it burned. I turned off the water and sat down heavily on the side of the bathtub. My T-shirt stuck to my back, and I felt a trickle of sweat dribble south toward my waist. I had thought I was okay with the insemination. But I was terrified.

The whole evening had been a hot mess. Seeing Keith and Tatiana. Cait, looking like the biggest bull-dagger alive in a crowd of black hipsters, crashing Rufus's party. Nona seeing us—and knowing that she would immediately blab to my mother. Gazing into the tub, I considered the alternative to walking into the bedroom and injecting the syringe full of sperm into Cait. Instead, I could lock the door, fill the tub with warm water, stuff pumice stones into the pockets of my jeans and drown myself.

"Honey, I'm ready," Cait called from the next room. Her voice sounded cheerful and melodic, like singing in the shower. She was giddy, a blissed-out teenage girl looking forward to her first date with donor 0901.

I walked slowly into the bedroom and glanced down at her.

She was lying on the bed covered with a sheet from the neck down, eyes closed. The room was lit with eight candles, which gave off the pungent smell of a waxy herb garden. In the dim light, Cait looked like a corpse, someone who had died happy. She had been lying in that position since we had gotten home from the party. It scared me.

"Are you sure this is the correct day?" I leaned down cautiously and moved my hand under her nose to make sure she was still breathing. I knew that she was set to ovulate tomorrow, since she had been charting her temperature and checking her cervical mucous using a book called *Making a Baby, Naturally* with the precision of an MIT physicist testing the formula for cold fusion. Apparently, she would be most fertile each month right before her temperature rose slightly above normal and when her vaginal discharge was the consistency of slippery egg white. Just to be sure, she was also using an over-the-counter ovulation testing kit. With all of this data under her belt, she had pinpointed tomorrow morning as fertility D-day. Plus, the sperm would only last so long.

"Yes, I'm sure we should do it today," Cait said quietly, moving her lips only slightly. She took a deep breath and exhaled, and I watched her chest rise and fall under the sheet.

"Okay then, I guess." Closing my eyes to calm down, I tried to calculate if she got pregnant today, when the baby would be born. Nine months from now is . . . I moved my fingers behind my back. Was I supposed to include between now and when the pregnancy is confirmed? Did the ninth month count in the calculation? Oh, forget it. I'll find a due date calculator in one of Cait's books or Web sites tomorrow; all I needed to know is that I would be a lesbian mommy more or less next fall.

"Angela, I'm ready." She opened her eyes, looked up at me and smiled.

Lowering my shoulders, I smiled back into the slate-gray

eyes of this woman I knew so well, but didn't really know at all. "Tell me what to do."

"Open the box and take out the sperm." Her eyes fluttered shut and she took another deep breath and blew it out noisily, her mouth relaxing into a crooked line.

As I used a pair of scissors to tear open the box, I couldn't believe you could actually get pregnant this way. It seemed like a cool high-school science project; would we make a baby and also win the Westinghouse Science Fair? My hands were shaking as I uncapped the canister and lifted the frosty vial from its dry-ice bed. I was surprised to see that it was slender and only a few inches long. It was capped with a brown top— brown for the donor's skin color.

"Now hold the vial in your hand, against your heart, to thaw it," Cait said softly, between deep inhales and exhales.

"Why against my heart?"

"It's a nice, loving way to unfreeze the sperm, don't you think?"

I loosened my grip on the vial, afraid it would shatter. Holding it on my chest, I felt it begin to warm and thaw. This gesture did seem very tender, like the anonymous man's sperm was actually a baby—well, a pre-baby—that I was protecting and nurturing. I liked that, and felt at one with the chilly, finger size tube.

"When it's thawed, pour it into that glass to breathe," said Cait, gesturing toward the nightstand at a cocktail glass that read OY VAY, I'M GAY, that she had pulled out of a grab bag at a Hanukkah party two years ago. A syringe, needle removed, lay next to the cup. "Then suck up the 'specimen' into the syringe."

I took the cap off the vial and poured the semen into the glass. It really wasn't a lot, maybe a couple of tablespoons. Was this really a complete "ejaculate," as the fertility counselor at

Gentex Labs had claimed? It had always seemed like so much more lying in the wet spot.

"I'm ready," said Cait, pulling the sheet down to reveal her naked body, legs spread. I grazed my fingers along her smooth, taut stomach and looked into her lovely face. It was angular and elegant, but softened by fine lines around her eyes and mouth. Squinting, I pictured Cait pregnant, imagining the boyish, wide-legged stride slowed by an unwieldy belly and full, heavy breasts. Smiling, I felt tenderness rush all over me like a blush.

As I stuck the syringe into the glass, I felt a slight tremor zigzag through my right hand. At the same time, my cell phone both vibrated and rang from the dresser a few feet away. The sound, loud and insistent, startled me, and my shaky hand banged into the glass, knocking it and the syringe off the edge of the nightstand. Cait and I watched with horror as the baby's daddy oozed across the hardwood floor.

"What happened?" Cait said, as she sat up in bed.

"Oh, my God." I covered my mouth, staring wide-eyed at the waxy sheen of the sperm coating the floor.

"Angela, what did you do?" She was standing next to the bed with her toe in a small puddle of sperm. Her eyes were round, full of tears.

"My hand was shaking . . . I . . . I don't know," I sputtered. I reached for her arm and pulled her away from the sperm. "I'm sorry, Cait. I think I'm scared."

"Of course you're scared. I'm scared, too." Cait sat down on the bed, sniffing and crossing her arms over her breasts. "But this is what we decided."

"You know how I feel," I said, sitting down on the other side of the bed, trying not to look at the sperm. I wanted to make Cait happy, and I couldn't stop her anyway. But I felt like I'd been first nudged, then pushed, then shoved into this. "I'm not sure if I'm ready."

"I can't wait for you to be ready, Angela." Cait's voice was low and scratchy as she wiped her face with the back of her hand, then pulled her arms tightly across her chest.

"What I think doesn't matter, so do it without me." I felt shaken, raw. I stood up, looking toward the door. I could walk right out of it and back into my old life. My real life, pre-gay, pre-baby-making.

"What choice do I have now?" Cait laughed, a throaty huff. She stood up, too, pointing at the sperm. "What are we going to do? Just leave the bloody sperm there drying on the floorboards?"

I looked at her, standing there, shivering in her nakedness. Yes, I was afraid, maybe more scared than I had ever felt, but was it fair to deny Cait her dream because of my uncertainty? She had planned and plotted her goal of motherhood down to this moment. It was not right for me to crush it, especially since I didn't seem to have a concrete dream or goal of my own. I looked down at the sperm, which was now mixed with a little dust. God damn it, I was not going to waste Cait's moment. Or her money. This ejaculate was not going to end up as the world's most expensive floor polish. I needed to get it together and get it in her.

"Cait, lie down." I spoke gruffly. Using two fingers, I plucked the syringe from the pool of semen, and dragged it along the floor, sucking in sperm.

"No, it's too late." Cait crossed her legs and set her jaw, turning her face toward the wall.

"Shut up and do it—now!" With the half-full syringe in one hand, I walked over to Cait and used my other hand to push her onto her back. "Spread your legs!"

"This isn't going to work, there's not enough in there," Cait said, opening her legs slightly.

"Listen to me. You've been a lesbian since *you* were a zygote, so you don't know jack about sperm." I pried open her legs, and used a Kleenex to wipe off the syringe. "Believe me, this is plenty for you to get pregnant." Cait's stony expression didn't change.

"Straight girls get pregnant looking at sperm," I insisted, ignoring her face. I stroked her forehead and saw it soften.

"Now relax, and go back to being Zen woman." I pushed play on the portable CD player on the floor near the nightstand. The room filled with the sound of some animal grunting rhythmically, accompanied by Latin-sounding acoustic guitar and flute.

"Cait, close your eyes, stop hyperventilating and breathe—come on, we can do this." I looked at her, and saw some of the tension ease out of her body. She began drawing in large, deep breaths through her nose, and pushing them out through her mouth, her lips quivering with each exhale.

"Ang?" One of her eyes had opened and she looked skeptically at the syringe. The solution inside was a bit gray. "Isn't our sperm contaminated?"

"As my grandmother used to say, 'God made dirt and dirt don't hurt.' " I leaned down, gave Cait's stomach a kiss and then moved my head toward her crotch. I pulled her legs farther apart and held onto her hip bone with one hand and guided the syringe gently inside her with the other. Cait's body stiffened, as I plunged the sperm in. I heard it gurgle inside her.

"Done." I tugged the syringe very gently out of her, and pulled her legs together. No point in letting the little bit we had left seep out of her. I felt productive and mildly satisfied. Was this how guys felt after they ejaculated during conventional baby-making?

"Good," said Cait, keeping her voice placid. She had relaxed and returned to her Earth Mama state. "Now, I want you to make love to me."

"Really?"

"Lesbianbabyhopes.com said it is best to have an orgasm from penetration right after insemination," Cait said. It causes the vagina to contract, like a vacuum, sucking the sperm toward the uterus."

"Well, okay," I said. "I'm going to wash my hands again."

As I walked by my dresser, I picked up my cell phone and looked down to see who the hell had called earlier. A 914 number—my mother. Sitting on the toilet, I listened to the message. "Hello, I am trying to reach Angela Wright." Pause. My mother spoke in the crisp, businesslike tone that she used for the phone. She had never gotten used to the concept of voice mail and sounded formal and officious whenever she left a message. She always began in the third person, as though the voice mail box were a real person, my electronic receptionist, putting her through to me.

"This is her mother, Mrs. Wright." Pause. "Angela, I know what's going on. Nona called and said she saw you on the train kissing . . . a woman." Pause. "What did you think? That I wouldn't find out that you are a . . . I can't even say it." Pause. *Sniff.* "Angela, listen to me. You must go back to your fiancé immediately. You are NOT a lesbian. No daughter of mine is gay. We do not do this kind of thing. How could you do this to your father? It will kill the poor man. Please call me right away so we can settle this."

I slammed the phone to the floor, and it bounced twice on the fuzzy rug next to Cait's bathtub. Fuck her. My mother wasn't going to tell me who I was or wasn't. Maybe I wasn't completely clear how I'd ended up standing at Cait's sink in Brooklyn rinsing semen from a sperm bank from between my fingers; but what I did know was, no matter what my mother thought, I was still going to march into the bedroom of my lesbian lover and make love to her until she writhed in the tangle of sheets, threw back her head and shrieked with pleasure as we created a little cardboard-colored grandchild that someday my mother might find in her heart to love.

Forty-five minutes later, Cait was asleep, snoring quietly. I gently lowered her legs to the bed and pulled the sheet and a comforter over her. I stood up quietly from the bed and walked into the kitchen.

Sitting at the table sipping a glass of water, I pushed my mother's phone call out of my mind and the image of Tatiana and Keith at the party drifted in. I felt sick with revulsion. I knew I should be open-hearted and happy that Keith had someone, but I wasn't—and not her. How come everything was so effortless for her? She got to have a cool European up-bringing, followed by good schools, a hot job and television and Internet fame. She was attractive, had a fabulous ward-robe, threw great parties, made her own sushi and was sched-uled to be a cover girl on my magazine. What did she need Keith for, too? She could not both be perfect *and* take my ex-fiancé. *Bite me, Tatiana.*

I stood up and pulled this week's grocery list from a pad at-tached to a corkboard and tore off a piece of paper from the bottom. Selecting a fine-point, felt-tip marker from a cup on the table, I wrote in plain block letters "Tatiana Braithwaite" and folded the piece of paper four times. Opening the freezer door, I stuck the paper in the back.

Yes, this was silly and immature and crazy, something I had read in a novel about Louisiana. But I wanted to freeze Ta-tiana out of my life. This was simply white magic—I hated that phrase, of course—low-rent voodoo. It was schizo to in the same hour, unthaw donor 0901 to bring a baby into my life, and stick Tatiana in the deep freeze to get her out. Still, I felt better as I pushed her name under a package of frozen tofu steaks.

Quietly, I stripped off my clothes and climbed into bed next to Cait, pushing myself into the warm part of her back. I put my arm around her shoulders, and lay my head on the pillow next to hers, settling in the itty bitty wet spot made by our dusty, store-bought sperm.

Chapter 26

Several months had gone by, and it was now bitter, dark, late winter. New York City was frigid under the spell of a cold snap, unrivaled since the turn of last century. Cait and I were snuggled under a blanket in the living room, but we were anything but cozy. Each of us was orbiting in our own parallel universe.

Computer in my lap, I was reading pornacopia.com, a sex blog. It was getting harder and harder to find good stories since Lucia and I had covered everything already. Plus, I had lost interest.

My mother would be horrified if she knew what I was doing. But she wouldn't, since we still weren't speaking, mired in our mother-daughter cold war. I hadn't returned her many phone calls, preferring to avoid her anti-lesbian diatribe. For the first time in forever, I had skipped Christmas dinner with my parents. I felt empty without them, like two organs were missing. Important ones, like my heart and lung. I just couldn't face her. But without my mother, it fell on me to ask myself— *What are you doing with your life?*

Next to me, Cait was reading a self-published manual

called *How to Boost Your Fertility*, as engrossed as if it were *Beloved*. In reality, she had already boosted hers, thanks to the fertility medication she had been zealously injecting into her hip for the past month. Tonight would be our fourth baby try, and we were both over the process. First, it was wildly expensive; between the sperm and its overnight delivery costs, doctor visits, fertility monitoring and injections, we were spending more than a thousand dollars this month. Keith should've been cashing in, rather than wasting his semen by recycling it back through his system. Of course, the downside of that would've been lots of little Keiths running around, probably trying to date each other.

I didn't know how much longer I could bear lying to the mailroom guys about the large, unmarked boxes I was receiving every month from Gentex. Each time they looked at me funny, as I babbled excuses—one month artwork, then Christmas gifts, then late Christmas gifts, then late Kwanzaa gifts.

Finally, it was difficult for Cait and me to handle the roller-coaster ride of desperate hope, followed by dashed expectations. Each month, she had locked herself in the bathroom when her period was due. I had listened to her whimper at the sight of spots of brown menstrual blood in her underwear or when the blue line didn't appear in the second box on the stick. Afterward, she'd unlock the door and we would clutch each other tearfully, our heads against the cold bathroom tile.

I understood why Cait was being so aggressive with the fertility meds; this process was stressful. She had pushed right past Clomid—the mildest, first-line medication for the infertile. Moving up the fertility food chain, she had insisted on being prescribed an injectible that had recently been approved by the FDA. Generally, this and other drugs of its type were reserved for women who were looking forty in the eye and near suicidal from years of "trying." For them, the ultimate goal was to mass produce buckets of eggs for a chance at in-

vitro as they raced to beat the biological clock before meno-
pause caused the whole system to sputter to a halt.

Cait was not even near that place, but her fear and impatience were real. We had flitted through three gynecologists
already, starting with the crunchy granola Amsterdam U doctor Cait had seen for years. When she said to Cait "be patient,
dear," I knew that would be our last appointment with her.
Next we had tried a physician in Borough Park, Brooklyn, who
accepted Cait's insurance. He seemed to be a favorite of the
Orthodox Jewish women of that neighborhood who were expected to produce a baby a year. Dr. Nixbaum, who was at
least seventy, should've retired years ago, since he seemed on
the verge of senility and blindness.

I figured something was wrong, when, during our visit, he
wasn't clear who the actual patient was. Squinting, he called
Cait "sir" several times and reached for my arm to draw blood.
I had snatched my arm away, and shoved Cait inches from his
wrinkled face shouting, "This is the patient!" Worse, in my
mind, he always wore a stained lab coat, accessorized with
black socks and white shoes, and smelled faintly of tobacco
and Scope. This seemed a sure sign that he was on the bottom
rung of HMO specialists.

Cait took advantage of him quickly and efficiently, bullying
him into the fertility medication though she wasn't technically
infertile, since she hadn't been trying for that long. After only
a bit of protest from him, he sighed and shakily scribbled the
prescription probably simply to get her out of his examining
room and move in another patient.

We had been to Cait's latest doctor—a very exclusive "fertility specialist" who practiced in an office on the Upper East
Side of Manhattan—two days ago. I hated our visits. In the
waiting room, I stare blankly at the other patients: nervous
women, hanging on their sullen husbands like pashmina. Quietly I reassured Cait she'd be pregnant soon.

And who did these people think we were—two women going to an ob-gyn visit? Who was I? Her supportive black friend? Her paid companion? Maybe these wealthy sophisticates, who flipped through *New York* magazine trend stories to stay "in the know," knew exactly who we were. Part of the "gayby" boom.

Near the end of the visit, after Cait had lain out—point by tedious point—why she needed fertility medication, Dr. Merrill had scribbled a prescription on his pad and handed it to her. Since she had begun the drugs, Cait's moods were erratic, and she needed constant comfort and coddling. Each night when I stuck my key into the door, I was unsure what to expect. Usually, her hormones haywire, she was teary and needy, though some days she was hostile and angry.

Most days her syringes and mood swings felt like a burden, and several times I had wondered if I had made a mistake leaving Keith. I had liked it better when Cait was seducing me, and I was careening between Harlem and Brooklyn having a lot of sex. Guilt had been a small price to pay for being a carefree object of desire. These days I loved Cait best when she was asleep. Relaxed and calm, I could enjoy the fantasy of her openly and playfully in a way I wasn't able to when she was grouchy and wide awake.

I looked at my watch—10 P.M. "Cait, it's time," I said, nudging her. According to the personal fertility awareness assessment sheet in the back of her book, Cait's most fertile hour of the day was right now. I went to the bedroom, which was lit by a table lamp, its shade covered by a rectangle of rust-brown cotton fabric. The herbal candles had melted into stiff, waxy puddles. Lifting the small vial of sperm out of its dry-ice bed, I thawed it quickly, in my hand, not bothering to hold it close to my chest. We also skipped letting it sit for a half hour and all the other rituals, except the orgasm. With Cait on her back, a pillow under her hips to elevate them, I shot the sperm into her. She pulled her thighs together and threw her legs onto the wall. I serviced her quickly, and then covered her with the comforter from the bed, and leaned down. "I hope this one's the charm," I whispered into her ear.

"Me, too," she said, closing her eyes tightly.

I sat stroking her head as she let the sperm do its duty, feeling alone except for the blank stares of several acaba fertility dolls parked in different spots around the room. I had surprised myself: I finally wanted this baby. The idea of her—or him—had started to feel real. Still, I felt abandoned and also overcome with sexual desire, free-floating and undirected.

Our sex life had taken a nose dive lately. It felt like we were already sexless mommies. Though much of Cait's energy was directed toward baby-making, my passion for her hadn't waned. At this point, I had become so used to looking at Cait's back at night in the darkness that it was like a familiar stone fence around her. What little she had left she gave to her students, her friends and GALS FREE. Had we become little more than roommates, companions, like two elderly English ladies sharing a household and reading poetry to each other after dinner by our fireplace? We didn't have to *pass* as affectionate friends, we were.

I wondered if that was why lesbians had all of those neutral names for their relationships—companion, partner, mate. Was "lesbian bed death," which I had learned about at the sex conference, inevitable? Did the comfort of being women together, in our case combined with baby-making, drive away the sexual feelings? Did we need a man—or a boi—dragging testosterone into the mix, to rev things up?

I felt ripped off, but knew it would be selfish to complain. I missed our all-day loving and the hunger in Cait's eyes when she looked at me. It felt unfair that she had brought me to such a high, showing me the revelation that love-making could be, and then snatched it away so quickly.

I kissed the top of Cait's head, and dimmed the lights in the room. I snuggled next to her in bed and dozed into a dreamless sleep.

The insistent ring of my cell phone jerked me awake. I glanced at the hazy numbers on my watch and was shocked to see that it was 11:27. A bit late for a phone call. Oh, God, was it my mother again? Had something happened to her or my father? I struggled out from under Cait, who protested sleepily, and ran to find the phone.

"Hello," I said after unearthing it from the bottom of my bag. I was breathing hard, almost gasping for breath.

"Angela, it's me." It was Mae, speaking urgently, her voice crackling with excitement. "I'm sorry to call you so late, girl. But I've got something to tell you."

Oh, God, I thought. I hated how that sounded. But it couldn't be my parents. Despite Mae's extraordinary access to the grapevine, she still wouldn't know about one of my parents dying before I did.

"What's going on, Mae?" I whispered. "Is it Keith? Has something happened to him?"

"No, it's Tatiana. She's dead."

"What," I said, gasping, my hand over my mouth as I loosened my grip on the phone. "What happened to her?"

"Do you want the official version or the truth?" Mae had raced right past grief to gossip.

"Official first."

"She died of a rare congenital heart condition." Mae sounded short of breath, too. "That's the official announcement on her Web site, and that's what will be in her *Times* obit."

"And, off the record?" I pulled out a chair and sat down at our kitchen table.

"She may have had a minor heart problem, but it was a drug overdose that took her out."

"Are you *kidding*? I can't quite imagine Tatiana running uptown in her good shoes to score crack or smack or meth or whatever—can you?"

"She didn't do street drugs—don't be a boob." Mae was impatient, just wanting to get to the punch line. "It was some kind of prescription stimulant. She apparently took too much and her heart basically exploded."

"She did not! My God. Do you think a doctor prescribed her that?" I instantly thought of my father, imagining how appalled he'd be at the idea of abusing prescription medication.

"Of course not. Does anyone get the good drugs from a doctor anymore? She got that shit from the Internet."

"What was it?"

"Hell if I know—what do I look like, a pharmacist? Some kind of upper, that's all I know."

"How do you know all this, Mae?"

"I'm scared of you," she answered, laughing huskily. The girl really never revealed her sources.

"Oh, my God. Mae, I think I know what happened to her." I rested my left elbow on the table, dropping my forehead into my hand.

"What are you talking about, Angela? How would *you* know?" she asked indignantly. I'm sure she'd been tempted to add "more than me!" "You weren't speaking to her. You said she stole your man, remember?"

"No, remember her party last fall? Well, I was snooping around her bathroom and found a bunch of bottles of pills in a drawer."

"I was going to say 'oh how tacky,' but you did have to spend a lot of time in the bathroom whenever you were around her." Mae gave a snorty laugh.

"Anyway, the pills I saw were called deso-something."

"What? Can you spell it?" Her voice sounded slightly muffled and I could hear rustling on her end.

"What are you doing?"

"Hello?! I'm logging on to my computer and looking it up in the *Physicians' Desk Reference* online. We're journalists, remember? Information is the name of our game. Besides, I need something to do. I'm much too hyped to sleep."

After a pause, she said, "Wait, I've got it. Desoxyn. D-E-S-O-X-Y-N. Does that sound right?"

"I think so, but I just got a quick glimpse of the bottles."

"Yeah, this is it. Listen to this: 'Desoxyn is in the family of methamphetamines . . .' " Mae read slowly, stumbling slightly over the last word.

"Methamphetamines? What is that? Like super-duper No-Doz?"

"Oh snap, I think it's stronger than that. I think it's like that stuff that all those people in the Midwest are getting addicted to. You know, hillbilly crack. This says that it's generally used as a stimulant, sometimes for weight loss. Oh, God—the drug is extremely habit forming, can cause irregular heartbeats and should not be used to combat fatigue or replace rest."

"Well, that sounds exactly like what she was doing, right? Upscale crystal meth," I said. Part of me felt posthumous awe that she actually had the guts to first do drugs, and then get addicted to them. I was such a chicken: drinking and maybe a little pot were my max.

"My God, this is so tawdry," Mae said, sighing.

"Well, I hate to say it, but I was always a little suspect of Tatiana's Superwoman perfection. This proves that no normal human being really has the time to make homemade sushi," I said, sucking my teeth slightly. "When's the funeral?"

"Day after tomorrow."

"Why so fast?"

"You know why: They need to get her in the ground, before somebody figures out what really killed her. She's a public figure, and it would be scandalous. Better to die a martyr of congenital heart disease than for everyone to find out Tatiana was living in the Valley of the friggin' Dolls."

"Hmmm, you're right. What do you think, Mae—should I go to the funeral?" I sat up, straightening my head. "I mean, I did, um, *hate* her."

"So what? Of course you're going. Everybody's going."

Chapter 27

On Friday morning, I entered the chapel at Sugar Hill Baptist Church, and looked around for Mae. I spotted her, or rather, I spotted her enormous black hat, with a half veil covering her eyes. That was the most modest part of her outfit. Her suit was cut daringly low, and she was showing a scandalous amount of cleavage—especially given the religious setting. Normally that kind of thing would be inappropriate at a funeral but okay for the funeral of someone you hadn't liked. I was one of the few without a hat; I refused to join the showy smackdown of black women in hats. Mae's crown was definitely one of the best. She could move to the semifinal round with the monstrosity sitting atop her head.

Mae must've felt my eyes boring into the back of her hat. She turned and signaled through the forest of headwear for me to sit by her. I hurtled my way through the crowd, and managed to squeeze into a pew between Mae and a woman I recognized from one of Tatiana's parties.

"Didn't I tell you, Ang?" Mae was whispering excitedly, her hand covering part of her mouth. "Everybody is here." It was true. I had spotted a former mayor of New York; the head of a cable network; half the editorial staff of a high-profile black magazine; and a conservative radio host accompanied by a woman who was probably his mistress. To my right were two state senators and the author of a book about the "mommy wars." With everyone wearing black—and except for the location—it could've been one of Tatiana's soirees. Her final party. The only person I hadn't seen yet was Keith.

The service was scheduled for 10:30, and it was now 11:15. Tatiana's body was lying in a satin-lined casket in the front of the room, and she was dressed in a tailored suit—Ann Taylored—silk blouse and pumps. With her hair done and her face beat to the usual perfection, she looked like she was taking a short nap after taping one of her TV segments. Not that she'd ever have needed a nap.

"Angela, walk up and pay your respects." Mae shoved her elbow into my side. "You better hurry up before this thing gets started."

"No, it's morbid. I don't want to get any closer to Tatiana than this pew." I was afraid of this ritual—the viewing—where everyone paraded to the casket to get one last look. Dead people scared me; I wasn't down with the circle of life thing.

"Get up there. Don't be such a chicken. She's dead, and I'm sure her laxative powers died with her."

"No, that's not it. Tatiana looks fine from here. I just don't want to go up there."

I folded my hands into my lap tightly and looked down. Maybe Mae would think I was engaged in silent meditation and leave me alone. Who's going to notice if I don't get one last look? Besides, only a few people seemed to be actually viewing. Because the service was running late, most people had already viewed. In fact, many folks seemed to have forgotten that Tatiana's dead body was in front of the room and were milling around in clusters, chatting, gossiping and exchanging business cards. She seemed little more than a prop, a macabre centerpiece, at a high-octane Manhattan social event.

"What are we waiting for?" I asked Mae. "Why do you think the service hasn't started?"

"The parents aren't here yet." As she spoke, she turned and craned her neck, brushing my face with her hat.

"Oh, that makes sense. They're flying in from Amsterdam, right?"

"I guess. Tatiana was always a little sketchy about her background. If my mother was European royalty and my father a prince, or diplomat or whatever, I'd keep that information front and center." Mae gave a short laugh. "Now get up, and go up and look at that girl, before they close the casket. If you don't go, people will think you were jealous, because of the Keith thing. Come on. I'll go with you." Mae stood up, and jerked me to my feet.

I followed Mae, walking toward the front with my head bowed. When we reached the casket, I looked up slightly, and there was Tatiana, looking peaceful and serene, free from the tyranny of multitasking. In death, she seemed truly plastic. Though I had facetiously called her a milk-chocolate Barbie, she actually hadn't really looked like the doll. But in death, she was an exact replica, glowing with a synthetic sheen. These days there were so many Barbies—veterinarian Barbie, WNBA Barbie, Cher Barbie, corporate executive Barbie, South African princess Barbie, differently-abled Barbie—that it wasn't so far-fetched that there could be cadaver Barbie. Tatiana could now be the model for the African-American doll.

Though it was difficult to look at her, I was glad I'd made the effort. The viewing ritual had grounded me, given me a sense of purpose, since I had no clear role or reason to be there. I wasn't a real friend, or colleague or relative—hell, she made me sick, physically and figuratively. But walking up to the casket, head bowed, gave me a feeling of belonging. Yes, I, too, was part of this collective grieving.

I pulled my eyes from Tatiana's perfect face, and looked around for Mae. She had somehow made another pass by Tatiana and was off to one side, near her head, chatting up Rufus Browne. He was wearing a tasteful black suit and light-blue open-collared shirt, one arm resting on Mae's shoulder as he admired her hat. As I walked toward them, there was some commotion in the back of the room, and just about every head whipped around to see what was going on.

To my surprise, Keith had walked in, supporting the elbow of an elderly woman in a thin raincoat and matching hat. They were trailed by an old man, coatless, wearing a worn black suit, about a size too big. The couple was clean and neat, not dirt-poor, but as country as you could get. They looked like they'd just gotten off Amtrak from somewhere way below the Mason-Dixon line, lugging cardboard luggage and shoe boxes of chicken and biscuits. They were also sobbing hysterically. I wondered who they were, maybe a couple of Tatiana's charity cases. Were there Save the Children-like sponsorship programs for aging country bumpkins?

Keith looked fantastic, dripping GQ, especially next to the couple. He was wearing a well-cut suit—probably one of those Tatiana had helped him pick out—and a new pair of glasses, these rimless. His haircut looked fresh.

Keith disengaged himself from the old woman, resting her hand gently on her husband's arm. He was so smooth and appropriate, it looked like Bill T. Jones had choreographed his move. Then he walked up to the casket, leaned over and whispered something into the ear of corpse Barbie, and gently kissed her stiff cheek. That caused a wildfire of whispering, sighing and sad tongue-clucking.

Oh, for God sakes. I know I shouldn't be thinking unchari-table thoughts in church—and I did have a girlfriend now—but that was so repulsive. How serious could they have gotten in so short a time? In death, Keith's relationship to Tatiana had grown more serious, elevated to grieving near-spouse. Red-eyed acquaintances were moving to the front to clutch his hands and hug him as though he'd lost a wife rather than a friend with benefits.

Oh, and look at him, eating it up, accepting condolences with a fixed, phony half smile. He had perfected the role of stoically devastated boyfriend. That pissed me off. I wanted to claw his stupid face. But then I noticed another feeling, walk-ing arm in arm with the anger: lust. Keith looked really good, and I liked that he was being less of a bore. That act could not be real. He was not a stodgy academic anymore, but a snappily dressed bad boy, and he wore it as well as he was wearing that expensive suit. Maybe that was why he was suddenly more at-tractive to me, and I started to feel tingly looking at him, a sensation that I had thought was as dead as Tatiana. Or maybe it was simply because I hadn't gotten "any" in so long.

I decided to speak to Keith, partly because I wanted to get a little closer, partly out of pride: I didn't want the others to think I was too freaked out and jealous to pay my respects to my grieving ex. Keith had moved to the opposite side of Ta-tiana—near her feet—so I'd have to view her again to get to him. I stood in line behind the older couple and got ready to walk by Tatiana.

But I stopped cold. In front of me, the old woman was down on her knees, her body convulsing with loud messy sobs. Her stockings were ripped, and a run was creeping up the back of her leg, moving toward the hem of her faded cotton JC Pen-ney dress. Oblivious, she pulled one of Tatiana's lifeless hands out of the casket, and pressed it to her mouth. "Peaches, baby,

Peaches," she wailed. The old man joined her on the floor, wailing along with her, "My baby, my baby, my baby girl, my baby daughter."

At that moment, to the relief of everyone in the room, Reverend Sheppard, Sugar Hill's minister, glided toward the couple, draped in a purple and black robe, his salt and pepper hair gleaming. He knew Tatiana well, since she was a benefactor of several of his community programs. He bent his knees and joined them on the floor, embracing them.

"I am so sorry for your loss, Mr. and Mrs. Braithwaite," he said, smoothing over the fact that neither of these people who were behaving like Tatiana's parents seemed to be a diplomat or a European heiress. He spoke in a booming voice that easily carried to the back of the church. "Tatiana was so special."

The old couple stopped sobbing, and looked at the minister befuddled. "Our name ain't no Braithwaite," said the man, his accent as thick as a ham hock. "I'm Reuben Johnson and this is my wife, Pearl. We from Prichard, Alabama. This is our baby girl, Peaches Johnson." If anyone had been talking, at that moment they stopped. My mouth dropped open and from across the room, Mae's eyes were large and round with surprise.

Tatiana—or rather Peaches—hadn't been the daughter of a diplomat and Afro-German heiress after all. Now that I thought of it, her accent had sounded a little Tina Turner-ish. She had built an elaborate genealogical house of cards to outrun a mundane, small-town childhood. She didn't expect to die, so she assumed her country parents would slip quietly into old age and then death, burying her past with them. *Ha, ha, Peaches*, I thought. *You are not European. You are not interesting. You are not special. You are just like so many of us: another black girl with down-South roots.*

My eyes darting from Peaches to Reuben to Pearl, I took a

deep breath and leaned heavily against the coffin. What was I doing? How could I continue to hold a pointless grudge? The girl was dead, and her parents were crying again, clutching Reverend Sheppard, sobs wracking their frail bodies. They didn't care who was in the room, their grief was real, their emotions profound. Tatiana had been loved deeply by these corn-pone parents who she was so mortified by. I felt ashamed, small-minded and mean-spirited.

Oh, my God—and responsible. Had I killed Tatiana by putting her name in the freezer? I hadn't wanted to kill her, just freeze her out of my life, but I had murdered Pearl and Reuben's beloved Peaches. All of a sudden I felt over-whelmed by my own emotions—fear, sadness, loss and guilt—and began sobbing myself. I felt like I had accidentally shot up a syringe-full of Cait's hormones. But maybe I needed a good cry; so much had happened to me in the last few months—the end of my engagement, my lesbianism, the stand-off with my mother, my impending co-motherhood—and I had had no opportunity to let it out. I was also crying for loss: the loss of Keith; the loss of my fun, sexy feelings for Cait; the loss of thinking love was so easy; and the loss of a more naïve and innocent version of myself. This was clearly not appropriate at Tatiana's funeral, but it was something I needed.

Oblivious to everyone in the room, I began to wail and moan, salty tears running onto my top lip. Sniffing and coughing furiously, I needed to blow my nose, so I stood up and began first walking briskly and then running up the aisle and out of the chapel. I knew every eye had moved from Pearl and Reuben to Keith's distraught-for-some-reason ex. Maybe people would think I had gotten "the spirit"—but I didn't care. For once, I really didn't give a damn what anyone thought. I had no idea it would be so freeing to act crazy. No wonder crazy people did it. I threw open the doors of the church, and felt refreshed by the stinging-cold air. Just outside to the left of the front doors, I bent over, weeping, great, gulping hysterical sobs. I felt a tap on my shoulder.

"Angela, what up?" Hard Tyme, Rufus's rapper brother, was standing near me in the shadow of the looming church. He didn't seem surprised by my hysterics as he took a pull on a huge spliff, and then clutched the joint in his eyeteeth. Gently he took off his bulky, black hooded parka and wrapped it around my shoulders, first removing a gun of some sort from the inside pocket. He shoved the weapon into the front of his slack jeans.

"Tyme, I I I I killed T T T A A A A–TIANA!" I blurted out loudly through the tears. "I I I I k i i i LLLLEd her."

"No, you didn't, baby girl. The bitch killed herself," he answered, taking another massive pull on the joint. He stared at me through hooded, bloodshot eyes. "Everybody knows that drugs are very, very bad. This is your mind on drugs." He spat into the snow and stomped it with the toe of his heavy boot, grinning lopsidedly.

"Y Y Y Y E SSSSS, I I I I I I did, Tyme!" I screamed, ignoring him. I felt weighed down by his heavy coat. "I I I I killed *her*. I froze her to death."

"Shit, Tatiana was already cold as ice; you didn't do nothing to her," said Tyme, thrusting the spliff at me and handing me a bandanna from his back pocket to wipe my nose. "You need this girl, take it." Holding the fat joint awkwardly, I inhaled deeply, which sent me into a coughing fit. Tyme banged on my back.

"This is good shit, but the first hit burns, then it's smooth," he said, shivering and rubbing his hands together. "Hit it again."

I obeyed him, though the last time I had gotten high, I had stumbled home without my panties, watch and keys. After a minute, I realized he was right. I did feel much better. I took another deep hit, and then another. Suddenly everything seemed very, very funny. I started laughing, first softly, then loudly. Doubled over, my crazed guffaw sounded more like a bray than a laugh. Tyme gently pulled the spliff from my fingers and put it back in his own mouth, inhaling deeply.

Chapter 28

"**A**ngela!" I thought I heard someone call my name. But the voice seemed to be floating somewhere above my head, maybe in the sky, in heaven. Maybe it was God. I felt a hand shake my shoulder roughly. I was being chosen, touched by God. I am Della Reese! Laughing even harder, tears rolling down my cheeks, I turned and stood face to face with not God, but Keith.

"Angela, what are you doing?" He stood next to me, his face stern, his brow furrowed. He was shivering and hugging his arms tightly around his waist. "Are you okay?" He turned to Tyme and said, "Hey, man," deepening his voice as black men do in each others' presence.

"Ang, come inside, you are *not* okay," Keith insisted when I didn't answer, and instead stared at him with a dreamy, unfocused gaze. He sounded irritable as he tugged my limp arms out of Tyme's coat and handed it back to him.

Keith pulled—dragged—me through the front doors of the church, and leaned me up against a wall outside the ladies' room. I was standing next to a poster announcing a faith-based weight-loss program illustrated with a drawing of a bearded, Christ-like person clad in shorts and a T-shirt and holding a plate of fish and fruit. The caption read: "What Would Jesus Eat?" I started laughing again, hysterically. That shit really was funny.

"Angela, what is wrong with you?" Keith had grabbed both of my shoulders and shook me frantically. "What was that scene you pulled in there? And you know you can't smoke dope, especially the kind of extra-strength dope someone like that Hard Tyme character must be used to."

Dope. What a funny, old-timey word. That was really so hilarious. Keith is sooooo old school. He's a dope. I couldn't stop laughing and even felt myself drooling. I leaned on him, my arms around him, giggling giddily.

"Cut it out," said Keith firmly, shaking my shoulders again, harder this time. Several people had come out of the chapel, their expressions turning quickly from sadness to disapproval once they heard my inappropriate laughing. Keith took a deep breath, looked around quickly, and then pulled me into the ladies' room, locking the door behind us.

"Keee-eeeth. I killed Tatiana, I killed Tatiana," I sang, through bursts of giggles. "I killed her, I killed her—la, la, la, la."

"Stop it!" Keith shouted, and slapped me across the face, not hard, but enough to knock the giggles right out of me. My God, what was happening? Had futzy Keith actually slapped me—again? Who did he think he was, the black Stanley Kowalski? Ike Turner? With Tatiana's fake Tina Turner accent, no wonder they had gotten together. Tatiana. Oh, God, she was dead. I began sobbing quietly again, moaning and coughing, my head buried in Keith's chest.

"Angela, you have to get a grip." He held my wrists in his hands and glowered down at me. As I looked up at him, I thought I saw something fighting past the rage; Keith looked sad and confused. I stood on my tiptoes and kissed his cheek. His eyes looked droopy.

"Keith, I'm sorry. I am so sorry," I whispered and kissed his cheek again.

"For what?" he asked, taking my face in his hands and pushing me away from his face.

"For Tatiana, for us, for Cait, for everything," I replied, looking into his eyes.

All of a sudden I missed him sharply, or at least I missed being with him. I imagined us sitting in our breakfast nook, the sun streaming through the blinds in lemony ribbons, passing sections of the Sunday *Times* back and forth across the table. I felt overcome with nostalgia and longing, and I kissed him again, my mouth moving from his cheek to his neck. Getting high always made me feel so alive, so conscious of my senses, so stimulated, so . . . sexually aroused, which was probably why I stayed away from it.

"Angela, please—you've got to get control of yourself," Keith whispered harshly as he pried my hands from his neck and pushed me away from him again.

I could hear Keith's voice, but it sounded muted and far-away, like he was speaking through the wrong end of a megaphone. Plus, I wasn't listening. Now that I had finally let myself go and lost control, I wasn't in any hurry to get it back. Instead, I was driven by some inner other person whom I didn't know well but seemed to be a very bad girl. A very bad high girl. I stepped toward him, pulling his arms around me and leaned in and kissed his mouth.

"Angela, no . . ." I stopped the words by pushing my mouth harder onto his. Pulling his head down toward mine, I began kissing him deeply and frantically. Finally, I felt his body relax and he kissed me back, roughly, his lips and tongue pressing into mine. I felt him pulling up my skirt, ripping my stockings and my underwear. I yanked open Keith's pants, and he pushed himself against me, my bottom perched on the cold sink—in the ladies' room at the funeral for the dead woman he had been dating. Only Lucia would fully appreciate the scene.

"Keith, I am so sorry." My voice was low, breathless and gravelly. I think the marijuana had not only unleashed my passion but also felt like truth serum. All of a sudden, with Keith's penis pushing inside me, I began unloading myself—my guilt. "I really did love you, Keith, I really did. Do you think you can ever forgive me?"

Keith grunted something. He was grinding his hips into mine. I groaned with pleasure as I tried to listen to what he was saying. Somehow he was thrusting, talking and panting at the same time. Had he learned that multitasking from Tatiana?

"I don't care, Angela," he said, panting harder, his mouth buried in my neck. "We don't have to keep talking about this. I'm over you."

"You are?" I asked, tearing at his shirt. Liar, no he wasn't. "I was afraid that you were totally messed up for life."

"You don't have that power over me." He took a deep breath, pushed it out loudly and thrust harder and faster, my bottom banging against the sink.

"Oh, yes." He was nearly screaming, trying to muffle the sound in my neck. He gave another hard thrust, and I felt him shudder.

"I realized you had lost your mind." He thrust again and again. "Why else would you start seeing that disgusting Cait person?"

"I'm so sorr—" I began, whispering loudly as I gulped air.

"Forget it, I have." He closed his eyes tightly. I pulled back, and looked at him closely. What I had thought was pleasure, looked more like anger, and I watched it drain out of him as his body sagged against mine.

Afterward, I leaned against the cool tile woozily watching Keith close his pants and listening to the faint sound of organ music. I felt something odd on some part of my body, but because I was still high and felt disconnected from my brain, I couldn't quite locate the feeling. It was watery, like rain, but more slippery, like an egg white, somewhere on my lower body. It was unfamiliar, yet I remembered it from my past. Oh, semen, that was it. As I stood there next to Keith, his semen was dripping steadily down the inside of my legs.

Outside the bathroom, I started to hear some hubbub, and it became clear that Tatiana's funeral was over. I yanked up my panties, now loose and baggy, and pulled down my skirt.

"I've got to find Tatiana's parents," Keith said as he smoothed the wrinkles out of his jacket. He turned away from me and glanced into the mirror. Gathering his dignity and straightening his tie casually, he looked like he was getting ready for work. Cautiously, he stuck his head out of the bathroom and looked around.

"Good-bye, Angela." He was speaking over his shoulder, raising his voice over the sound of one of the toilets gurgling. "Thank you. I feel much better now."

Making sure no one was watching him, he squeezed through the door without looking back. I followed him a few minutes later. I felt dazed, both my mind and body fried.

"Mae!" I shouted, waving when I spotted the top of her hat. She pulled herself away from the crowd of mourners and walked over with Rufus trailing her.

"Oh, baby, I wondered what happened to you. You're still upset. Look at how red your eyes are." She pulled me into her arms, embracing me sympathetically. "What the?" she began as she sniffed the pungent odor of high-test ganja clinging to my clothes.

"Can I talk to you a minute in the bathroom?" I said, slurring. My tongue felt dry and heavy as I ran it across my parched lips.

"I'll be right back, Rufus." She blew him a little kiss, which brought a half smile to his lips. Mae and I slipped back into the ladies' room.

"Listen my girl, I don't know what you've been doing, but you smell like Reggae Sun Splash," Mae said, scolding me. "I'm not even going to ask you how you ended up getting high at a funeral. Now, I love you and I hope you're okay, but, you're right, that Rufus is a sweetie. We're going out for brunch now, so you need to get yourself together." She put her hand on the door.

"Mae, I had sex with Keith." At that moment the elastic from my panties gave out, and they slipped to the floor.

"OhmiGod." She took a sudden intake of breath. The room felt close and smelled like sex. She looked down at my crumpled heap of underwear, and then, using the heel of her shoe, kicked them to the side. They skittered into a corner underneath the sink.

"Come here." She spoke softly, pulling me toward her into another hug. "I know you're upset and seem deranged. Let's talk later, okay?" She smiled at me nervously, and pressed her cheek to mine.

"Wait, Mae, I didn't use anything, you know what I mean?" My head was spinning and I leaned against the paper towel dispenser.

"Angela, um, so what? Keith never shoots his wad, so to speak."

"Well, he did this time." She wrinkled her brow, her mouth forming a surprised "0." "Mae, I hope to God I'm not pregnant."

"Pregnant?" I watched Mae's face as her expression moved from sternness to concern to alarm. "I hope to God you don't have HIV."

"Of course I don't have HIV—this is Keith's virginal sperm, not some guy I picked up in a club."

"You don't know who he's been with since you broke up."

"Yes, I do—Tatiana." I said it stubbornly. Mae was being ridiculous and paranoid. "And he wore a condom with her. I saw the package on the table next to the bed when I caught them doing the nasty."

"You don't know who *else* he was with. Unless you've been carrying his dick around in your purse . . ." She had moved into lecture mode, and was shaking her finger in my face.

"That's gross, stop it." I pushed her finger away, though I could feel the muscles in my stomach clenching with fear. "Can we deal with one problem at a time?"

"All right, listen to me," Mae replied hurriedly as she dug through her purse. "Take these."

"What are they?" I stared down, blinking and trying to concentrate on the round purple pill case in her hand.

"Angela, what is wrong with you? These are birth control pills." Mae spoke quickly. "Well, I guess you haven't seen any of these babies in some time." She opened the dispenser and pressed it into my palm.

"Now listen to me: I need to GO, so I'm giving you the whole package. You need to take two now, and then two more in twelve hours. If you take them like this, they work like morning-after pills. Got it?" She was speaking rapidly as she moved toward the door and toward Rufus.

"Okay, I think I understand," I said as I tried to digest the information. I closed my fist around the pills. "Now go." I gave her a shove into the door.

"Call me, okay?" Mae said as she left.

After the door closed, I stood at the sink groggily fingering the dispenser. I was a little embarrassed to admit this to her, but I had never taken "the Pill." I had become sexually active not all that long ago, and had been scared into "using a condom every time." I guess Mae used both. That was like her, such a Girl Scout: always prepared. I pictured her in a little green uniform, a birth control pill badge on her sash.

Blearily, I stared down at the pills. They were a mystery to me, but really very pretty, so many different colors. I guess that doesn't matter—color. We're all one color under God, and so are these pills. *One pill makes you larger/And one pill makes you small.* I started laughing again and dropped my arms. The pills clattered to the floor.

Catching my breath, I got down on all fours, and scooped up several pink pills and shoved them into my mouth. I picked up the rest of them and threw them into the garbage. Uck, dirt don't hurt, but this is unsanitary. Leaning over the sink, I washed the pills down with several handfuls of water. I could feel them sliding past my tongue, down my throat, into my stomach, into my genitals. *Good pills, that's right, get rid of that little baby that's probably growing inside me. Good-bye little baby AngelaandKeith.*

Something beeped; my phone was announcing a message. I scrolled down, and squinted woozily at the 914 number—my mother. Oh, God. But instead of my mother, I heard my father's baritone.

"Hello, Angela. How are you?" Like my mother, he had never gotten the hang of voice mail, and always sounded formal, uncomfortable, like he was reading from a script whenever he left a message.

"I'm just calling to say hello. Is everything okay out there?" Pause. "I haven't heard too much from Mom. I miss you like crazy. I don't know what's the matter or what's going on, but please give your mom a call. Daddy loves you and your mom loves you."

I bent over the sink and started laughing again, and then crying—the same release. Looking down, I caught a glimpse of my panties in a silky puddle underneath the sink and sobbed even more.

By the time I got myself home, it was early evening. Cait was sitting in the living room, shuffling through a stack of flyers with Roscoe curled up at her feet. As I walked in, she looked up at me and smiled.

"How'd it go?" Her expression turned to concern once she got a good look at my bloodshot eyes and disheveled clothing. "I know your friend was more a frenemy, but it's always hard when someone dies young."

"Yeah," I grunted, and kissed the top of her head quickly and then moved toward the bedroom. I didn't want to get close enough for her to sniff the bouquet of sex and pot that clung to my clothes and skin. Wasn't that ironic: When she had been my undercover lover, I had pulled the same sneak-sneak routine with Keith. Now they had switched places, and I was pulling the same okey-doke on her. I was a mess. A dirty, smelly, lying, guilty mess.

"What you up to?" I asked, taking a step away from her.

"Just trying to nail down the details for a GALS FREE guerrilla action," she replied. Her foot was resting on top of a box of the group's T-shirts. "The sex conference was such a success, and now we plan to—"

"Uh, Cait, sorry, but . . ." I said over my shoulder, cutting her off, "I . . . really need a shower."

As I stripped off my clothes, I started to cry again. Standing naked in our bedroom, I picked up my phone and punched in my mother's cell number.

"Mama, Mommy," I whispered into the phone when I heard my mother's crisp hello. "I miss you so much."

Chapter 29

I walked up the steps of the Rainbow House, the epicenter of multicultural extracurricular activities at New Amsterdam U. Many of the campus's activist and affinity groups held meetings there. It was located on a side street, a few blocks from the university's main campus. During a hasty phone call earlier—now a couple of days after Tatiana's funeral—my mother had explained that she was conducting interviews for her transgender documentary here, and suggested that I meet her after work so we could talk. With its brightly colored "painted lady" front, copied from the classic Victorians in San Francisco, the three-story house looked like an actual rainbow. It stood out garishly from the gray brownstones and brick buildings on the rest of the block.

"May I help you?" An exotic beauty with long, straight hair, inky black eyebrows and velvety skin was sitting at a desk in the corner of the room. Next to the telephone, a sign read "Zulena Carlyle, assistant director."

"Yes, I'm looking for Janet Wright. She's . . ." I began, glancing around the room nervously. I was feeling more and more afraid, but I also knew it was time for a family détente. With my life coming unhinged, I needed my mother.

"Oh, yes, I'm so excited that she's here," Zulena replied. Her perfect smile nearly blinded me. "She's shooting in the conference room. Down the hall to the right," she said, gesturing with long, elegant fingers.

Pushing open the door quietly, I tiptoed toward the back of the large room where my mother was conducting an interview with a taut-lipped, fortyish black woman. Hearing the sound of the door opening, Stephen, my mother's camera assistant, an unpaid New York University student who waddled behind her like an imprinting duckling, moved his eye from the viewfinder on the bulky camera and pressed his finger to his lips. I walked toward him and peered over his shoulder to watch my mother at work.

She was sitting in a chair across from the woman, their knees almost touching. My mother was leaning in, listening intently, her eyes squinting slightly. The woman was sitting back a bit, her arms folded loosely across a red wool dress, a kente ribbon pinned to her chest. My mother was nodding, punctuating each tight little head bob with an "ummm" or "yes."

"Mrs. Woods, tell me about the Rainbow House," my mother said, smiling and shuffling through a small stack of note cards on her lap.

"It used to be the *Umoja* House, created for the *African* descended students here on campus." Mrs. Woods had the precise diction of a former high school English teacher. She sighed deeply and her arms dropped from her chest to rest lightly on one crossed knee. "Back then, if you were a black student at New Amsterdam, this was the place to be."

"What has happened?" My mother leaned her head toward Mrs. Woods, whose straightened hair looked sleek, almost wet, next to my mother's thick, unruly natural.

"Diversity." Mrs. Woods spit it out like a curse word. Her rich voice was now animated. "That's what happened. The downsizing of blackness in exchange for some vague concept of multiculturalism."

"Uh-huh, yes, sistah." My mother's head dipped up and down. She'd edit that out to assure her "objectivity."

"How are you managing?" My mother moved her arm gingerly past the black wire attached to a microphone that was clipped to the neck of her blouse and placed it lightly on Mrs. Woods's shoulder.

"Not well. The administration forced us to change our name to something more 'inclusive,' which also explains the god-awful, undignified paint job." Mrs. Woods had grown lively now, forgetting about the lights and the soft whir of the camera. "They redistributed our budget, now the bathroom's the last straw."

As quickly as my mother had placed her hand on Mrs. Woods's shoulder, she hastily moved it away. "What is wrong with your employee, Zulena, requesting gender neutral restrooms?" Zulena, the stunning assistant director at the front desk.

"Disgusting." Mrs. Woods was speaking loudly, her eyes bulging. "He can't use the ladies' powder room."

"Help me understand." My mother straightened in her chair, pulling away from Mrs. Woods.

"I am not doing my business with a man in the room—period—I don't care what kind of surgery she says she's going to have." My mother nodded toward Mrs. Woods, who couldn't seem to settle on a pronoun for Zulena.

"These gay groups with all their money and their rich alumni are trying to take over." Mrs. Woods had definitely forgotten she was in front of the camera. "I loved that boy like a son. Why is he doing this to me? I mean, Mrs. Wright, what would you do if your child came to you with this trash?"

"I would love her because she's mine, that is what you do with a child, isn't it?" My mother looked at Mrs. Woods, her eyes hardening. She turned her head slightly toward the camera, and I felt a surge of hope. Had my mother tried to meet my eye, to communicate that she now understood what I was going through? I took a deep breath and blew it out quietly, willing myself to relax.

"It's not natural." Mrs. Woods raised her chin, crossed her arms tightly across her chest and moved her body away from my mother. The interview was over.

"Thank you, Mrs. Woods." My mother looked at Stephen and made a little cut sign across the front of her neck. Stephen switched off the camera and removed his headphones. Mrs. Woods snatched off her microphone.

"I thought you were on my side, Mrs. Wright, I thought you were someone I could trust." She shoved the microphone into my mother's hand. "You just wanted to make me look foolish. Why would you do that to another sister?"

"Zulena is a black woman, too, even if you don't think so." My mother wound the microphone cord around her hand, turning her back on Mrs. Woods. She was finished with her; no need to be sisterly anymore.

"Listen, you made me sound so narrow-minded, but that's not who I am." Mrs. Woods was breathing hard, nearly panting. "We have to draw the line on this thing somewhere. And there are others who don't agree with this bathroom thing, including some of the gays. Let me get someone else for you to interview."

"I'll talk to whoever else you have after I interview Zulena." My mother smiled at her indulgently, as she removed the microphone from her blouse. Mrs. Woods hurried off. I heard a door slam in another part of the office.

"Hello, Angela." My mother spoke to me with the clipped tone she used on camera; she had given Mrs. Woods more warmth. "Stephen, why don't you take a walk and get something to eat? I need to have a talk with my daughter."

My mother seated herself in the same chair she had used to interview Mrs. Woods, and pulled the other chair closer to her. "Tell me, what's going on?"

"Mother, you know what's going on," I answered stubbornly.

"Angela, are you gay?" She looked at me, biting her lip. I noticed an expression in her eyes that I had rarely ever seen— fear.

"Do you want the truth? Do you want to really hear what I have to say?"

"I want to hear you say that it's not true." She interlaced her fingers nervously in her lap as she spoke.

"I can't say that." I looked down at my own hands, small and long-fingered like hers. "All I can say is, I don't know."

"Are you seeing that woman, the white woman Nona saw you with?"

"Yes."

"You need help, Angela." My mother's voice was raspy, suddenly bordering on shrill. "We'll find you someone to talk to, someone black."

"Stop it, Mother. You're not even trying to understand how I feel." I shifted my eyes to my feet; I could no longer look at her.

"What is there to understand?" She hugged her arms to her body. "I thought I'd raised you right; but obviously I did something wrong."

"Mom, nothing's wrong." I shook my palms out in front of me, and spoke through gritted teeth to keep from screaming. "Love is not wrong."

"Angela, do not be so naïve," my mother snapped. "You are part of a community, *we* are part of a community. We have a responsibility to our people. This isn't who we are."

"This is who I am," I said, pushing my palms against my

temples. "I have a responsibility to myself." My mother lowered her head and covered her eyes with her hands.

"What I don't get is why you understand what Zulena and Ronald and your other interview subjects are going through, but not me," I continued. Standing up, I grabbed her wrists, pulling her hands from her face.

"What's happening to them is wrong." Tears were pooling in the corners of her eyes.

"What you're doing to me is wrong. I heard you telling Mrs. Woods that you should love your child no matter what. You're a hypocrite. What you really meant is that you'll love me unless I'm gay."

"That's not what I said." My mother wriggled out of my grasp, and placed her hands on the sides of my face. She looked at me pleadingly. "I will love you no matter what, but I don't want you to destroy your life."

"I'm not destroying my life, Mom. I'm living it." I jerked my face away from her, and took a step back, turning slightly. Stephen walked into the room, a paper bag in hand. My mother rearranged her face back into the professional mask.

"Hey, what's that noise?" he asked, looking at the two of us. Voices were coming from down the hall. Was that singing?

"What's going on?" My mother stood up, and began walking down the hall toward the sound. Stephen picked up his camera and fell in step behind her. Relieved, I followed them.

We passed several dark offices and meeting spaces, before finding the ladies' room—marked with a childish drawing of a woman with a triangular lower body and an old-school flip 'do. Startled, I looked down at a carpet of bodies lying outside the door. Cait was in the middle flanked by Lindsey and Jules from the sex conference and six other women wearing GALS FREE T-shirts and buttons. Eyes closed, they were loudly humming "We Shall Overcome."

"Cait?!" Her eyes fluttered open to meet mine. "What's going on?"

"Hey, Angela. You remember the protest I've been trying to tell you about?" she said, smiling up at me. Her eyes moved toward Zulena, who had entered the room and was standing at my side looking both embarrassed and afraid. "We were trying to figure out when to have it, but once Mrs. Woods let us know that the media was here . . ."

Just then, I heard the double click of heels as Mrs. Woods entered the hallway in front of the restroom.

"See, Mrs. Wright, I told you I'm not alone in this." Mrs. Woods was speaking breathlessly. "This group of women also doesn't want him in the *ladies'* room." She pointed at Zulena who had now tucked herself behind me.

"Make sure you get this on tape, please," my mother said quietly to Stephen, gesturing toward the protesters with her chin. He turned on his camera and began shooting. "Angela, move out of the shot," my mother said testily. I ground my fist into my hip and stepped to the side.

"What's happening here?" a deep male voice boomed from behind my mother and Mrs. Woods. Oh, God, not Keith, too. He walked in surveying the scene quizzically, his glasses on the top of his head, a stack of papers under his arm.

"Keith, Keith, son." My mother moved toward him and encircled him in a hug. "Angela, look—Keith's here."

"Hello there, Mama Wright—good to see you." Keith smiled back at her warmly. "What are you—"

"You know Dr. Redfield, who sponsors the African Diaspora Society?" Mrs. Woods looked from Keith to my mother and back again. "It's such an important organization for our black students."

"Thank you so much, Mrs. Woods," Keith said, as he loosened his tie slightly.

"Anyway, Keith, I'm so glad to see you. This is wonderful." My mother held onto Keith's hand as she reached toward mine. Even with so many bodies in the room, I was chilled to the bone. My body felt immobilized, frozen into place. Cait sat up, confused.

"Why don't you two go find someplace to talk?" My mother said cheerfully to Keith and me. "Give me a minute, and I'll join you. I'm sure we can get everything worked out if we all sit down together."

"Mama—no!" I shouted, pulling my hand out of hers.

"Oh, Mama Wright, have you met Angela's *lover?*" Keith said, pointing down at Cait. He looked like he was going to begin a lecture, and explain, point by tedious point, his side of the story. Then he stopped, leaned down and kissed my cheek. The spot where his lips touched me stung. I felt queasy. Was I pregnant with Keith's baby? Or was his spiteful display making me ill?

"Oh, I guess not," he continued with a mean little smile. "I'll let Angela introduce you."

Finally realizing what was going on, Cait blinked and dislodged herself from the GALS FREE crew, her eyes moving from Keith to my mother to me.

"Is this your mother?" Cait pulled herself to her feet and knocked her shoulder into Keith as she walked toward my mother. Mom was standing stiffly, her mouth open slightly. "*Janet*, I am so honored to finally meet you," Cait said, her eyes shining.

Tentatively, but with real emotion, Cait put her arms around my mother and pulled her into a deep embrace. Every part of their bodies was touching—breasts, hips, toes. My mother always carefully kept her back arched during a hug to avoid the inelegance of chests and pelvises pressing against each other. She didn't care for physical contact with people she wasn't close to, but Cait was forcing their bodies together.

As I watched Cait and my mother, I tried to catch my breath. Without noticing, I had been holding it. In the eerily still room, my labored gulpy breathing now seemed thunderous, the only sound outside of the whir of Stephen's camera. Despite the quiet, one word screamed in my head, screeching over and over like a car alarm—"Janet, Janet, Janet."

Even worse than being hugged by a stranger, my mother hated being called by her first name by anyone she didn't know. Like many black women of her age and upbringing, she used this formality as a weapon to command respect and fend off the corrosive slights that could, little by little, erode her dignity. I remember introducing her to a college acquaintance who shook her hand and asked, "May I call you Janet?"

"No," my mother had replied frostily. "You may call me Mrs. Wright." Cait didn't know. She looked happy to grab hold of some new part of me.

Finally, without speaking or even looking at Cait, my mother untangled herself and turned her back, leaving Cait standing uncomfortably alone.

"Come with me, Angela—now," my mother said over her shoulder as she stomped toward the door. She walked by Stephen who was still shooting, moving from the protesters to Zulena to Mrs. Woods to Keith to my mother, to Cait to me, not sure where to focus.

I wasn't sure either. As my eyes moved from one to the other, I realized that I didn't know what to do, where to go, who to go with. Worse, I felt like I had lost a grip on who I was. Standing in the Rainbow House, ground zero of the modern melting pot, where race, gender, sexual and cultural identities collided, I realized that I was now extremely uncomfortable in the worlds I had lived in uneasily at best. I had relished being a black woman, my mother's daughter. But my mother was ashamed of me, insisting that by loving a woman I was rejecting "our people."

But was I really a lesbian? And if I was, did that mean that I would not only lose my "black card," but also end up motherless? Cut loose from my family, would I simply create a new one—Cait, me, our cardboard-colored baby? Or babies—was I pregnant, too, with little AngelandKeith? Was I really a journalist, even though I couldn't interpret or communicate the facts of my own story? I felt as lost and out of place as Zulena, longing for compassion and support from someone, anyone.

"Stephen, turn off the damn camera!" I heard my mother bark. "Angela, are you coming?"

"No, Mother," I said quietly. I turned to Cait, "Come on."

"Well, I should stay, actually," Cait began, looking toward her GALS FREE compatriots, who seemed in limbo without her.

"No, you shouldn't, actually," I snapped at her. "You need to leave now. And, by the way, what you're doing is absurd, so knock it off," I said, pointing my shoe toward her friends, lying there like sleepy children arranged in a neat row for a nap.

"You know nothing about this, Angela . . ." Cait said tartly, her brows knitting together in little peaks. "These people and their demands are holding the lesbian movement hostage. Why do women have to fight for men's rights?"

"Maybe you need to broaden your definition of women," I said harshly. Cait was startled by my vehemence. "You're not fighting for anyone's rights, you are simply oppressing people like Zulena. Your thin-sliced queer 'values' make no sense to anyone. Get off your high horse and admit you're being narrow-minded because you don't like the way she dresses. Leave her and let her be her own damn self—whoever that may be."

I grabbed Cait's arm and pulled her toward me. Pressing my hand into the small of her back, I held it firmly in place as I pushed her toward the hall. As I walked by Keith, still standing there rubbernecking, I leaned toward him and hissed into his ear, "By the way, asshole, your favorite poet, Langston Hughes, was a gay man."

As we passed my mother, I glared at her pointedly. "And, Cait, please meet my mother, Mrs. Wright."

Chapter 30

I hung up my coat and sat on the couch. I didn't think I'd ever felt so tired. I didn't feel angry at Cait anymore, just worn out. Cait sunk down next to me, exhausted, too, her weight depressing the corduroy cushion. I let my body slide closer to hers, pressing tightly against her.

"Let's just stay right here, just like this," I said, throwing my leg over hers. "I never want to leave this apartment, this room, this couch."

"Angela, that's the problem," Cait said, resting her head on my shoulder. "We can't lock ourselves away in here, hiding from everyone. Keith, your friends, your mother. That is who we're hiding from?"

I nodded. "This is hard, Cait, harder than I thought it would be." I felt a catch in my throat as I spoke and swallowed hard. "Mae and I used to joke that 'men are dogs, let's go ahead and be lesbians.' But it's not that easy."

"Oh, no, don't tell me you're on the verge of being a 'has-bian,' " she said, teasing. As she spoke, she stroked my hand with the tips of her fingers. "But, really, it may not be as hard as you're making it."

"Easy for you to say, but it's different for me." I sat up and pulled away from her slightly. "Here, with you, everything feels fine. But in the real world, my world, I'm not comfortable being a lesbian."

Cait nodded, looking at me steadily. I tried to see what was in her eyes.

"I don't expect you to understand this, Cait," I continued, hurriedly, afraid of her silence. "You're so comfortable in the world, you know who you are."

"Angela, it hasn't been easy for me, either," Cait said. Smiling faintly, she disengaged her fingers, and gently placed her hand on top of mine. I flicked my index finger against the nubby grain of the couch.

"I'm afraid, too," she said, looking over at me. Her voice was halting, tentative. "I can't have the world I want, so I guess I've tried to create my own."

This time, I didn't say anything, but snuggled closer to her. I had become so used to Cait barreling ahead, heady, headstrong and hardheaded—whether it was her political activities, our relationship, baby-making. But at this moment, she wasn't on some polemical bandwagon, and I liked this more thoughtful, diffident side of her.

"I want a safe place, too," she continued, looking at me intently, willing me to understand. "A world where I can bring my baby into. Our baby."

"But you can't have your corner of the world by shutting out others, Cait," I said. "The way you treat the transgender folks is beneath you."

"Why can't I have a world without men?" she began, but stopped as I shook my head. "Okay, let's agree to disagree. But, Angela, maybe you should listen to your own advice. It's time for *you* to be your own damn self—whoever that may be."

It was true. I was tired of this silly passing. Passing for black, passing for straight, passing as a lesbian, a twisted, 21st-century version of some tragic 19th-century mulatto in a

Charles Chesnutt novel. I was sick of the divided life I had been leading, always hiding, worried that someone would "read" me. I craved just being my own damn self.

"Do you really want me to be myself?" I hated the way I sounded—small, needy and terrified, just how I felt. "Do you know who that is?"

"You mean do I know the part of you who doesn't know how beautiful you are? Who has a hair crisis most mornings? Who's a stubborn mama's girl? Who's cheap. Who uses that ancient cell phone? Who has no poker face? Who can't dance?"

"I can dance, when I'm relaxed," I said, frowning at her.

"I love all that, plus the parts that are funny and adventurous, and sexy and spirited, and smart and easy to be with." She kissed my forehead and I felt her smile. "All of it adds up to you."

"Cait, are you sure?" I put my arms around her, breathing in her soapy scent. "It doesn't always feel like it. Sometimes all you care about is making a baby."

"I'm sure of you," she said, nuzzling her face into my neck. "I always have been. I want you to be part of this family I'm trying to create. Why else do you think I agreed to that donor?"

"Not because of the haircut."

"No, silly. I was hoping the baby might look like you. Like us." She lifted her head and kissed my cheek, before resting her forehead on my shoulder. "But it doesn't feel like I'm ever going to get pregnant."

"Yes, you are. Yes, *we* are." Wrestling away from her, I looked at the calendar on my watch. "Hey, what day is it? Isn't it time for your period?"

"It's day thirty."

"Let's test," I said, sitting up.

"Maybe I should wait, give it one more day. You know it's more accurate first thing in the morning. I'm sure my period will come tomorrow." She was looking down at her knuckles, weakened by the monthly disappointments.

"Oh, come on. Let's be hopeful for a change." I took her hand and pulled her to her feet. "I'm going to be right here with you."

We sat in the bathroom, me at her feet, as she tore the wrapper off the little plastic stick. She gripped it in her hand, shaking slightly. I pried her fingers off the stick, opened her legs and put it between them. I didn't breathe, as I listened to her urine splash onto it. I looked up at Cait. Her eyes were squeezed shut. She looked like a little girl making a wish.

"I can't take the disappointment," she said. As I stared at the stick, I could see one line clearly in the control window, as I watched the urine edge its way toward the pregnancy window.

"You know I love you, right?" I said. With my hand over the little box, I shook the stick twice, like a thermometer.

"Are you sure you're ready to be a mother?" Cait asked, her eyes still shut. "A lesbian mother? You can't hide or pretend or pass with a baby, you know."

"I know." I squeezed the stick and closed my eyes, too. "I'm ready, no matter how long it takes."

"I love you," said Cait, tensing her body and squeezing her fists, too. "I'm ready."

I opened my eyes and looked down. Two lines.

"Hey, we're pregnant!" I said, climbing onto her lap.

She opened her eyes and shrieked. Cait threw her arms around me, and I felt her grasp tighten as her body shook with sobs. "I like it when you say 'we,' " she said, drying her eyes on my shoulder.

A few minutes later, we were still sitting on the toilet, my legs straddling hers, the pregnancy test on the floor in front of us. Finally, she began to dislodge herself.

"I've got to call my GALS. They'll be so excited." She

squeezed my arm and stood up. "No, I know exactly what I want to do right now—go for a ride on my bike. Come with me?"

"No, you go," I told her, reaching up to kiss her. "I'll be right here when you get back."

Cait skipped as she left the bathroom. She hurdled over a dozing Roscoe and pulled open the front door. Her hand on the knob, she stopped and turned toward the coatrack. Smiling at me, her dimple denting her cheek, she yanked the helmet off its hook and tugged it onto her head. As I stood watching the door close after her, I felt something damp dripping lightly down my right thigh. I opened my jeans and looked at my leg—blood. Thank GOD. The right one of us was pregnant.

As I pulled my pants closed, I felt my cell vibrate in my front pocket.

"Hello, Daddy," I said as I cradled the phone to my ear. "Yes, I'm listening. . . ."

Chapter 31

My father looked over his shoulder as he eased his car into a space in front of Hell's Kitchen Hair-itage House, the beauty salon on 45th and Tenth where my mother was getting her hair shaped and deep conditioned. Though it was after 10 P.M., the place was jumping.

"Come on, Angela," my father urged gently as he unbuckled his seat belt. He had picked me up in Brooklyn, Mae along with him, insistent on brokering a truce between my mother and me. "This is for the best."

"No." I folded my arms, crossed my legs and burrowed deeper into the slippery leather seat.

"Angela, please." He turned and touched my shoulder. "You just need to talk to your mother. I don't know what this is about between the two of you, but you all need to get everything straightened out. Your mama loves you. We can fix this thing." He turned toward Mae, who was sitting next to me, his cloudy gray-brown eyes pleading.

"Girl, get out of this car—now!" Mae leaned over me and pushed the door open on my side. Hoisting her foot up, she jammed a spiked heel into my hip and shoved me halfway out the door. "Go talk to her. We're all sick of the mama-drama. Angela, it's time for you to be a big girl and deal with this."

"ALL-RIGHT!" I got out slowly and slammed the door, just missing Mae's foot. My father on one side of me, Mae on the other, we walked up the steps and into the Hair-itage House.

It was standing room only in the second-floor shop, packed with sisters "of a certain age." Draped in plastic African-inspired gowns, their hair in various states of done-ness, they sat under dryers, flipped through magazines, shouted to each other over the Motown oldies blasting through speakers mounted on each wall. Many munched on fried rice and lo mein, complimentary to customers after 9:00 P.M.

"Hey, Dr. Wright—how you feeling, sir?" shouted a young woman sitting at a desk crammed into a corner of the room. "Your wife's in the VIP area. Go on back."

"Thank you, Miss Wanda," my father said in his usual gracious tone. He smiled and bowed slightly.

Mae and I followed my father through a short, narrow hallway and opened the door to a large private room in the back. My mother was sitting in a plush, brown-and-tan velvet chair, wearing a delicately embroidered gown, her hair covered in some kind of thick green goop. Next to her, in an identical chair, Nona was eating shrimp fried rice with a pair of chopsticks lashed together with a rubber band. She seemed to be wearing a stocking cap on her head. Across the room, a young attendant was humming quietly to Freda Payne's "Band of Gold," as she meticulously sewed clumps of straight black hair into a wig that was sitting on top of a Styrofoam head, spray-painted light brown. "I'm Bonita." She looked up briefly and waved.

"Hello. Hello, ladies," my father said as he leaned down and kissed my mother's cheek, careful to avoid getting conditioner on his face. "Look who I brought. Maybe you can have a little talk."

"Oh, Chester, I didn't expect to see you, at least not so soon." Nona dropped the chopsticks and touched her head, embarrassed. "I'm just having my, umm, hair touched up." She looked sheepishly at the wig. Mae and I stepped from behind my father.

"Hello, Mae," my mother said, nodding toward my friend. "Angela," my mother said, cutting her eyes toward me. Her voice was crispy. "Nice to see you girls. Anything new, Angela?"

Mae elbowed me. "Say something, Ang," she murmured in my ear.

"No, Mother." I spoke just as coolly as she had. "Nothing has changed."

"Well, then, pull up a chair, maybe you girls should get your hair done," my mother said, wiping conditioner from her forehead.

I crossed my arms as I watched my mother glance at me, before adjusting her reading glasses and picking up a copy of *O* from a pile of magazines. I avoided her eyes, looking instead at the copy of *Désire* magazine underneath. On the cover, Tatiana—Peaches, or whoever she really was—was standing between the other two women, her eyes bright and animated. She was turned slightly and a bit more forward and taller. Even in spirit, Tatiana was trying to shoulder the others out of her way. Lucia had let me know that the blogger babes cover was the bestseller of the year. The dead celebrity rule still held.

The door opened, and Donny Epperson walked in, his long legs squeezed into Ultrasuede pants. He was the owner of the Hair-itage House and had been taking care of my mother's hair for two decades. Donny had seen her on television and insisted on providing her with hair care for life, on the house. His own hair was combed back in soft gray waves. He wore a turquoise wife beater, and his ropy arms glistened with sweat.

"Mizz Janet, Mizz Nona—family—Hel-lo." He grinned at everyone, breezily ignoring the tension in the room. His silver bracelets jangled as he ran his fingers through my mother's hair. "You're ready for a rinse. Come with me over to the sink, and we can get this stuff out of your hair. One of these days I'm going to update your look," he said brightly, falling comfortably into the old joke. He was always threatening to cut off my mother's hair. She pushed his arm away affectionately.

"Listen, excuse me," Nona said, looking at me. "Angela, I know this is between you and your mother, but we're all family here, and I really feel the need to say something on her behalf." Nona looked like a mean old turtle with the cap on her head.

"Angela, your mother and I are Christian women, God-fearing, churchgoing women, so we really cannot condone your lifestyle, honey. Do you understand that?" The room became suddenly very quiet. Bonita looked up from Nona's wig, Mae turned her head sharply, my father's brow knotted in confusion and Donny turned off the water and stopped spraying my mother's hair.

"I mean, Angela. Your mother is trying to do what's best for you. Homosexuality is a sin. That's all there is to it. The Bible says it, it's the truth, that's the end of it. You can't argue with God."

"Mizz Nona, tell me, where does the Bible say that?" Donny spoke in a low purr, studying my mother's hair as he toweled her dry.

"Baby, Leviticus 1:22, Old Testament. Look it up yourself. Homosexuality is an abomination and can't be tolerated under any circumstances."

Donny draped a clean towel over my mother's shoulders

and squeezed them gently. He turned from her and walked over to the desk where Bonita was sitting. Scooting her legs to the side, he reached underneath and pulled out a worn copy of the Bible, pink stickies peeking out from a number of pages. Putting on the reading glasses strung around his neck on a beaded chain, he turned the tissuey pages.

"Okay, Mizz Nona, you have been enjoying my free shrimp, am I right? Now here also in Leviticus, but a little later in chapter 11, verse 10, it says that eating shellfish is an abomination. There seems to be a lot of abominating going on up in here." Donny touched his fingers to his temples lightly and looked up at Nona questioningly. My mother and father were listening intently and Mae's hand was covering her mouth.

"Listen, Donny, what you're doing is blasphemous. Stop using the Bible that way, boy. The Bible says that man should not lie with man. That is clearly an abomination. God made Adam and Eve, not Adam—" Nona was getting agitated, raising her voice and gesturing.

"That is so tired. We all know that the Bible doesn't say anything about Steve," Mae said.

"What, you're a lesbian too, Mae? Listen, sis—I understand. There are so few good men out there." At the word "lesbian" I glanced at my father. He blinked twice.

"I didn't say I was a lesbian, but I also didn't say I wasn't. That's my damn business, excuse my profanity." I looked over at Mae, her head cocked slightly to one side, her jaw set, and smiled at her gratefully.

"Nona, I've been doing your hair for I don't know how long and for just as many years you've been complaining about your ex-husbands." Donny flipped through the pages again, squinting through his half glasses. "I'm reading Matthew 19:3: Is it lawful to divorce one's wife for any cause? Verse 9 says 'whoever divorces his wife, except for unchastity, and marries another, commits adultery. I think that goes for divorcing husbands, too." He looked at Nona over his glasses, as she squirmed slightly.

"So are you with me? Divorce and remarriage equals adultery and adultery equals—guess what?" He continued glaring at her. "Chalk up another abomination for you."

"Don't judge me," Nona said, standing up from the chair.

"It's not me who's judging you, sweetheart." Donny continued paging through the Bible. "It's God's judgment that's harsh. I'm going back to Leviticus now. If a man commits adultery with the wife of his neighbor, both the adulterer and the adulteress shall be put to death. It's right here in the Bible."

"Stop it, now." Nona said loudly. She pursed her lips and slapped her hand on her knee. "You are my boy, but homosexuality is still a sin, and if you practice it, you're going to hell."

"Seems like we'll all be there together, Mizz Nona." Donny walked over to me and placed a hand on my shoulder. It felt solid.

"I am a God-fearing man, and I've been teaching Bible study at my church for as long as anyone can remember. Massa kept our people enslaved by quoting Ephesians, 'slaves, be obedient to those who are your earthly masters, with fear and trembling, in a singleness of heart, as to Christ.' Using the Bible any way you feel like by picking out parts that suit you then ignoring the rest was wrong then and it's wrong now."

"But Donny, I'm not talking about you. You're a good person, even though what you're doing is sinful. I don't have any problem with you."

"I have a problem with you, Mizz Nona." He reached over and picked up the wig stand, fingering the strands of hair while staring down Nona.

"Listen, I . . ." Nona began. Touching her head, she

glanced at my mother. My mother looked stricken for a moment before quickly composing her features.

"No, you listen," said Donny, continuing to look hard at Nona. "You can think whatever you want, but when you are in my house, you need to show some respect for who I am. Understand?"

"Well, yes," replied Nona, staring nervously at "her hair."

"Perfect." Donny removed Nona's wig from the stand and draped it over his left hand. With his other hand, Donny slipped his Bible back under the desk.

"Are we all okay here?" Donny looked around the room. Everyone seemed shaken. "Does anyone want some herb tea? Well, I know I do. Come on now, everyone, let's get some tea and leave the family here to talk things out." He planted a kiss on the side of Nona's face, threw an arm across her shoulders and steered her out of the room, shooing Bonita out with them.

Mae looked over her shoulder at me, before following them. "Be strong my sistah," she mouthed.

"Well, are we okay?" my father asked, moving his eyes from my mother to me. "I think I'm getting an idea about what's going on here. But the only thing that's important to me is that we are okay here."

"Are we, Mom?" I held onto my father's arm as I looked at my mother. "Do you think I'm going to hell?"

"No, Angela, of course not, don't be ridiculous." My mother gave a tense laugh and looked down at her hands. "I don't think you're a sinner, that's not why I'm upset. I just don't understand what I did wrong. How could this happen to . . ." My mother had dropped her usual in-control tone. Her voice was filled with anguish.

"To you, Mom?" I stared at her sadly. "This isn't about you, it's about me." I looked over at my father as his eyes shifted from me to my mother. He was folding and unfolding his beefy hands behind his back. I hated that he had to hear this.

"Okay, then I'll just say it: What is wrong with you?" My mother gripped the arms of the chair, the veins showing on the tops of her hands. "I don't want you to be like this. This is not what I wanted for you. You are not a lesbian."

"Janet, nothing is wrong with Angela." I'd never heard my father raise his voice. Though I knew he loved me with a quiet fierceness, he didn't like conflict or loudness and preferred to wait until emotional messiness settled back into place.

"I don't know too much about gay or lesbian, but I know my daughter. Nothing is wrong with her. This is the bright, beautiful little girl we brought up. Stop talking about Angela like she's somebody else's child.

"Now let's end this," he continued, looking back and forth between my mother and me. "You girls can work out the details later; I don't need to be in it. But we are a family. Now come on." He tugged me over to where my mother was sitting, leaned down and pulled the three of us together awkwardly.

"Come on now." His voice was forceful as he tightened his grip on the two of us. My mother's soft, damp hair brushed against my cheek. After several seconds, she looked up at me, her eyes watery.

"Angela, baby, I love you. I love you so much." She pulled me toward her, crushing my face in the gown. "I don't want you to be a lesbian, but I love every part of you with every part of me. I'm ashamed that you don't know that. I always have."

That's all I ever wanted from my mother, for her to step around herself and all those people who adore her and love me—all of me. I started to cry softly, and she hugged me tighter.

"I love you, too, Mama," I said, my voice muffled in her shoulder.

"Mizz Wright, I love being part of this family moment, but it's getting late." Donny had walked back into the room, followed by Mae and Bonita. Nona trailed a few steps behind, her hair back in place. "I got a roomful of women out there waiting to get pretty. Are you ready for me to cut that hair off?" He pulled a pair of scissors out of his back pocket and moved them over the top of my mother's head.

"Yes, Donny, cut it." She patted my back and turned to him. "Get rid of it."

"What?" Donny looked at her with surprise. All of us did.

"Cut it off—all of it." My mother's voice had turned no-nonsense again. "There is no reason for me to be having the same hair that I did twenty-something years ago. It's my damn hair, but sometimes it gets in the way."

I stepped away from my mother as Donny shakily grabbed a handful of hair. As he clipped, it fell in damp, fuzzy clumps around the bottom of her chair.

"God, I didn't know how good this would feel." She took my father's hand, kissed it, and then held it to her cheek. He rested his thick, solid arm on my shoulder. Mae looked at me and mouthed "oh, my God!" Nona gave a little wave from across the room.

Bonita moved toward the door carrying the extra hair that hadn't made it into Nona's wig. My mother stopped her as she passed her chair, and touched the shiny hair.

"Where does this hair come from, Donny?"

"That comes from . . ." Donny walked over to the sink to rinse the remnants of my mother's wooly hair from his hands. Half of her head was covered in soft, steely curls, the other remained wild and unruly. "Oh, I don't know where it comes from. But that's real, human hair, not that mess that come from yaks or llamas or whatever. And who cares where it comes from? It's mine now." Mae raised an eyebrow skeptically.

With Donny's back to the sink, Bonita leaned down, her lips to my mother's ear. "Mrs. Wright, I'm a member of Trans Action, and we're really proud of you for what you're doing . . . you know, your documentary. Thank you." She was whispering, speaking quickly, her lips so close to my mother's ear it looked like she was kissing it. "I know where that hair comes from if you're interested. It involves a village in Bangladesh, a hair broker and a factory in Queens."

My mother turned around to look toward the sink. Donny was still trying to scrub off all of the little hairs that were clinging to his arms so he could finish my mother's head. My mother's eyes were bright with excitement, her interest definitely piqued.

"Angela, get me my notebook and a pen from my purse. This is a good story for me." She spoke in a commanding stage whisper, pointing to her bag tucked underneath the chair, without looking up.

"For you?" I squinted at her, leaning on the arm of the chair. I reached down and swatted her hand lightly. "No, I think it's a good story for me."

"Angela, maybe it could be something we work on together." She smiled at me, pulling me close and kissing my hair. Then she bent over and retrieved her bag herself.

Epilogue

Cait eased the baby gently from her breast, and kissed his forehead before handing him up to me. I dabbed his mouth with a nubby towel, and nuzzled my face against his. I loved the feel of our son's warm, milky breath on my neck.

"Stop staring at Cait's tits, you big perv," Mae said, punching Rufus's meaty arm. The two of them, dressed and accessorized in their Sunday best, had stopped by to take little Homer out for a walk. Rufus even had a felt fedora and old-fashioned walking stick.

"Girl, please," replied Rufus, but he looked sheepish. Cait raised an eyebrow and winked at him as she pulled her shirt closed. "Sorry, Cait. I couldn't help it."

"Men," I said, moving Homer to my shoulder to burp him. I thumped his back and was rewarded with a burp.

Cait stood up from the couch, and rubbed noses with the baby. She had been freaked out at first, insisting that the itty bitty penis that appeared on the sonogram was a smudge, wayward foot or a birth defect.

"Cait, get over it—we're having a baby man." I had kissed her forehead as we both stared at the blurry protrusion on the screen. Later I had caught her pulling the wrinkled sonogram photo from her backpack and bragging to her GALS FREE friends about the size of his male organ. "Well, at least my little man is going to be a *real* man."

"Girls, cut the cord already," Mae said impatiently as she fitted the cloth baby carrier onto Rufus, enlarging the straps for his big frame. "Give me my godson."

I handed Homer to Mae. He gurgled and gave her a toothless smile as he reached toward one of her earrings.

"Come on, Homes, your Auntie Mae is going to take you out of this estrogen den," she said, dodging his tiny brown fist and expertly fitting and snapping him onto Rufus's chest. "By the way, girls, nice outfit."

That morning, Cait and I had dressed Homer in his best clothes—an unstained white shirt, preppy argyle sweater vest, khaki pants, matching jacket and suede baby lace-up boots, all gifts from Mae. At the last minute I stuck a little silk knitted cap on his head that my mother had picked out for him earlier this year. The two of us had been poking around hair processing factories in Southeast Asia, collecting interviews and footage for our documentary.

"Ang, don't you think this would be cute for the baby?" my mother had said. It was the first time she had acknowledged that I would be a mother soon.

"Yes, Mom, it would," I had answered, choking a little on the words. The little hat stuck in her bag, we had stood together, holding hands, our temples touching. It was much easier to get close to her without all that hair. "Thank you, Mama."

She and my father had come to the hospital the day Homer was born. My mother hadn't looked Cait in the eye, but she had been civil and had almost smiled when Cait called her "Mrs. Wright," and handed the baby to her. She had held him tight to her chest for a long time, and blinked when I told her we had named him Homer, after her grandfather. Afterward, I had seen my father tapping the nursery glass window and waving at his grandson, my mother standing behind him, looking over his shoulder.

"Good-bye, ladies," said Rufus cheerily. Mae stuck a large, zipper lock bag with the baby's "things" into her purse and then linked her arm through his. "See you in an hour or two."

With our arms around each other, Cait and I leaned down into Rufus's chest and kissed our son again.

"My God, women," Mae said, tugging Rufus toward the door and blowing kisses to us. "You're gonna turn Homeboy into a mama's boy."

"Hey," said Rufus, pulling Mae back and somehow managing to herd all of us together into a messy embrace. "Aint nothing wrong with that."

PASSING FOR BLACK

Linda Villarosa

ABOUT THIS GUIDE

The suggested questions are intended to enhance
your group's reading of Linda Villarosa's
Passing for Black

Discussion Questions

1. What does the title, *Passing for Black* mean?

2. In what ways does Angela "pass"?

3. Who else is passing?

4. Imagine Angela's life in the years beyond the end of the novel. What does the future hold for her?

5. Did Angela love Keith? Did he love her?

6. How are the male characters portrayed in the novel? Does the author give them a fair shake?

7. What is Angela's relationship with her mother like, and how does it change?

8. Is Cait capable of raising a black male child?

9. Angela accuses Cait of excluding transgender men and women from "the lesbian nation." Her response is, "Why should we include everybody? Why can't there be a space and a day and an event just for us, for women, without penises all over the place?" What are your thoughts?

10. Mae encourages Angela to stay with her fiancé because of a shortage of black men. Is the so-called black male shortage real or overblown?

11. Mizz Nona takes it a step further when she warns that "career success is *all that*, but you can't get ahead if you leave your man behind." Are men intimidated by successful black career women? What has your experience been?

12. At one point Angela says, "though I had been black-born-black for almost thirty years, every day I wrestled with the tyranny of striving for authenticity." What's your reaction to her statement?

13. Tatiana is a complicated person—beautiful, black and conservative, among other things. What do you think of her?

14. Suzy G, the sex activist, thinks that anonymity heightens sexual pleasure. She says, ". . . you're judging your lover using senses beyond vision, so you're aren't prejudiced by race or age or hair color or looks of any kind. And no one's judging you, so your self-consciousness melts away. Unknown flesh is more interesting." What has your experience been?

15. How did you feel when Mizz Nona and Donny used the Bible to alternately condemn and defend homosexuality?